RS   H92

T

Comes the Hunter

Also by Geo. W. Proctor

Enemies
Walks Without a Soul

Comes
the Hunter

GEO. W. PROCTOR

A DOUBLE D WESTERN
DOUBLEDAY
New York London Toronto Sydney Auckland

A DOUBLE D WESTERN
PUBLISHED BY DOUBLEDAY
a division of Bantam Doubleday Dell Publishing Group, Inc.
666 Fifth Avenue, New York, New York 10103

DOUBLE D WESTERN, DOUBLEDAY,
and the portrayal of the letters DD
are trademarks of Doubleday, a division of
Bantam Doubleday Dell Publishing Group, Inc.

Library of Congress Cataloging-in-Publication Data

Proctor, George W.
Comes the hunter/Geo. W. Proctor.—1st ed.
    p.   cm.—(A Double D western)
1. Kiowa Apache Indians—Fiction. I. Title.
PS3566.R588C66   1992
813'.54—dc20   91-26953
CIP
ISBN 0-385-41803-5
March 1992
First Edition

10   9   8   7   6   5   4   3   2   1

To Lee Goggins—

For sitting me down atop a mountain called High Lonesome and giving me the privilege of reveling in the night sky.

Comes the Hunter

One

COUGAR—a musky, wet effluvium of mountain cat permeated the air. Thick and heavy, the feline scent forced its way into Clay Thorton's nose, clogging his nostrils.

Pa! Whispered desperation floated on the soothing spring breeze that caressed the banks of the San Antonio River.

Cougar—the rancher ignored the intruding voice. Clay's head jerked from side to side searching for the source of the overpowering odor that sought to smother him with every shallow, quick breath he drew into his lungs.

Nothing. He saw nothing except cottonwood boughs swayed by the warm breeze.

Icy needles pricked over his body as cold fear coursed through his veins. There was no mistaking the overwhelming odor. Once a man smelled clawed death, he did not forget the scent. Clay knew it well; he had encountered it often in the Guadalupe Mountains bordering Texas and the New Mexico Territory, but never here beside the serenity of the San Antonio River.

Pa! The urgent whisper carried on the wind persisted.

San Antonio? Clay Thorton's thoughts stumbled. Why was he standing by the river? He had not visited Central Texas since—

Pa!

The ground beneath the rancher's booted feet quaked, dissolving into a quagmire of running browns and greens. The tall cottonwoods that lined the river's banks shimmered violently before they dissipated into a sky churning like a maelstrom.

Pa!

The demanding whisper came directly from the center of the

whirling chaos that filled Clay's mind. The voice belonged to his son Martin!

The rancher's eyes blinked. A dream of yesterdays spent beside the San Antonio River near the town bearing the same name faded. Around Clay, shadow-cloaked junipers and pines thrust toward a sky sprinkled with stars that faded before an encroaching purple hue of predawn.

The scent of cougar still hung heavy in the air—heavy and near. Clay went rigid, fearing the slightest movement might attract the mountain lion. Shy by nature, the cougar shunned the places of men. Here in the basin of the Guadalupe Mountains, called the Bowl, was the cat's domain. He and his son Martin were the intruders.

"Pa!"

Clay's gaze darted across the cherry-red glow of the campfire's dying embers. Beneath a thick, black tangle of sleep-tousled hair, Martin stared at him, eyes wide and round with panicked fear.

The source of that fear left Clay's mouth as dry as the desert encircling the Guadalupes. His heart felt as though it had lodged in his throat. Curled between the fifteen-year-old boy and the radiating heat of the embers lay a cougar!

Were it not for the panther's size, the rancher could have imagined it no more than a common house cat, its head nestled between chest and arm and tail wrapped about its body while it slept beside a stove. However, the mountain cat was big. At that moment it appeared the largest cougar Clay had ever encountered. Enhancing its massive size was the animal's proximity to the rancher and his son.

The bone-chilling, predawn cold of the spring morning had brought the cat into the camp and the company of man—which it usually avoided, Clay realized. The warmth of the flickering embers drew it like a candlebug to a flame. *Only these coals*, the rancher thought, *will not kill like a candle flame burns a moth*.

"Pa—"

Martin's words were abruptly hushed by a warning shake of his father's head. Clay silently mouthed to his son, "Keep still."

The boy nodded. The cautious accepting motion of Martin's head did not disguise the doubt Clay saw reflected in his son's eyes. That same doubt trembled through every inch of the rancher's body when he edged back the blankets of his sleeping roll and pushed to a less than steady elbow.

Clay's pale blue eyes shifted from left to right while he searched for something that might—

My rifle! His gaze homed on the barrel of a rifle that leaned against his saddle a yard from where he lay stretched out on the ground. He glanced back at the puma and his son, then reached out.

And froze with arm outstretched, fingers a mere inch from the rifle.

The cougar moved! The panther lifted its broad feline head to open slitted eyes that focused on Clay. The rancher purposely let his gaze dip to the ground while keeping the mountain lion at the periphery of his vision. The last thing he wanted was to provoke the cat. Eye-to-eye contact would signal a blatant challenge to the lion.

The puma's head moved from side to side, before its eyes returned to the rancher. Without warning the head arched back, and its mouth opened! Not in a scream of attack, but in a lazy yawn. Imitating its harmless cousin, the house cat, the cougar stretched front and back legs to their limit—an action that fully exposed the recurved claws hidden in each of the four padded paws—before its eyes closed, and its head returned to the ground. The great cat slept once again with its cream-colored belly exposed to the embers' warmth.

Clay silently sucked in a breath and expelled it as a soft hiss in an attempt to quell the tremors of his body and quiet the pounding of his heart. Slowly, his fingers withdrew from the rifle barrel.

He could not trust himself with the Winchester, nor with the Colt holstered on his right hip. He did not like to admit it, but he was afraid, both for his son and himself. He considered himself handy enough with sidearm and rifle, but no one had ever accused him of being a shootist or a crack shot. Even with only ten feet separating him from the cougar, he could not rely on the accuracy of his eye or trigger finger. If he missed, the risk of hitting Martin was too great.

Avoiding his son's eyes and the questions they contained, Clay once more glanced around the small camp, uncertain what he sought, less sure that it existed.

Beside the saddle near his head, the twisted form of a weathered, gray cedar branch jutted from a pile of fallen tree limbs he had gathered last evening to fuel the fire through the night. He drew in another steadying breath. Perhaps there *was* a way . . .

Slowly reaching out, Clay's fingers closed around the morning-chilled wood. Gently, ever so gently, he pulled outward with a silent prayer on his lips that the pile of wood would not collapse like jackstraws when he extracted the limb.

His heart again doubled its pounding when the branch snagged itself amid the jumble of firewood. Easing the limb back into the heap, he gave it a slight twist and pulled outward once more. This time the three-foot length of cedar slipped free.

He allowed himself a quick glance at Martin, read the questioning on the boy's face, then tightened his grip on the branch. The rancher inched closer to the glowing embers in a sideways motion that was half wiggle and half scoot. He extended the branch to bury its end under the closest ember. He flipped the limb upward.

The coal popped up, its surface burning hotter as it jumped into the air. Two feet it flew—straight up—only to drop back to the smoldering remains of the campfire.

Clay whispered a curse as his gaze shot to the cougar. The cat did not move, its sleep undisturbed by the falling ember. Clay thrust the cedar branch back into the coals.

The second ember he flipped upward sent a shower of sparks cascading behind it as it arched three feet into the air to descend. It dropped to the ground and rolled to a halt two feet from the out-stretched mountain lion.

The rancher wasted no energy on further curses. For a third time he poked the branch into the embers, selected another glowing coal, and flipped upward with a flick of the wrist.

Like a miniature comet the ember streaked outward then curved downward. It hit the ground, careened off a rock half-buried in the ground, and rolled a full two feet, finally coming to rest against the dark pads of the panther's right forepaw.

In a single pounding heartbeat, the cougar came alive. The great cat leaped to its feet spitting. Without pause to locate the cause of its sudden pain, the mountain lion bounded from the camp, screaming in rage.

Nor was the puma the only one to take to its feet. Both Clay and Martin came out of their bedrolls, scrambling for footing. The younger Thorton snatched up an old army carbine resting on the ground beside his saddle. Martin cocked the weapon.

As his son hefted the rifle to shoulder, Clay leaped across the mound of embers to reach out and grasp the barrel of the weapon. He shoved the muzzle toward the ground. "No need for killing."

"Pa?" Martin's face twisted in puzzlement. "That cat might have gone after one of us."

"But she didn't," Clay answered. "She was just trying to keep the chill from her bones. No reason to kill a man or a beast for that. Put the rifle away, Son."

"But—" Martin's eyes lifted. His gaze followed the fleeing cougar silhouetted against the pink golds that pushed away the night sky. With an uncertain shake of his head, he eased down the hammer of the rifle. "I guess you're right. But that cat sure enough scared me."

"Scared me plenty, too. But scared ain't reason enough for killing." Clay smiled and squeezed his son's shoulder. "A man who meets up with a cougar and doesn't get a scare put in him is a damned fool. And I don't remember me or your ma raising you to be a fool."

"I reckon not." Martin grinned sheepishly at his father, then looked back at the mountain lion, that disappeared amid a stand of piñons. "Didn't know cougars came as big as that."

With a shrug Clay replied, "Cats are like men, I guess. They come in all sizes—some big and some small."

"What if she comes back? Only this time she ain't looking for a warm fire?" Martin rubbed his arms to fight off the morning's chill.

"What if's can drive a man crazy. If she takes it on herself to come looking for us, we'll handle that when it happens." The fear sparked by the cougar's unexpected visit to the camp receding, Clay felt the cold seeping through the jacket he wore. He nodded to the smoldering embers of the dying campfire. "Martin, get some flame into that, and I'll put on a pan of coffee and cook up some bacon to go with those biscuits your ma packed away for us."

"You just struck yourself a bargain," the boy answered while he laid aside the rifle.

"Then get to it," Clay urged. "We've a day's work ahead of us this morning and another one waiting when we get back to the house."

Two

CLAY THORTON pulled a wide-brimmed, dirt-stained hat from his head. He wiped the sweatband with a handkerchief and ran a hand through a head of brown hair thinned by thirty-five years before tugging the hat back on.

He glanced at a glaring yellow sun that rode a hand's length above the horizon. With a shake of his head, he peeled off his jacket and tucked it beneath the bedroll tied to his saddle. The morning was barely an hour old, and the heat had begun. Nor was there a hint of a cloud in the sky that promised a brief respite from the relentless sun.

He surveyed the rich vegetation surrounding him. Here in the Bowl of the Guadalupes there was moisture, plentiful enough for grass and trees—real trees, not just the junipers that most Texans called cedars. Maples with their palmated leaves grew in the basin. He admitted they were not as prolific as the piñons or even the ponderosa pines, but maples did grow here.

To be certain, the Bowl could not rival the dense Piney Woods of East Texas. Yet the abundant life Clay found here always seemed like nothing short of a miracle to the rancher. It was as though God had reached down into the desert and dipped a finger amid the rugged Guadalupe Mountains. Where His fingertip brushed the ground the Bowl sprang to life as a sign that even amid hell His gentle presence was to be found.

Wiping a shirt sleeve across his forehead, Clay reminded himself that it was also cool in the Bowl. The real heat would hit when Martin and he rode out of the Bowl, back into the desert.

Something we'd best be about, he thought when he shifted in the saddle to glance at the nine mares and foals that grazed on the ankle-deep grass to his left. He let his gaze travel in a circle about him again. *What's keeping Martin?*

A little smile came to his lips. One mare and colt were still missing from the twenty animals he and his son had brought to the Bowl two weeks ago for the spring grass. The mare was a blue-spotted Appaloosa Clay had purchased as a yearling in El Paso two years ago from a mountain man come all the way down from the Canadian border. Clay gave the filly to Martin on his thirteenth birthday.

The pride Clay had seen on his son's face only had grown as the boy haltered and then saddle-broke the young horse. This spring that pride doubled. The Appaloosa threw her first foal—a colt with a spotted rump to match that of his momma's.

A rustle of underbrush drew Clay's attention to the right. Martin reined a bay between two cedars. The boy led the Appaloosa mare, rope looped around her neck, on his right. The young colt trotted behind its mother.

"Found her about a mile up yonder," Martin called to his father. "She didn't shy when I rode up to her. Let me drop this rope over her head without batting an eye."

"Little wonder! You've treated her like a house pet since I brought her back from El Paso. Never seen a horse more pampered." Clay waved on his son. "Bring her along. We've got a long ride 'fore we get back to the house."

Martin pulled beside his father's buckskin. "Ten miles ain't that far. No more'n two hours."

"That's if these mares don't take a mind to give us a run. Like as not, they won't like giving up this grass for the high and dry." Clay clucked his gelding forward.

"Saw five elk among some pines about a half mile from here," Martin said. "Think we might come back up here before summer and try for one?"

"Maybe next year. Give 'em another season to get their numbers back."

Clay remembered the days before the War Between the States, before the Butterfield opened a way station at the foot of Guadalupe Peak. The elk had been plentiful when his father had first taken him hunting in the Bowl. He had been no more than a boy then. Although the Butterfield-Overland Stage only ran through this country for about a year, until the U.S. Army opened Fort Davis hundreds of miles to the south, it brought men into an area once inhabited only by his family and Indians. Those men had carried empty bellies and rifles. In a matter of a few years they had all but killed off the elk they found in the Bowl. Now Clay refused to hunt them, preferring to let their numbers swell again.

From the corner of an eye, the rancher saw the disappointment on his son's face. "That ain't to say we can't slip off one day and try our hand at a deer. Whitetails are always plentiful hereabouts."

A smile washed over Martin's face. "I think I can handle that. Just remember what you said. I intend to hold you to your word."

"I'll remember. Now, why don't you take that spotted mare of yours up ahead and start on home? I'll fall in behind these others and make certain they follow," Clay directed his son.

The boy was only fifteen, the rancher reminded himself. Although Martin already stretched a full inch over Clay's five-foot-ten height, he still had some living to do before he was a man. Still had a mite to learn about the land and how it was apt to turn on a man who misused it.

It was a lesson Clay had learned after the Civil War when those in the east suddenly found they had a taste for Texas beef. He had watched the ranchers drive in herds of longhorns to the grasslands around El Paso. The grass had been waist high for as long as men could remember. In a mere year the grass disappeared, overgrazed. Only sand and rock remained. The desert that lurked beneath a grassy disguise had returned. Nor did it give any hint of allowing the grass to take root again.

Around the Guadalupes grass was as sparse as water. Clay ran only two hundred head of cattle over the two sections he called the Sweet Water Creek Ranch. Those beeves were constantly shifted from one parcel of land to another to prevent overgrazing.

This was the desert; Clay had never deluded himself that it was anything else. He kept his stock, both cattle and horses, at a level the land could support. Nor did he keep any goats or sheep as did some of his Mexican neighbors. Both animals grazed too close to the ground, often eating all the way to the roots of fragile grass plants.

It was this respect for this unforgiving land that kept Clay from grazing the Bowl except in the spring when the grass was young and hardy enough to recover from the mares and foals and in the fall before the first killing frost, after the grass had gone to seed. One full season of grazing, even a few horses or steers, might transform the lush Bowl into desolate rock and sand like the terrain that now encircled El Paso.

Clay could not ignore a tug of regret when he thought of the massive herds run by Texas ranchers on the grass-rich plains far to the east. He had watched many of the dirt-poor hands he had ridden the Chisholm Trail with after the war become rich almost overnight. They would drive a herd up from Mexico, stake a claim to a portion of the grasslands, fatten the steers, then drive them north to the railhead in Kansas to sell to the eastern meat packers.

That life might have been his—money, a big home with furniture brought west from places like New Orleans and St. Louis, and fine clothes for his wife and children. Such a life also would have carried a price. He would have had to give up this land.

The hint of amusement upturned the corners of Clay's mouth. At times it seemed damned foolish to place any value on land that most sane men would refuse even if it were given to them. But it was here that his parents had settled, his father more interested in prospecting the mountains for gold than ranching. And it was here his mother had died, giving birth to the only child she was to bring into the world. Buried beside her now was a husband who was killed twenty years ago by an Apache war chief named Red Shirt. Clay had been the same age as Martin when he had dug that second grave with his own hands.

Alone and scared, Clay had done the only thing he knew to do. He accepted the one thing his father had left him as a legacy—the land—dug in, and survived.

More than just survived, he admitted with a touch of pride. He had made a life for himself and his family. Although many of the fineries found to the east were missing, he was working on correcting that. His horses were starting to pay off.

Clay's slight smile widened when he remembered the two men who had traveled all the way from Corpus Christi and Jefferson last fall. Each purchased one gelding, saddle-broke and trained for cutting cattle—at a price of two hundred dollars a horse. That totaled four hundred dollars! Some dirt farmers in prosperous East Texas could not claim such a handsome profit off cash crops like cotton.

Those two men promised to be back this year—with friends. And there was Señor Díaz in El Paso who had already promised to buy

three horses as soon as they were broken and trained. It had taken
time, but Clay's reputation as a horseman was slowly spreading. If
all went as planned this year, he would have the money to travel
east to buy a blooded stud. A good stallion would breed speed into
sturdy cowponies known for their endurance.

"Pa."

Martin's voice intruded into Clay's plans for the future.

"Pa"—Martin turned in the saddle to look back at his father—"I
also saw Indian sign back among the trees."

"Apache or Comanche?" Clay asked.

Indian sign had been rare since the attack on Manzanita Spring a
year ago in 1869. Clay had tracked for the army that day when they
had come upon a Lipan Apache band only a few miles from where
Martin and he now rode. The fighting had been fast and furious.
When it was over, the few Lipans who survived escaped into the
Guadalupes.

The newspapers, especially those that came west from Jefferson
and Austin hailed the battle as the final defeat of the Apaches in
Texas. Clay was not as certain as those writers. Apaches still wandered across the border from the New Mexico Territory. Although
they were few in number, there remained the possibility one or
more bands might decide to return to the lands that had been their
home long before white men first came to this portion of Texas.

"Couldn't tell." Martin shook his head. "Only saw what was left
of a small fire. Looked to be at least a week old. Couldn't have been
big enough for more than one or two braves."

"Probably just that. A couple Apache braves came over the
mountains into the Bowl," Clay said. "All the same, keep an eye
peeled just in case."

"I'll do that." Martin's right hand lightly brushed the stock of
the carbine slung from his saddle.

Clay looked down at his own rifle as though to make certain it
remained securely looped about his saddle horn. He resisted the
urge to check the six loads in his holstered Colt. The pistol's cylinder always carried full loads, and the rancher kept a spare cylinder,
also carrying six shots, tucked away in his saddlebags. It was far
quicker to pop a fresh cylinder into a six-gun when there was a
need than trying to reload each chamber.

For an instant his gaze dropped to the pommel of a hunting

knife sheathed on his belt. An uninvited shiver worked up his spine as memories he would have left forgotten wedged into his mind.

With that very knife he had killed the Apache Red Shirt, extracting a bloody revenge for the death of his father. After burying his father beside his wife, Clay had tracked the young war chief for six months. And he had found him.

Another shiver coursed through the rancher as he remembered the morning he had ridden into Red Shirt's camp and brazenly challenged the Indian. By all rights, Clay realized, he should have died that day, his scalp tied to a lodge pole outside a wickiup. But the warriors who had followed Red Shirt for almost two years had grown weary of bloodshed. They had slowly abandoned the war chief, one by one leaving him to return to the bands from which they had come.

Only six wickiups stood in the Apaches' camp. The braves and squaws who awakened to find a foolish white boy waiting to greet them were too shocked to react to his presence. The same shock left Red Shirt's chest swelled with overconfidence when that boy spat a challenge in his face. Clay had seen the gleam of certain victory when Red Shirt drew a hunting knife. The gleam flickered and died, replaced by disbelief when Clay ducked beneath the warrior's first, wide, testing attack and drove his own blade into Red Shirt's chest.

As the war chief dropped to the ground, Clay turned, mounted his horse, and rode away. Had that camp been larger, even by only a few wickiups, Clay was now certain he would never have been able to leave. Some brave would have taken his life to avenge Red Shirt's death.

Instead, he later learned, the Apaches had given him a name that day—Fears-Not-Death. The story of Red Shirt's death spread among the Apaches, and they left Clay Thorton alone. Only a white man protected by mighty medicine could do what he had done and ride away unmolested.

Drawing a deep breath, Clay pursed his lips and exhaled in a sharp hiss. The past was past; nothing was gained by dwelling upon it. He did not convince himself. Although the Lipan Apaches had been driven from the region, Comanche raiding parties occasionally used Guadalupe Pass as they drove south to the Mexican border.

Clay stared to the point of the small herd of mares and colts.

Martin rode there, his head occasionally turning from side to side as he peered about the country through which they rode. With luck the Indian tales of Fears-Not-Death still protected them this day, and Martin would not have to dig a grave for his father as Clay had done twenty years ago.

The thought came as a silent prayer both for Martin and himself.

Three

"DADDY!" Sarah ran from the open door of the stone ranch house as Clay and Martin herded the horses into a corral constructed of cedar posts.

"Martin, close 'em up and make certain they've got plenty of water," Clay called to his son. "They'll be wanting it after two weeks in the Bowl. It's a mite hotter and drier here."

The younger Thorton nodded to his father as Clay reined his buckskin around and tugged the horse to a halt. The rancher stepped from the saddle, squatted with his arms held wide, and swept his seven-year-old daughter into them. He hugged her close, savoring the tightness of her arms about his neck when she returned the embrace.

"Daddy, I missed you." She kissed his cheek.

"I hope so." Clay held the young girl in his arms when he stood and started toward the house and the slender woman who stood framed in its doorway. "The only good thing about a man having to be away is being missed. That's why he comes back home. If he ain't got someone missing him, he might as well just keep riding on to somewhere else."

"I wouldn't like that," Sarah answered. "I don't even like it when you have to be gone overnight."

"You can add my don't likes to that, too." Elizabeth Thorton stepped from the door and into the sun. A welcoming grin spread over her delicate oval face.

Clay's gaze took in his wife as he placed Sarah on the ground. Elizabeth stood a hairsbreadth shorter than her husband. Her hair, the jet black of a raven's wing, had only a few random strands of gray intertwined here and there. The blueness of her eyes was as bright and deep as it had been when he had first seen her working as a clerk in her father's dry goods store in San Antonio. Sixteen years later, Clay found himself wanting her as much as he had that long-ago summer morning—if not more.

"I wasn't expecting you two back till late this evening. I haven't put anything on the stove." She reached his side and kissed his cheek.

The smell of flour and yeast hung about her, belying her words. Elizabeth had been baking bread. Beneath those comforting aromas of the kitchen wafted the hint of the lilac soap Clay had purchased for his wife the last time he had ridden into El Paso.

"That ain't the kind of a kiss a man expects to welcome him home." Clay slipped an arm around Elizabeth's waist and eased her to him.

Her lips met his willingly for an instant, then in a heartbeat, she pushed away. "Clayton Morgan Thorton, that's no way to be acting in front of the children."

He grinned. The hint of a smile on her lips and sparkle in her eyes spoke more than her words. The kiss pleased her as much as it had him. "It's only the way I feel."

She arched an eyebrow. "It wasn't your feelings I was asking about. It was your stomach. I've got some biscuits left from breakfast and some bacon if you're hungry."

"Martin's apt to be wanting something, but a cool drink to wash away some of the dust in my mouth and throat would do me fine." Clay tightened his arm around her, noting Elizabeth made no attempt to pull away.

"Sarah, you run along to the kitchen and fetch those biscuits and bacon. Take them to your brother," Elizabeth ordered their daughter, "while I pour your father some water."

Under the watchful eyes of her father, the seven-year-old trotted off to a ten-foot-by-ten-foot stone structure attached to the ranch house by a breezeway. "She's going to be a handsome woman, Elizabeth. Each day she looks more and more like you."

"It's a good thing." Elizabeth's arm went around Clay's waist once they entered the house. "We wouldn't want a young woman looking like you, would we?"

"And what's wrong with my looks? I can think of several—"

She muffled the rest of his words with a long kiss that left them clinging to each other. She rested her cheek on his shoulder. "Sometimes I feel like it has to be a sin for a woman to care for a man the way I care for you."

He nuzzled her hair and lightly kissed it. "There's nothing sinful about what we got. It's good—only good."

Her head lifted, and her gaze met his. "It is good, isn't it? Even after all these years together."

"Still good." He tenderly kissed her lips. "But there ain't no reason to be talking like we was all old and gray. It hasn't been all that many years."

"Hasn't it?" She turned him around and pointed outside where Sarah stood at Martin's side while her brother wolfed down a biscuit sandwich. "Those are our children out yonder, Clay. That's a son who's a growed man and a daughter who'll be looking for a husband in less years than you want to imagine."

A sudden somber tone to his wife's voice caught Clay by surprise. Her eyes shifted to the floor, and she eased away from him to retrieve a pitcher of water on the table when he looked at her.

"Is there something wrong, Elizabeth?" He looked back at his children.

There was no way to deny they were growing—and their parents slowly aging. Clay shook his head. In his mind, his thoughts, he still felt as young as the day he had brought Elizabeth to their home. Yet there was no ignoring a receding hairline and the few strands of hair that barely covered a balding spot at the back of his head. Nor could he overlook a stomach once taut and firm that now threatened to sag toward a middle-aged paunch.

"Nothing more than what usually bothers me when you're gone. I just get on the pensive side—start thinking about things." Elizabeth handed him a fired red-clay cup colorfully painted with Mexican designs.

"Things?" Clay drank deeply, enjoying the coolness that washed the desert dust from his throat. "What things?"

His wife gave her head an uncertain shake. "All sorts of things, like the thoughts women have when they are girls."

His brow creased, unsure of what she spoke.

"I guess a man doesn't have those kind of thoughts." She smiled, but there was a hint of sadness in that expression. "When a girl's young with what beauty she'll ever have, she worries more than just about finding a man to love and who'll return that love. She worries about how she'll keep his interest when the years start to leech away her youth."

He drained the last of the water and set the cup aside. Taking her hands, he met her eyes with his gaze. "Elizabeth—"

"Clay"—her hands squeezed his—"it's just that what I've had with you is good, and I get to wondering if it's the same for you. More than you just feeling tied down and having to take care of a family."

"Far more." He wished for words, fancy words like those he read in books. Words never came easy for him, especially when he wanted to describe the feelings that moved within his breast. "Elizabeth, I wouldn't want to have it any way but the way we've had it together. A man—this man—couldn't ask for more."

He drew her close, enfolding her in his arms. Her mouth lifted to his, and he kissed her, trying to focus all the feeling he held for this woman who was his life in that kiss. His desire stirred as it had for sixteen years whenever they kissed.

Apparently Elizabeth felt the rise of his passion. She arched a questioning eyebrow when their lips parted. "Clay Morgan Thorton, I've got the thought that you've got more than just a little spooning on your mind."

He smiled and nodded toward a door on the left of the ranch house's main room that led to their bedroom. "It would be like old times, Elizabeth, back when there was nothing more important than our loving."

A pleased smile answered his, and her blue eyes shifted to the bedroom door. Reluctantly she shook her head. "That was a long time ago, before we had two children who might come bounding into the house at any moment. And before you had cattle and horses to attend."

"The stock can wait, and we can shut the front door to keep Martin and Sarah out," he suggested.

Again she shook her head. "There's a time and a place for everything, but this ain't the time for what's on your mind. Go on with you. You've got your chores, and I've got mine."

Clay shrugged and heaved an exaggerated sigh. "Reckon you're right. But it would have been a nice way to spend the afternoon."

Elizabeth lovingly kissed his cheek. "And what would the stage do this evening when it came rolling in?"

"When you're right, you're right. Best be about my chores." Clay abandoned his attempts at an amorous afternoon.

Since the end of the war a man named Shiner had run a stage line between Santa Fe in the New Mexico Territory and El Paso. The Sweet Water Creek Ranch served as one of the few way stations in the long stretch of arid terrain between Albuquerque and the stage's final destination. The line only ran one coach a week. For keeping a fresh team of horses ready and waiting and for the meal Elizabeth prepared for the passengers, Clay collected ten dollars a stage. The hard cash was often all he saw in the long months between the sale of his steers or a horse.

Drawing his hat brim down against the sun, Clay stepped outside. He made a mental note that when time permitted he would add a covered porch to the front of the house. Three years had passed since his last addition to their home—Sarah's room built at the back of the house beside the room he had constructed for Martin.

A porch, a real porch, he realized, would require wood, cut and milled boards. Flat rocks piled atop each other and mortared together with adobe, the main building material for the ranch house, would not do for a covered porch. Those boards would cost greenbacks, unless he could find a merchant needing a horse broke in trade.

"Pa?" Martin called to his father. "Is it all right if I cut Misty and her colt out from the others? I'd like to keep 'em in the pen beside the barn the next couple days until we take 'em to pasture."

For a moment Clay considered admonishing his son for overpampering the Appaloosas, but let it slide. Martin's displayed pride in his own stock was a good sign that he was maturing. "Do what you like, but don't take all day with it. Stage comes in this evening, and it'll be needing a team of eight ready for the harness."

Martin nodded and pointed to the Appaloosa colt. "Think he'll bring a handsome price when he's old enough?"

"Reckon he will. Spotted-rumped horses are rare enough in this country, and a lot of folks got an eye for 'em," Clay replied. "But it's still a while before he'll be ready for a buyer."

"If he's ever ready for a buyer," Martin said.

Clay peered questioningly at the boy.

"I've been thinking about keeping him," Martin added. "He's got the looks of a good pony. Maybe my own saddle horse."

"Like I said," Clay commented when he turned to the barn, "there's still a while before he'll be old enough to sell. We'll cross that bridge when we come to it."

The answer seemed enough to hold Martin, who made no further comment. Clay had been expecting this. He hoped that when the time came to sell the Appaloosa colt Martin would have a choice. The hard facts of the matter were that the money the colt could bring to the family might outweigh all other considerations, including Martin's desire to keep the animal.

"Clay!" Juan Morales stepped from the barn and waved an arm.

Clay grinned when he saw his neighbor. Although several years his junior, the Mexican rancher was the closest thing to a friend Clay could claim in this barren land. An inch shorter than Clay, Juan appeared at least twice the rancher's weight. That girth came from muscle and not fat. A neatly trimmed mustache crawled on Juan's upper lip when he returned the grin.

Behind Juan came three cousins—Augusto, Ernesto, and Manuel, each greeting the rancher with a "Señor Clay" and an acknowledging tilt of his head.

Clay welcomed them, calling the four men by name, then asked, "What brings the Morales clan by this sunny day? I didn't expect to see y'all till day after tomorrow to help move my stock closer to the creek."

Juan Morales, his wife, five children, three cousins, and a various assortment of aunts, uncles, and in-laws, who came and went on a sporadic basis, were Clay's closest neighbors. The Mexican ran a spread ten miles to the south.

Occasionally during the year, especially in the long spring and summer months, Juan and his cousins helped out on the Sweet Water Creek Ranch. When there was money to be made, they were paid. Usually their payment was in kind; Clay and Martin often rode the ten miles to the Morales ranch to help run Juan's stock. The trade-off was equally beneficial in a country where ranch hands were as scarce as hen's teeth.

"María's mother has come to visit." Juan spoke of his wife's mother. "Me and my cousins were in need of a rest from all the little jobs she finds for us."

The three younger men who stood a step behind the thirty-year-old Mexican smiled sheepishly and nodded their heads. It was Ernesto who said, "We are hunting rabbits for the stew."

Clay grinned. "Reckon you found a whole passel of them in the barn."

"As many as we found on the ride here, my friend." Juan's chuckle was echoed by his cousins.

Augusto added, "It is strange how the rabbits they shied from our trail. On other days they seem so plentiful. It's hard to keep your horse from stepping on them. But today"—Augusto threw up his hands and shrugged as though totally perplexed by the situation.

"Ain't that the way it always goes?" Clay played along. He had met Juan's mother-in-law during her last visit two years ago. He had been ready for any excuse to get away from the rotund woman after ten minutes.

Juan glanced back to the barn, which, like the ranch house, was constructed of flat rocks held together with adobe. "When Elizabeth told us you and Martin were up in the Bowl, I realized there would be a stage running through this evening. We were just checking on the horses. We were going to have them ready in case you and the boy got hung up looking for the mares and foals."

"One of the team has thrown a shoe and three others have loose shoes," Manuel said. "I was going to light a fire to heat the shoes."

Clay heaved an inward groan. Blacksmithing was backbreaking work, but it was something a man who settled so far from a town had to do for himself. "I'd appreciate that. I'll handle the loose shoes first, give the fire time to get hot enough to heat iron."

Ernesto pointed to four water barrels that stood outside the barn. "They are almost dry. Want that Augusto and I should fill them?"

Clay nodded his approval. "Get Martin to lend a hand."

Until the stagecoach reached the natural water basins of Hueco Tanks, over fifty miles to the east, the only water it would find would be in the two barrels it carried. Water in the desert was more important than a fresh team of horses. With sufficient water men could cross the hundred miles of desert to El Paso on foot if need be.

"I'll bring out the first horse," Juan said when he turned to the barn.

Following his friend just inside the structure, Clay stepped into a small tack room, its walls hung with harnesses, bridles, rope halters, and four saddles. The latter were all Mexican-made, with broad horns to solidly hold a rope when its opposite end was looped about the neck of a stubborn steer.

From a wooden peg, Clay took a leather apron and placed his hat on the empty peg. The apron, which covered him from chest to the knees, was now slick and stained from years of use. In a corner of the tack room he lifted an oblong wooden box from the floor and quickly rummaged through the prongs, files, and hammer within to make certain all his tools were where he left them. Martin had a bad habit of forgetting to return tools to their proper place.

At the bottom of the box he found a cracked coffee mug half-filled with horseshoe nails. He made a mental note to send an order to El Paso for more with the stage driver. The box also held ten horseshoes forged by a smith in the border town. Although having the shoes shaped saved work, he still had to fit them to a hoof. That meant fire, bellows, anvil, and hammer. He softly cursed. The desert was hot enough without having to work with red-hot iron over a blazing fire.

Outside, Juan stood holding a haltered bay gelding. "Right hind on this one. The shoe is pretty loose. You might have to put on a new one."

Clay gave a noncommittal grunt in reply while lifting each of the gelding's other three hooves and checking the shoes before examining the hoof Juan mentioned. "Shoe's still in good shape, but it's too loose just to tack back on. It'll have to come off."

Balancing the horse's ankle on a knee, Clay used the hammer's claw to pull out the four nails still holding the shoe. He tossed it aside and used a file to smooth the hoof.

"Sam Dunton is putting together a drive," Juan said. "He is talking about heading north the second week of May."

"Mmmmm." Clay half-listened while he placed the old shoe atop the filed hoof, and judged how much the curved sides would have to be hammered in to fit the hoof. He gave an approving nod. A few taps would do the trick. He would not have to fire the shoe.

"He has ten ranchers interested," Juan continued while Clay stepped outside the barn to where Manuel had set a small anvil beside the fire he stoked. "He asked me to see if you were interested?"

"What about you? Spring rains'll have your stock ready for a drive." Clay worked at the shoe with the hammer, lifted it for inspection, judged it slightly off on the left, and gave it two more sharp raps before returning to the horse.

"My cousins will go with my stock," Juan answered. "I will stay here and take care of the ranch."

"If they'll take my stock and not me, I'm interested." The shoe was a close-enough fit. Clay began to nail it in place, careful to avoid driving into the quick and leaving the horse lame.

"Dunton needs hands as well as cattle for the drive," Juan said.

"I can't leave here," Clay said around the nails he held at the side of his mouth. He now understood the reason for his friend's unexpected visit. "Not with the stage and my horses."

Juan tilted his head toward the rancher's son. "What about Martin? He is old enough, and he handles himself well."

Clay caught himself before he said, "But he's only fifteen." He remembered all he had done at the same age. A trail drive was almost a Sunday picnic in comparison. Martin was old enough for the drive, and he did know his way around cattle and horses.

"I'll have to think about it." Clay drove in the last of the nails, cut off the sharp points which protruded from the hoof, and began to file them smooth. "Have to see what Elizabeth thinks of the idea. And, of course, what Martin has to say."

"I would not take long doing that," Juan said. "Word is there is talk of quarantining all cattle coming into Kansas from Texas. Dunton thinks we need to get our cattle north before they pass some half-assed law that will cost us steers and money."

"I've heard rumors of quarantines because of Mexican fever." Clay released the hoof, straightened, and rubbed the small of his back.

"They call it Texas fever in Kansas," Juan said as he led the gelding to a stall at the back of the barn. "While they want the beef, they think Texas steers are causing all the sickness."

Clay shook his head. If it was not one of a thousand things in the cattle business, it was another waiting to rob a man of his livelihood. Mexican fever, as Texans called it, or Texas fever did not matter; it was still splenic fever. "I thought they'd proved it was ticks that caused the fever and not cattle."

"That is what some doctors are saying." Juan brought another bay from a stall. "But saying is not proving as far as those in Kansas are concerned."

"Damn!" Clay sucked at his teeth and spat. He didn't want to think about a trail drive. But Juan was right. He had to make a decision. A quarantine could tie up a herd for months. "When does Dunton want an answer?"

"He said next week, if possible." Juan halted the horse beside his friend.

"I'll tell Elizabeth the situation, then talk with Martin." Clay bent to look at the horse's hooves. "I'll get back to Dunton first of the week."

He pressed a thumb into the soft flesh beneath the animal's ankle, and the horse lifted its right foreleg. Clay stared at the hoof for a full five seconds before his mind focused on the fact that its shoe was securely in place. He let the leg drop and picked up the left foreleg and tried to get about the task at hand. His thoughts still wandered back to Martin.

The rancher had never seen himself as a mother hen when it came to his children. Yet, as he considered the possibility of his son leaving on his first trail drive, Clay's mind was assailed by a thousand doubts and an equal number of reasons why the boy should not go. To be certain Martin was almost a fully grown man, but the life he had faced in his fifteen years was far different from what Clay had experienced at the same age.

A trail drive carried a score of ways to rob the most experienced cowhand of his life. That was the root of Clay's uneasiness—the very real possibility that Martin might not return from the drive north. Clay had helped bury more than one man along the cattle trail, men drowned in river crossings, poisoned by snakebite, crushed beneath the hooves of stampeding steers, or cut down by Kiowa arrows.

Did all fathers face such fears when staring at the fact that it was time for their children to leave home? Clay's lips pursed, and he sucked at his teeth. He did not know; the men he called friends rarely spoke of their families, except to brag about their children's accomplishments. They kept what was in their hearts locked inside.

"Momma! Momma!"

Clay released the hoof and glanced back to see Sarah run toward the house. She carried a bowl with chicken feed streaming from it. The rancher looked up at his friend. "That old red rooster has it in for my girl. Chases her out of the chicken pen every time he gets a chance."

Juan chuckled. "My father had a rooster when I was a boy that thought its purpose in life was to tear an inch or three of hide off my legs whenever he saw me. I prayed to the Holy Virgin for the day my father would let a younger rooster rule the roost and we would have the old one for Sunday dinner."

"I can recall a—"

"Clay! Clay!" Elizabeth called to her husband, urgency in her voice. "Clay, you better come out here—right now."

The rancher stood straight. "I'd best see what the problem is. Be right back."

Juan nodded. "I am not going anywhere."

Clay walked outside the barn, eyes squinting against the sun's brightness. A few feet beyond the door to the ranch house, Sarah clung to her mother, arms wrapped tightly around Elizabeth's waist. "What's wrong? That ol' red tear into Sarah again?"

Elizabeth's head snapped around. Her eyes were wide and her facial features taut. Her right arm jerked up to stab a finger toward the north. "Clay, we've visitors coming."

The rancher frowned. Visitors were a rarity this far in the desert. He turned, shielding his eyes with a hand, and stared to where his wife pointed. His heart doubled its tempo. He blinked to make certain the sun was not playing tricks on him. It was not . . . Indians! There was no mistaking them, and they were headed directly for the ranch.

Four

"ELIZABETH, get Sarah in the house and stay there," Clay ordered, watching his wife respond without question. The danger of Indian attack was a real part of life for all families dwelling west of Fort Worth. Every man, woman, and child knew what was expected of them when the time came to face the fear that inhabited their every waking moment.

"Indians," Clay called out while he hastened back to the barn. "Get your rifles and make sure they're loaded and ready."

Martin and Juan's three cousins abandoned their appointed tasks and did as told.

Inside the barn, Juan stood holding two rifles and Clay's hat. "I saw them. I thought you would be wanting this."

He handed the rancher his rifle when Clay tore off the leather apron and tossed it inside the tack room. "You make out how many there are?"

"Nor if they are Apache or Comanche," the Mexican answered. "Too far off. But no doubt they are Indian."

"No doubt," Clay agreed, moving back outside with Juan behind him.

Without difficulty Clay located the band again. A small cloud of dust rose behind the approaching Indians. They were a half mile from the ranch and coming on slowly and deliberately.

"Martin, you and Ernesto and Augusto get over by the house. If there's trouble, duck inside." Clay waved the three toward the ranch house.

A man never liked to divide his strength, but there was a strategy in the rancher's orders. With three men inside the house, Juan,

Manuel, and he would take to the barn if it came to a fight. That way the men in the house could keep attackers off the barn's roof, the only portion of the structure vulnerable to fire, while those in the barn did the same for the house.

Besides catching the braves in a crossfire, Clay thought.

"They do not seem to be in a hurry getting here." Juan peered at the approaching band. "That is a good sign. Maybe they do not come to cause trouble."

Clay silently agreed—with doubts. Apaches and Comanches were well-known for their tricks. The obvious was never obvious with such sly fighters.

"They are slow because most of them are on foot," Manuel said. "I can only make out five riders. The rest are on foot."

"On foot?" Clay's brow creased with doubt.

"*Sí,*" Juan confirmed.

Clay saw them now. Manuel was right. Five of the Indians were on horseback. The rest followed behind the leaders on foot. "Looks to be at least ten braves wearing out moccasin leather."

"Or more." Juan tried to count aloud the braves he saw on foot. He began three times before giving up with a curse. "They keep moving about behind the riders. It is hard to make out one from the other."

"They are Apache," Manuel said. "Lipan."

Clay nodded. Even at a quarter mile, he saw their long-sleeved shirts, traded or taken from whites in raids. Beneath flapping breechclouts the braves wore leather moccasins that ran from their feet to their knees. Their long black hair was held from their copper-hued faces by knotted headbands of brightly colored cloth. None of those faces was streaked with the paints of war.

"I'll be damned if I can figure out what they have on their minds." Clay shook his head. "I've never seen Lipans act like this."

"No need trying to outguess them, my friend." This from Juan, who double-checked his rifle. "They will be here soon enough."

Their methodical pace unwavering, the Lipans came within a hundred yards of the ranch house and halted. For several minutes they stood staring at the rifle-armed men as though waiting for some reaction. Clay and his companions held their positions, weapons ready as they returned the Indians' stares.

"Fears-Not-Death." An ancient voice hailed Clay by the name the Apaches had given a fifteen-year-old boy.

An old brave, hair streaked with running silver, nudged the side of a sorrel pony with the heels of his moccasins. The horse took three strides forward, and the old brave drew him to a halt. In Spanish, the Lipan said, "It is I, Crow-Who-Flies-Far. I come to speak with you, not to harm you or your family or your home."

"Crow-Who-Flies-Far! Sweet Mother of Jesus!" Juan's words came as an awe-filled whisper. "I thought he was long ago dead."

"It doesn't seem to be that way, does it?" Clay replied. "Else that's his ghost sitting out there on that pony, and he's come to haunt us."

Neither Juan nor Manuel smiled at their friend's weak attempt at a jest. Clay didn't blame them. Crow-Who-Flies-Far was a legended war chief among the Lipans and feared by every white and brown man in Texas living west of the Pecos River.

While a young Clay Thorton sought to avenge the murder of his father, Crow-Who-Flies-Far gained a name for himself by terrorizing settlers who came from the east to claim the land around Fort Davis. Nor was his name unknown to farmers along the Rio Grande —often a favorite target of Crow-Who-Flies-Far and his warriors.

Like Juan, Clay believed the old Apache chief to be dead, killed in the raid on Manzanita Spring last year. The rancher was certain he had seen the old brave ridden down by a young private. Obviously his eyes had lied.

Holding his rifle before him so that the Apaches could see it, Clay took three steps forward. "There are many who believed Crow-Who-Flies-Far to be hunting with his ancestors. I am surprised to see him at my door."

A dry sound that imitated a chuckle came from the ancient chief's throat. "There are many Texans and Mexicans who would wish me to be in the company of my ancestors, but I do not live to fulfill their wishes."

"My eyes are wide and can see that." Clay spoke in Spanish, a language the Apaches had learned from the earliest European explorers. "What is it you want from Fears-Not-Death?"

"I and those who travel with me have come a long way." Crow-Who-Flies-Far lifted an arm and swept a hand toward the Guadalupe Mountains. "Two days we have come from beyond the mountains to talk with you. We will leave as we have come if you will not hear my words."

Clay did not doubt the old brave; an Apache did not lie. However, he often chose not to speak the whole truth. If the rancher did not parlay with them, the Lipans would turn and walk away.

Until they're out of sight, Clay thought. After that twenty Apaches were apt to do anything. He was certain whatever brought the Lipans over the mountains was important to them. They would not leave without getting it—or trying.

"I will talk with you, after we have shared tobacco and coffee," Clay called back to Crow-Who-Flies-Far. He then said to Martin. "Get me my cigars and some matches from the house. Tell your ma to put on coffee—a lot of it."

"Twenty," Juan said softly beside Clay. "There are twenty of them in all. Two carry spears, and five have bows. I see no firearms —pistols or rifles."

Clay nodded. A quick perusal of the braves proved Juan correct. However, each brave who stepped forward did carry a hunting knife. An Apache with knife in hand was as capable of spilling blood as one holding a rifle. Although they were less likely to start anything with such sparse arms, especially when the men they faced carried rifles and pistols.

"Without being obvious about it," Clay said to Juan and Manuel, "take a look around and make sure Crow-Who-Flies-Far ain't trying to pull a fast one. That he just wants to talk doesn't mean there ain't another band sneaking up on us who would like to have our scalps hanging outside their wickiups."

"We shall do that, my friend," Juan answered. "It would be like Apaches to try such a deception."

"These are not braves." Manuel leaned close to his cousin. "They are no more than children."

The three men had been too concerned with the Apache numbers, weapons, and intent, to notice the age of the Apaches following the old war chief until Manuel mentioned it. Now that Clay's gaze traveled to the Lipans' faces, the rancher saw how young the Indians were. At least ten of the twenty who approached the barn were younger than Martin. They could not have been more than thirteen or fourteen.

Clay found himself releasing a cautious, silent sigh of relief. As savage as they were when fighting an enemy, Apaches did not bring children on blood raids. The age of Crow-Who-Flies-Far's warriors also explained the dearth of weapons among the Lipans. Children

did not carry rifles, lances, and bows. Those the Apache reserved
for the males of their bands who had reached manhood.

"Pa, here's your cigars and matches." Martin handed his father a
cardboard box half-filled with twofers a stage driver had brought
from Santa Fe.

Taking the smokes, Clay said softly, "Move on back to the house.
Stay close to your mother and sister."

The rancher watched his son edge away, eyes on the Indians, who
drew their horses to a halt and dismounted. Martin positioned himself in the breezeway that connected the kitchen to the house. Elizabeth had their son's rifle to protect her should a fight erupt.

"It is good that you will talk with us, Fears-Not-Death." Crow-
Who-Flies-Far handed his horse to one of the young Lipans. "It is
an honor when one who is such a great enemy of the People allows
them to enter his home and talk in peace."

The ancient warrior settled cross-legged in the sand and motioned for the older braves to do the same. When they were seated,
Clay followed their lead. The younger braves with the horses moved
back a few yards and stood silently, watching their elders.

All except one, Clay saw out of the corner of an eye. The brave
was neither a child nor an Apache.

In spite of his general appearance, the brave wore leather leg-
gings and shirt, both bearing the beadwork of a Kiowa, ally of the
Comanches who ruled the far-sweeping plains to the north. Taller
than most Apaches, the brave also lacked the stocky build of a
Lipan. He was lean and sinewy, his movements gracefully slow and
determined like those of a cat. Also unlike an Apache, his facial
features were sharp and distinct, as though chiseled from a block of
flesh and blood. Pox marks pitted his high cheeks. His dark, red-
rimmed eyes constantly shifted like the eyes of a man who checked
to make sure his actions went unnoticed.

Clay caught himself before he gave an involuntary shake of his
head. How had a Kiowa come to be with Lipans? Neither Comanches nor Kiowas were known for their friendship to the Apaches—
especially hated were the Lipans, who once scouted for early Texans in their battles against the Comanche bands.

To find a Kiowa among Apaches left a knot in Clay's stomach. It
was more than wrong; it was unnatural like sheep inviting a coyote
into their fold. Although the rancher would never compare
Apaches to meek sheep.

Clay glanced at Juan and tilted his head toward the Kiowa in Apache disguise. The Mexican's eyes widened then narrowed. Juan looked back at his friend and gave his head a little affirmative tilt, silently signaling he would watch the brave.

"It is also good an honored enemy such as Fears-Not-Death would share tobacco and coffee with those of the People," Crow-Who-Flies-Far spoke, drawing Clay's attention from the Kiowa.

"Often braves of the Lipan Apaches have ridden to my home and been welcomed as friends," Clay answered as he lit a cigar, puffed twice, and passed it to Crow-Who-Flies-Far.

The old war chief's references to "honored enemy" held a double meaning, Clay recognized. First, Crow-Who-Flies-Far sought to compliment the rancher and gain his ear. Secondly, the aging war chief verbally probed to test Clay's mood, to discern if the white man was receptive. Clay had assured him he would truly listen by mentioning the friendly encounters with Lipans during his long years in a land the Indians once considered their own.

After taking two deep draws off the cigar and exhaling the blue smoke, Crow-Who-Flies-Far passed the stogie to the brave beside him, who, in turn, repeated the action. So the cigar and two more smokes made their way around the small circle. Martin eventually brought a pot of coffee and mugs. At the same leisurely pace, each Indian drank two cups of coffee.

Time and again, Clay found himself quelling the impatience that rose within him. It was not the Apache way to hurry things. Talk would come when it was time for talk. Until then the Lipans considered it rude not to enjoy fully the hospitality shown by a host, even if that host was white-skinned.

Crow-Who-Flies-Far cleared his throat and spoke, "Your words are true. I cannot count on my two hands the times Fears-Not-Death has traded with the People when times were lean."

Traded for and given the Lipans steers in harsh winters and droughts that sucked moisture from the land, Clay thought. Not charity but safety had governed the rancher's actions. It was far better to deal openly with hungry Apaches than to deny them and have braves raiding the herd.

"Times are lean again, Fears-Not-Death," Crow-Who-Flies-Far continued. "The winter on the other side of the mountains was bitter. The land is new to us. We do not know it, nor does it know the People."

While Clay listened to the ancient chief speak of the harsh winter with its snow and ice, he began to understand why Crow-Who-Flies-Far had come and why the braves he brought with him were so young. There were no older, experienced braves; these were all who remained. The once proud Lipan band driven from Texas during the attack at Manzanita was no more.

Crow-Who-Flies-Far confirmed this as he told of a raging blizzard that separated the survivors of the band. Those who lost their way were never found. Lost, too, in the harsh storm were the Apache horses—some breaking their tethers and running away, others eaten when braves could find no other meat to fill the bellies of their starving children.

"It is the long, cruel winter that brings us back into the land of the Texans, risking the anger of the long-knives with their blue shirts." Crow-Who-Flies-Far spoke of the certain death the Lipans would face should they encounter an army patrol out of Fort Bliss. "My people are in need of meat. If our children are to live, they must eat until we can find others of the People."

Those others the Apache mentioned, Clay knew, were the Mescalero bands who roamed the lands beyond the Texas border in the New Mexico Territory.

"And horses, Old One." This came from the Kiowa, who stood at the corral containing the mares and foals Clay and Martin had driven down from the Bowl that morning. "A brave must have a horse if he is to hunt and keep the cooking fires supplied with fresh meat."

Crow-Who-Flies-Far's head snapped up, and he stared at the young brave. Clay saw both anger and hurt hanging around the old man's eyes. Both stemmed from the Kiowa's words—words spoken from outside the council circle as though attempting to usurp the power of the band's chosen leader.

Clay understood enough Apache to catch the gist of Crow-Who-Flies-Far's sharp reply to the brave. In less than polite words and tone, he told the younger warrior to keep in his place and contain his words. The Kiowa grunted and said nothing else.

Crow-Who-Flies-Far turned back to Clay, but before the old man could speak, the rancher asked, "How is it that a Kiowa travels with the People?"

"He who was Kiowa and now is of the People is called Coyote Man," the old chief replied. "After the fight with the bluecoats following the melting of the ice last year, my people fled across the mountains. After our wounds were healed and our braves could ride, we traveled north searching for a land that would welcome our wickiups."

From Crow-Who-Flies-Far's description, Clay judged the surviving Lipans traveled to the fringes of the Texas high plains, the Llano Estacado—a dangerous territory for Apaches. It was there that the Antelope-Eater bands of Comanches made their home. Where there were Comanches, Kiowas usually could be found.

"The Kiowas attacked our camp," Crow-Who-Flies-Far said. "Coyote Man was taken as captive. Before he could be given to the squaws to be tortured—as befitted one as cowardly as to be born a Kiowa—he escaped the rawhide bonds that held his arms and legs."

During that escape a coyote entered the Lipan camp, the old man said. "A coyote with foam running from its mouth and teeth bared. The coyote charged a chief called Pronghorn-Eater who had awakened early that morning and sought to relieve himself. Coyote Man saw this. Instead of running, he faced the coyote with a spear he had taken and killed the animal. For saving his life, Pronghorn-Eater adopted the Kiowa and gave him his name. Coyote Man now walks as one with the People, Comanche and Kiowa. He has proven to be both a great hunter and warrior."

Crow-Who-Flies-Far paused and looked back at the Kiowa, who walked to the pen beside the barn and stared at Martin's Appaloosa mare and colt. "Coyote Man still carries many of the ways of those who gave him breath. He has yet to learn to respect those whose experience greatly outweighs his own."

Simply put, Clay realized, the brave's bones would now be bleaching in the sun if an Apache war chief had not been caught with his pants down when a mad coyote had run into the Lipans' camp. Luck often made strange bedfellows and, it appeared, equally strange adopted sons.

Or that was what Crow-Who-Flies-Far wanted Clay to believe. Somehow the rancher could not swallow the chief's tale. It came too easily from his tongue—as though the Apache expected to be questioned about Coyote Man and had carefully prepared a yarn to explain the brave's presence. However, Clay realized the old chief would add nothing to his story.

"We talked of meat and horses before Coyote Man spoke," Crow-

Who-Flies-Far brought the conversation back to the reason the Lipans had traveled to the ranch. "We would trade with you for both, Fears-Not-Death. We have brought skins."

The chief waved a hand to the young boys holding the horses. Immediately they lifted two bundles from the backs of the ponies, brought them to Crow-Who-Flies-Far, and spread them on the ground.

Carefully, like a man examining the confirmation of a blooded horse, Clay lifted each of the ten deerskins the Apaches brought in trade. Once a valued commodity, the hides had lost any real price as whites pushed farther and farther into the lands once solely inhabited by the Indian bands. Of what use were harsh, rough buckskins when wool and linen were available at dry goods stores? Deerskin might make a decent pair of moccasins but lacked the endurance of bull hide when it came to a pair of sturdy boots.

"These will buy you three steers," Clay finally said after enough time to display he appreciated the finest of the hides.

"And ponies?" Crow-Who-Flies-Far asked. "We also came to trade for ponies."

Clay shook his head. "I will not trade for horses."

Giving food to a band already crushed by soldiers and a killing winter was one thing. Starvation was no way for any man to die, no matter what the color of his skin. Horses were another matter.

"You see all the ponies left to our band." Crow-Who-Flies-Far waved an arm to the five mounts. "Our braves must have ponies to hunt."

Still Clay refused. Although, he was certain the Lipans would use mounts to hunt, he also knew horses would give the Apaches long legs. A man with four legs beneath him instead of two had the ability to ride long and far. With Apaches that meant the ability to attack ranchers on both sides of the border. Clay would be no part of that.

Fully for half an hour, Crow-Who-Flies-Far pled for mounts in his own fashion, speaking of starving children and squaws, of his dying band. Clay simply refused the old man, steadfastly standing his ground. The Apaches could have meat for their children, but no horses for their braves.

"We have five rifles back in our wickiups," Crow-Who-Flies-Far revealed. "We will return with them for the ponies."

If the Lipans were willing to admit five rifles, Clay thought, that meant they had twice that number in their camp. Those rifles meant dead ranchers. Again he refused.

From Crow-Who-Flies-Far's expression, the rancher realized the chief knew he had played his only hole card and it was not enough. The Lipan nodded. "Then we shall trade for cattle. Four steers, not three."

It was robbery. Crow-Who-Flies-Far knew it, and the Indian knew that Clay knew it. Had the afternoon not been growing late, Clay would have haggled as the Lipan Apache expected. Instead, the rancher gave the deerskins a quick once-over again and nodded his acceptance. "Four steers for the hides, you've struck a deal."

Crow-Who-Flies-Far could not hide the shock on his face, even with the quick nod he made in reply. "Will you ride with us to pick the beeves?"

Undoubtedly the Lipans had scouted the herd before coming to the ranch, ready to take what they wanted should Clay have refused their trade. Under normal circumstances, Clay would have gone with them to select the steers. Today a stage was due, and he still had a team to prepare.

"You may pick the cattle you wish," he answered, "as long as they are steers. No cows or bulls."

"No cows or bulls," the Apache repeated. "It is agreed."

The time for talk past, Crow-Who-Flies-Far pushed from the ground, the rest of the braves rising with him. "We will go now."

"May your journey back to your camp be a safe one," Clay said, watching the Lipans turn to leave.

"It is said that you sell horses to other white men." Coyote Man spoke. He turned from the small pen to face Clay. "Is that true?"

The rancher's gaze met the brave's piercing dark eyes. The Kiowa's stance, his tone, the way he held his body spoke of contempt. Clay nodded. "I sell horses."

"I would buy a pony." An amused smile curled one side of the Indian's mouth as though his words were some private joke. Coyote Man opened a single button on the belly of his black wool shirt. He eased a hand inside to withdraw a small leather pouch that he balanced in an outstretched palm. "I have the white man's gold— five of his round coins."

Clay wondered about the unlucky rancher or wayfarer who had once carried the money pouch before the Kiowa had looted it from his dead body.

"Five of the white man's gold coins to buy an Indian pony for one of the People." The smile remained on Coyote Man's lips when his head tilted toward the Appaloosa mare. "I would have this pony or the colt with the spots on their backsides."

A cold spike of dread drove into the base of Clay's spine as he caught a hint of where the Kiowa attempted to maneuver him. He said nothing, but continued to stare at the brave.

"These are not white men's ponies." Coyote Man shook his hand, letting the coins in the pouch jingle as though he hoped the sound would tempt the rancher. "Such ponies are mated by Indians in the woods of the far north lands. I know, for I have seen them before—once by the river waters of the great mountains to the west."

Clay had heard of the Nez Perce tribe, who supposedly had given rise to the Appaloosa breed. What surprised him was that the Kiowa apparently had encountered the Nez Perce or at least others who had. From his description, Coyote Man had traveled all the way to the Rocky Mountains. A strange journey for a plains raider.

The Kiowa gave the pouch another healthy shake. "I will buy one or both from you. They do not belong with the white man."

Clay sucked down a steadying breath to make sure his tone was strong and clear. "The mare and foal are not for sale."

"The white men sell all things," Coyote Man pressed. "I have the white man's money, and I would buy them in the white man's way."

"No." Clay shook his head. "The horses are not mine to sell."

Coyote Man's smile widened to a pleased grin. "If the ponies are not yours, then you have no claim to them. I will take both mare and colt."

Boldly, with complete disregard for the rifles held by white man and Mexican, Coyote Man pivoted sharply and leaped onto the small corral's fence. Leisurely, as though he challenged Clay and the others to stop him, he climbed.

A second of doubt froze Clay where he stood. His first reaction was to shoulder his rifle and shoot the would-be horse thief as he would any man he caught trying to steal one of his horses. This was not any man; Coyote Man was accompanied by nineteen Lipan Apaches. Gunfire would ignite a fight—a bloody fight Clay was certain the Kiowa was determined to start.

A blur of motion shot forward on Clay's left. Martin, rifle tossed aside, ran straight for the brazen Kiowa. A yard from the pen the boy launched himself into the air to tackle the brave about the waist with both arms. "Touch either of them horses, and I'll kill you."

Together, Kiowa and boy spilled to the ground. Martin groaned, air driven from his lungs, as his back slammed into the ground with the full weight of Coyote Man atop him. He could not keep his grip as his arms flung full wide.

The Kiowa reacted instantly. Muscles flowing with the fluidity of a cat, Coyote Man rolled from the boy and sprang to his feet. In one smooth motion his right hand dropped to his waist and freed a hunting knife from its sheath. A victorious brave ready to put a quick end to the fight.

"Stop!" Elizabeth's voice rang out with unquavering strength. "Move one more inch toward my son, and I'll put this bullet right through your heart!"

Coyote Man halted. His head snapped around to stare at the woman who stood sighting down the barrel of Martin's discarded carbine. His grin twisted to a contemptuous sneer. This was, after all, a woman, a mere white woman, who stood against him.

"I mean it." Elizabeth shouted, her tone as steady as the rifle she held. "I'll put this bullet right through your heart. I swear by God, I will!"

It was doubtful that the Kiowa understood the English Elizabeth spoke. But Clay saw the hatred in Coyote Man's eyes that said he fully understood the carbine, as well as the rifles Juan and his cousins cocked and lifted.

For seconds that seemed to stretch into hours, the Kiowa's dark gaze shifted between those rifles and the boy on the ground. Then, with a disgusted grunt, he spat to the sand, sheathed the blade, turned, and walked away, heading westward without a glance over his shoulder.

"His blood is that of the Kiowa, not the real People." Crow-Who-Flies-Far's voice sliced through the uneasy silence.

Clay's head turned to the old war chief. The simple statement was as close to an apology as he could expect from the Apache.

"We will go now and select our steers." With that Crow-Who-Flies-Far mounted his pony. He waited until the others had done the same, then reined to the west with his band following.

Clay turned to Juan. "Get Martin on his feet and dust him off."

When the Mexican stepped toward the boy, Clay crossed from the barn to the ranch house where Elizabeth stood watching the

Lipans depart. The carbine remained firmly nestled in the hollow of her shoulder, and her finger still lay wrapped about the trigger.

"You can put that down now," he said gently. "They're gone. They won't be giving us any more trouble."

He saw a tremor of relief shoot through his wife's delicate frame. For an instant she hesitated. She then lowered the carbine and handed it to her husband. "I would've shot him if he had gone for Martin."

"I know that." Clay slipped an arm about her waist and drew her close to lightly kiss her forehead. "So did he."

Elizabeth's gaze followed the Lipans and the dust trail that rose to the air behind them. "Are you sure they're gone?"

"Sure," Clay answered. "They got what they came for. They won't be bothering us again today."

Her hand found his and squeezed it tightly as she led him through the door to their home. Inside, she reassured their daughter that everything was all right, then sent the girl outside. "You and your brother stay away from the house until me or your pa calls you. We need some time to be together right now."

Clay did not question his wife when she closed and barred the door. Nor was he surprised as she took his hand again and escorted him into their bedroom. Sixteen years of marriage had taught him the full meaning of the glow he now saw in Elizabeth's blue eyes.

When she turned from closing the bedroom door, he took her in his arms and kissed her deeply. In all those years, their lovemaking had been most passionate after they had faced and stood down danger together. It was as though the intimate union of their bodies was a reaffirmation of the life that coursed through their veins.

As their lips parted, Clay lifted his wife in his arms and carried her to their bed. From outside came the clank of hammered iron. Clay smiled as his mouth returned to his wife's lips. Apparently Juan understood their need for privacy and tended the blacksmithing.

Five

CLAY STOOD at the open door of the ranch house and gazed across a land shadowed by a gibbous moon. His eyes lifted to the sky and the stars that burned steadily there. He knew the names of some of the shapes they formed in the heavens. That fuzzy patch of stars hanging about two hand widths above the eastern horizon was called the Manger. Higher was a sickle shape and triangle; that was Leo the lion. Although, the rancher admitted that neither constellation looked anything like their names.

"See anything?"

Elizabeth edged behind him, her hands resting on his arm. The warmth of their lovemaking hours ago still felt as though it radiated from her palms and fingertips. It was a good feeling that left Clay with the desire to snuggle close to this woman who stood at the center of the life he had built.

"Nothing but stars," he answered. "Not too many of them. The moon's bright tonight."

Her hands tightened on his arm. "Come to supper. You aren't going to make the stage get here any faster by standing at the door looking for it. We've got company, and they're hungry."

"So am I." He smiled at her. "I ain't had a bite to eat since morning."

With Elizabeth on his arm, he turned back into their home's main room. It was simple and spacious when compared to the soddies and lean-tos used by most ranchers living on the plains: a full fifteen by fifteen feet square. A fireplace stood on the back wall with two rocking chairs set in front of it. The walls were lined with adobe mud, whitewashed and scrubbed clean. Here and there wooden shelves, filled with books and nicknacks, were pegged to the walls. Three doors led from the room, each opening on a bedroom.

The last two rooms Clay had built for each of his children. There should have been a fourth bedroom, but their second child, a boy they named Jonathan after Elizabeth's father, had died of a fever less than a month after his birth. The child now rested beside Clay's mother and father.

In the middle of the room stood a table, around which Juan, his cousins, Martin, and Sarah waited. The legs of the wooden table sat inside tin cans half-filled with kerosene, a measure designed to keep insects from climbing from floor to table top and sharing the family's meals.

And the insects were numerous. There was no way to keep them out of a house in the desert where the cool of the stone structure offered refuge from an unmerciful sun. The wooden floor did nothing to help the situation. Scorpions liked to hide beneath the boards during the day and come out at night to hunt.

The latter problem and their painful stings might have been eliminated with a packed-earth floor to the house. Elizabeth would have no part of an earthen floor. She said a house was not a house unless there was a floor on which to place a rug. So Clay had brought boards from El Paso for that floor as a gift to commemorate their first anniversary.

The floor, after fifteen years and two growing children, was more than a little worn, Clay realized. He added it to a growing list of things to replace when the horses began to bring in money. He refused even to think *if.* The horses would pay off; he was certain of that.

"It is not unusual for the stage to run late," Juan said when Clay seated himself at the head of the table. "They might have run into some bad weather. I noticed storm clouds on the northern horizon before sundown."

"Guess I'm still a mite edgy from our Lipan visitors." Clay accepted a large bowl of pinto beans from Elizabeth and ladled them onto his plate. He crumbled a wedge of cornbread into the soup before slicing two rings of onion atop it. "The day's been long. I'm ready to put it and myself to bed."

He saw Elizabeth's eyes rise to him and the slight blush that colored her cheeks. He reached beneath the table and patted her knee. Her blush widened.

"It has been a day for Martin, too." Ernesto grinned across the table at the boy. "First, he awakes to find that he is sleeping with a puma, then he decides to take on a Kiowa brave with his bare hands."

"Aye, this one has turned into much man." Manuel, who sat beside the boy, slapped Martin's back. "Someday they will sing songs about his bravery and his deeds."

"I'd rather they'd write songs about how he outlived Methuselah." Clay lifted a spoonful of beans to his mouth.

"When the women hear those songs, they will flock about our young Martin and give to him their hearts," Manuel continued.

Augusto laughed. "With luck they might give him more than their hearts."

Juan shot a disapproving glance at his cousin, reminding the younger man that they ate among mixed company. Augusto's face went somber, and he returned to his meal, leaving any further off-color comments unspoken.

"I wasn't being brave." Martin's eyes downturned in obvious embarrassment. "I was just protecting what was mine. I wasn't going to let that Indian take my mare and colt."

Juan looked at the boy. "Often bravery is no more than a man standing up for what is his own." He paused as though assuring himself Martin understood his meaning. He then added with a wink. "Just make sure you stand up and are not laying on your backside in the sand."

Juan's comment even brought a smile, although touched with chagrin, to Martin's face. "I reckon I did act a mite rash this afternoon. But I couldn't think of anything else to do."

The problem, Clay thought while he studied his son over the edge of a coffee cup, was that Martin did not think at all. Although he admired the boy's display of grit, his brash action very well could have started a bloody fight with the Apaches. Coyote Man had been baiting them, seeking an open confrontation. Martin had snapped up that bait hook, line, and sinker. Had the brave not been of Kiowa blood, Clay was certain that Crow-Who-Flies-Far and the other Lipans would have come to his aid without batting an eye.

Later, Clay told himself. He would talk to his son later and hopefully impress on him the importance of thinking out a situation before he acted. At the dinner table with a house full of guests, who were impressed by his courage, was not the right time. A father's comments would appear as a reprimand or an attempt to belittle Martin's action.

"Clay,"—Elizabeth rested her hand on his wrist as he set his coffee mug on the table—"I think I hear something."

The dinner conversation died away. Heads turned to the open doorway and cocked slightly. The distant jingle of harnesses sounded in the night.

"It's the stage!" Clay pushed from the table. He heard the hollow pounding of hooves and the creaks and groans of metal and wood as the coach moved over the rocky terrain. He frowned; apprehension crept along his spine. "Something's wrong. The driver's bringing her in too fast. He's driving the team hard."

Everyone within the house followed him outside. The brightness of the moon revealed the stagecoach, a dark silhouette against the sandy terrain, a half mile from the ranch house.

"The man driving that team is a madman," Juan said over Clay's shoulder. "The ground is soft, too sandy. If a wheel sinks in, he will overturn the rig."

The rancher agreed, but there was nothing he could do. He was not driving the team. "Martin, get the lanterns and let 'em know we're here waiting."

Clay scanned the night-shadowed country behind the stage, searching for the cause of the driver's haste. Nothing, he saw nothing, but there was no doubting the man at the reins was in a hurry.

"I'll clear the table and prepare for the passengers." Elizabeth took Sarah's hand and led the young girl back into the house.

"We'd best get to the barn and ready the team," Clay said when his son came back carrying two blazing lamps. "If that driver's in such a rush, he won't be wanting to stay around here and visit long."

Juan and his three cousins had two horses in harness when the coach shuddered to a halt before the barn's open double doors. The pungent smell of horse sweat from the lathered team bit into Clay's nostrils.

"Thorton, we got trouble, man! Bad trouble." A short man with a mustache that drooped all the way to his jawline tossed the team's reins down to the waiting rancher with his left hand.

"Indians?" Clay recognized the driver, Cotton Evans, a man who usually rode shotgun rather than at the reins. This night he sat alone in the driver's box. "Martin, unhitch the team and get 'em inside. Give 'em water, but not enough to flounder 'em."

"Ain't no rush, boy," the driver said when he scooted to the edge of the box. "We ain't goin' nowhere quick. Agggahh!"

The groan jerked Clay's head up. A pained expression twisted Cotton's face as he muttered a string of curses. The rancher also saw why the man had used his left arm with the reins. He cradled a broken right arm in a makeshift sling made from an undershirt.

"Ain't no redskin done this." Cotton let Clay help him from the driver's box. "We was back about fifteen miles when the right front wheel hit a rock 'bout the same time the left 'un slipped into a pothole. Next thing I know I was a-flying through the air head over tail. Came down smack-dab atop a boulder 'bout the size of that there barn. That's how I got this." He nodded to his arm.

"Get yourself into the house, and I'll be along soon as I help the passengers out of the coach," Clay said. "That arm needs settin'. I'll tend it soon as I get the passengers settled inside."

Cotton shook his head. "It ain't all that easy, Thorton. I ain't the only one what's got things broken. Two of my passengers got broken arms, and another's leg's busted. You see, I wasn't just thrown off the box; the stage overturned. It was hell back there." Cotton paused and swallowed hard. "Hurt wasn't all we got. Ken Weaver was kilt. Neck broke when he was throwed from the stage. I got his body inside."

The rancher now understood why the stage's shotgun had been at the reins. Ken Weaver usually took the driver's seat on the Santa Fe to El Paso run.

"Guess we were lucky we didn't bust a wheel or axle," Cotton continued as he stepped to the side of the coach. "My six passengers who weren't hurt were enough to get us righted again. These old celerity wagons might be rough ridin', but they're lightweight. If this had been a Concord, odds are we'd still be walkin' in to your place. One of them fancy Concord coaches weighs a ton or more."

Clay stopped the man when he started to throw back the canvas that covered the stagecoach. "I'll take care of this. I've got some neighbors visiting. They'll help with the passengers. You get in the house and tell Elizabeth what's happened. Tell her to get ready to help with the doctoring."

Another grimace of pain crossed Cotton's face. He didn't argue, but simply tilted his head in acceptance and walked toward the house.

Calling to Juan and his cousins, Clay opened the wagon's canvas flaps, tied on the outside to cut the trail dust entering the coach. Six men piled out to help another two with arms in slings.

A passenger pointed to a man laying on the coach's floor. "Mr. Oliver there is gonna need a litter or something. He ain't able to walk with his leg busted and all. Ridin' in here damned neared kilt him."

"We'll take care of him. Y'all go into the house. There's hot food and coffee inside." Clay pointed to the ranch house's open door and gently nudged one man forward. The others followed as the man stumbled toward the house's entrance.

Inside the coach, the injured Mr. Oliver was stretched out beside the body of the stage's driver. Oliver's head lifted and he grinned at Clay. "I ain't hurtin' all as bad as that McGery let on. Had me a pint of whiskey tucked away in my coat. It cut the pain right nicely."

The whiskey had been at least a hundred proof if Clay judged correctly from the smell of the man's breath. The rancher did not condemn the man's action. Oliver's leg needed to be set before he was moved. That meant handling the task right in the stage. With the man half-drunk, Clay's job would be easier.

"There's a torn tarp folded in the corner of the tack room," Clay said as Juan came from the barn.

In turn, the Mexican signaled one of his cousins to retrieve the tarpaulin before running to Clay's side. "Holy Mother, that is Ken Weaver. Is he hurt bad?"

"About as bad as it gets," Clay answered. "He's dead. Help me get him out of here."

Together they dragged the body forward, lifted, and placed the dead stage driver on the tarp Augusto spread on the ground. While Juan and Augusto wrapped and tied the body in the heavy canvas, Clay walked behind the barn. From a small stack of boards, he selected an assortment for use as splints. In the tack room he gathered two burlap grain sacks and sliced them into strips before he returned to the stagecoach and Mr. Oliver.

There he had Juan climb in and hold the man's shoulders. Clay then carefully took the man's broken leg. He steeled himself against the man's cries and pulled the leg outward until the broken ends of bone slipped together. With alacrity, he splinted the leg with two long lengths of board and tied them securely with five burlap strips.

Clay turned to the three Morales cousins. "Let Mr. Oliver get his breath back, then help him in the house. There's a pile of mesquite and oak branches beside the kitchen that Elizabeth uses for kindling. Take a look and see if there's one long enough and strong enough for this man to use as a crutch."

"Juan,"—Clay waved to his friend from the coach.—"That's one down. We've got three broken arms inside that need tending."

CLAY'S GAZE moved about the main room of his home while he sipped from a steaming cup of coffee. It looked more like an army field hospital than a family dwelling. Although there had been only four broken bones in the wreck, not one of the nine passengers escaped without a collection of cuts, bruises, scraps, and bumps.

Elizabeth, Sarah, and Martin had attended each of the passengers with soap and warm water and sulfur powder to fight infection. About the heads of two men were bandages cut from blue floral flour sacks. Sacks, Clay realized, Elizabeth had been saving to use for a new dress for Sarah. Material for a daughter's spring dress was yet another item he added to his growing mental list of things he needed to purchase.

With a bowl of soupy pinto beans and cornbread in his good left hand, Cotton Evans crossed the room to stand beside Clay. The stage's shotgun lifted the bowl to his mouth and drank from it like a mug. He chewed at the beans a few seconds before swallowing. "Reckon all this was a mite more than you were expecting, huh?"

Clay smiled and nodded, then took another sip of the coffee. This whole day had been more than he expected.

"I also guess you've been thinking over the situation and realize I ain't in no condition to be driving that stage outside," Cotton went on. "Not with no broken arm. Nearly turned the coach over twice trying to get here."

Elizabeth arched a questioning eyebrow when she walked to the table to refill one of the passenger's coffee mugs. "Perhaps one of these men can handle a team, Mr. Evans."

"Not likely, ma'am." Cotton shook his head. "These are merchants and store clerks for the most part. Lucky if any of 'em could even sit on the back of a horse."

Elizabeth's face set firm and solid. She drew a heavy breath. "My husband can handle a team of horses."

From his wife's tone, Clay recognized she did not like what he had to do, but she also accepted it was expected of him. It was his responsibility.

"Reckon how I knew that, Missus Thorton, and I guess that was what I was trying to get around to asking of your husband." Cotton took another gulp from the bowl. "Can you cut loose from here for a few days?"

Few days! Clay silently cursed the conclusion to one of the longest days in his life. It was a full eighty miles from the ranch into El Paso —with no way station in between. That meant a team had to be paced slow and easy. Pushed hard, the horses would die from the desert heat. A man on foot could travel almost as far in a day as could a team pulling a stage loaded with nine passengers.

The only water to be found on the journey was at a mountainous stand of upthrusted granite called Hueco Tanks, so named because of basin-like depressions in the rock that served to collect water from rain and dew. Even after reaching the tanks, there was still another thirty miles of desert to Fort Bliss and El Paso.

Two and a half days to the Rio Grande, a few hours' sleep, then a two-day ride back on horseback; Clay tallied the five days he would be gone from home. No matter how he examined it, he did not like it. There were too many things that needed to be done here, especially if he was going to send Martin and his steers on the Dunton trail drive. And that was a matter that still needed settling in his mind.

Yet, there was no way to avoid his responsibility. No one else could drive the team. He had to take up the reins, like it or not. "I'll need time to get my gear and a saddle horse for the ride back."

Cotton smiled. "What about a shotgun? Ain't no way I'd be much use to you. Couldn't handle a scattergun or rifle with just my left hand. Could probably fire a shooter, but I doubt I'd hit much."

Clay had not considered that. Cotton's broken arm eliminated him when it came to riding shotgun, nor did the rancher relish having a merchant or clerk sitting beside him. "You're asking a lot."

"The line'll pay him—and you," Cotton said. "Fifteen dollars for sure, and they're likely to kick in expenses for meals."

Fifteen dollars was not bad pay for five days. Clay took another sip of coffee. "I'll talk with Juan."

"The Meskin?" Cotton frowned. "I was thinkin' you'd maybe take your boy there. He seems able to handle himself well enough."

Clay did not have time to be bothered by the man's personal problems with Juan's skin color. "Ain't a man I'd rather trust with a gun at my side. Best hope that your fifteen dollars appeals to him. If it don't, you'll be taking the stage to El Paso by yourself."

By the expression on Cotton's face, Clay could tell that the man knew there would be no discussion of the subject. Clay drained his mug, placed it on the table, and left Cotton still trying to manage his supper with one hand.

Juan listened to Clay's proposition. The Mexican did not hesitate to nod his acceptance. "Fifteen dollars is like the icing on the cake, my friend. You forget that my mother-in-law is in my home. The stage line will be paying me to get away from her."

Clay laughed. "I hadn't looked at it that way, but I guess you're right. Martin and I'll go out and see to getting us a couple of mounts for the ride back."

Starting for the door, Clay turned back to his friend. "I've got another favor to ask of you."

"*Sí,*" Juan replied. "What is it?"

"You think you could convince one of your cousins to stay over until we get back?" Clay whispered. "I ain't expecting trouble, but I'd feel better knowing there was someone here to give Elizabeth and Martin a hand if something came up."

"The Lipans bothered me also," Juan replied. "I will ask Augusto to stay. "He can make himself a pallet in the barn. He will understand."

Clay felt a breath of relief slip from his lips. "Thanks. Tell Augusto that I'll make it worth his while when the line comes through with our pay."

"You do not have to do that," Juan assured him. "He has no more liking for Maria's mother than I. Besides, Elizabeth will feed him well."

"Thanks again," Clay called to Martin and walked outside to where the stagecoach waited.

. . .

CLAY HANDED COTTON EVANS a corked jug when the man stepped into the coach. He nodded toward Mr. Oliver, who lay sleeping on the floor of the stage. "I think he might have had the right idea. The ride's not going to be easy. Use this sparingly. It'll help cut the pain."

A grin spread across the shotgun rider's face as he securely clutched the jug of whiskey to his side with his good arm. "Me and the others will appreciate these corn squeezin's. I'll see they're shared fairly. They'll make the ride go a mite quicker."

The rancher was uncertain that alcohol would speed the journey into El Paso, but it certainly would help dull the pain of four broken limbs. He only wished he had another half-dozen jugs. He would rather have four passed-out drunks on his hands than men wishing they were dead with every bone-jarring rock the stage's wheels hit.

"Let us tie off the canvas from inside," Cotton requested when Clay pulled down the heavy tarp flaps that served as door and window shutters for the celerity wagon. "I heard you had some redskin visitors today. If some of their brothers decide to pay us a call on the road, I'd just as well be able to get these flaps open from inside."

Clay agreed. In spite of his own request for Augusto to stay on the ranch while he was away, he did not think he would ever see Lipans this side of the border again in his lifetime. Crow-Who-Flies-Far's tale had been one of a dying people. If the Lipans survived, it would be by joining a Mescalero band in the New Mexico Territory. After that, the Lipans would soon adapt and change. In a short span of years they would be Mescalero themselves—the term Lipan something they would use only when they spoke of half-remembered ancestors.

A twinge of sadness wiggled uncomfortably through Clay at that thought. He walked around the stagecoach double-checking the two barrels of precious water lashed to its sides and the two horses tied behind. Saddles and bridles for the ride home were stashed in the canvas-covered boot along with the body of the man who had held the reins in the driver's box only a few short hours ago.

The rancher wished there were a more dignified way to bring Ken Weaver home to his family in El Paso. There was not. The lightweight celerity wagon, as its name implied, was built for speed, not hauling cargo. Clay would make certain the man's body was removed from the boot and laid out properly before his family saw him.

"Pa—" Martin approached his father as Clay completed his circuit of the stage and team to assure himself all was ready for the desert haul. "You certain you don't want me to come along with you?"

Clay reached out and squeezed his son's shoulder, realizing how much a fifteen-year-old yearned to visit a civilized town, even if that visit would consist of a few quick hours. "I wish you could. But you've got a mother and a sister and ranch to see after. Maybe next time."

Martin's understanding smile failed to hide the disappointment that the night could not conceal. "I'll take care of things. You can depend on me."

"I know I can." Clay squeezed his son's shoulder again. He glanced to Juan gathered with his cousins, each with requests for items they wanted brought from town. "Soon as you four finish your wheeling and dealing, we can head out."

"A minute or two more, my friend," Juan answered, with a wave of a hand.

Clay placed his left boot on the stage's single step to climb into the driver's box, then pulled it back. Elizabeth hurried from their home.

"Here, you forgot this." She handed him a drawn and tied leather pouch. "I took two twenty-dollar pieces out from under the board in the bedroom."

The United States Government might have forced Texas to lay aside its constitutional prohibition and open banks after the War Between the States, but Clay and Elizabeth put no trust in them. Their savings were kept in a box under a board at the foot of their bed.

"I got your list in my pocket." He patted the buttoned pocket on the left breast of his shirt. "I'll pick up everything I can."

"Sugar and books are the main things," she said. "Books especially. Martin and Sarah have been through the four we have twice already. And don't go wasting good money on those penny dreadfuls you like so much. Our children ain't going to learn nothing about the world from them."

Clay failed to mention that the colorful adventure yarns he favored had not cost a penny in years, but sported a price of a full nickel. "I'll do what I can. It ain't always easy to find books in El Paso, not English printed books, that is."

"You'll find them if you look hard enough. I'm not going to bring up my two children to be ignorant savages." She leaned forward and softly kissed his lips. "You be careful, now. I don't want anything to happen to you, Clayton Morgan Thorton. After all these years, I've grown accustomed to having you around."

Smiling, Clay returned the kiss. "I'll get the books." He climbed into the driver's box and called down to Juan, who still took orders from his cousins. "If you're going with me, you'd better climb aboard, 'cause I'm on my way."

"I am coming." Juan said a hasty good-bye to Ernesto, Augusto, and Manuel then scrambled into the driver's box beside his friend. "What are you waiting for? El Paso is a long way to the west, and it is not getting any closer with us sitting here."

"When you're right, you're right." Clay grinned and unwrapped the reins from the stage's brake lever.

He called out to the eight-horse team, lightly popping the reins to their backs. The team lunged against their harnesses, and the stagecoach rolled to life. As he turned the horses westward into the night, he mentally estimated the time it would take to cover the ground ahead.

By daybreak, they would be down the steep winding grade of Guadalupe Pass and onto the white salt flats below the mountains. He would give horses and passengers an hour's break then. After that he would move as quickly as possible. The vast stretch of alkaline white was no place for man or beast when the sun rose to its midday height. Not if staying alive was what mattered. And it mattered more than anything else to Clay Thorton.

Six

CLAY THORTON chuckled aloud while the buckskin he sat astride slowly plodded up Guadalupe Pass beside Juan Morales, who sat atop a brown mare.

"What can one find so funny in a newspaper, my friend?" Juan asked with an eyebrow arched cynically. "I read one once. All it had were notices of new taxes the United States Government felt were needed for its people to pay. That and promises from the politicians in Austin, which they never keep."

The rancher looked up from the folded newspaper he had read off and on the past two days to help break the monotony of the long ride from El Paso. For the most part, Juan was right when it came to the paper's contents.

There was an article on someone called Boss Tweed in New York City, who supposedly was running a corrupt city government. Two reports of congressional debates around something called the "Force Act" filled one whole page of the four-page newspaper. This act, according to the paper, sought to stop groups such as the Ku Klux Klan from preventing "Southern Negroes their rightful place at the polls." There was also a mention of President Grant planning something called the Civil Service Commission to hire governmental employees.

"From what I read here, you and me have done gone and got ourselves in the wrong line of business." Clay tapped a finger at the article he had just finished. "Back east they're talking about forming a professional baseball league called the National."

"Baseball?" The Mexican's forehead wrinkled in question. "What is this baseball?"

"You know, we saw those boys playing it two summers ago when we helped Sam Dunton bring that herd in from San Antonio."

"Base—*Sí!* I remember. They were throwing a small ball and trying to hit it with a fat stick, a club."

"When they hit the ball, they ran to those sand-filled sacks that they called bases, remember?" Clay asked.

"I remember. It seemed like a silly thing to be doing." Juan shook his head, then studied the pass that rose for hundreds of feet above them.

"If this story here ain't lying, it might not be all that silly," Clay answered, gaze scanning the pass. He saw nothing except a single buzzard soaring high overhead.

"How is that?"

"Well, it says some businessmen in different cities in the east are going to pay men to play this baseball game against each other to see which team is the best," Clay said.

"If it's a game," Juan asked, "why do they have to pay these men?"

" 'Cause then they can charge people to come and watch them play." Juan's perplexed expression irritated Clay. Sometimes his friend seemed unable to grasp anything that did not directly apply to his ranch. Perhaps Elizabeth was right. Martin and Sarah needed the books packed in his saddlebags to learn what other men did in different parts of the world.

"That seems silly, too," Juan said. "Why would anyone want to pay hard-come-by money to watch men hit a ball with a club?"

"It doesn't matter why, just that they do," Clay answered, holding his exasperation in check. "It says this National League is going to start playing next year."

"Grown men playing a children's game?"

Clay ignored his friend's question. "It also says here that the men who play are expected to make around fourteen hundred dollars. That's for a season that lasts from the middle of March to the middle of November."

"Fourteen hundred dollars!" Juan's eyes widened with interest.

"That's what it says. A man named George Wright got paid for being something called a shortstop. He was playing for a team in Cincinnati, Ohio, called the Red Stockings. Says the Red Stockings were the first men to get money for playing this game."

"Fourteen hundred dollars," Juan repeated. "What we could do with that, no, my friend?"

Clay read aloud part of the article pertaining to the clothing the baseball players wore, chuckling about the shortened pants dubbed "knickerbockers." "A man wearing short pants with long red socks like that would get laughed out of any town in Texas. Doubt a baseball league like this National would make it here. No fully grown man would ever be caught dead dressing like that."

"Fourteen hundred dollars," Juan said, a faraway quality to his voice. "Maybe you and I should look into this baseball game. How hard could it be to hit a ball with a club and then run to sacks filled with sand? We could maybe get our own team of men and have people pay us to watch them play this silly game."

Clay drew a deep breath and rolled his eyes, trying to remember why he had brought the news article to Juan's attention in the first place. He slipped the folded paper into the sleeping roll tied behind his saddle. The last page of the paper he saved for tonight or tomorrow in the privacy of his own home.

"We should stop and let the horses rest," Juan said when they reached the top of the pass. "Water would do both them and ourselves good. We don't want to have them dying on us so close to home."

Clay agreed, although he found himself hard-pressed not to keep riding. Home lay but ten miles ahead along a path that wound through the hills lying at the foot of the Guadalupe Mountains.

Dismounting, the rancher removed his hat and wiped his sweat-glistening forehead with a shirt sleeve. He then unlooped one of two canteens from the saddle horn. The first had been emptied four hours ago. He untwisted the cork and took one mouthful that he held in his mouth while he poured half the water into his hat and allowed the buckskin to drink. The rancher swallowed and rationed himself another mouthful before giving the horse the remainder of the water. He finally replaced the hat atop his head, enjoying the few drops of water that trickled down his neck.

Juan pulled a cigar from his pocket, stuck it in his mouth, then yanked the stogie from between his teeth, and stared at it a moment before returning it to the pocket. "Too dry for this. It would have my mouth feeling like a bowl of sand after two puffs."

Clay watched his friend upturn his final canteen and let the few remaining drops trickle into his mouth. The rancher did the same

with his own canteen before shoving the cork back into the neck
and draping the empty container over the horn.

"Looks like we might get some rain." Juan tilted his head to the
craggy mountains on their left.

Dark clouds gathered above El Capitan and Guadalupe Peak.
Occasionally the distant rumble of thunder rolled in, although Clay
saw no flash of lightning.

"Doubt it." Clay shook his head as he stuck a foot in a stirrup to
swing into the saddle. "The mountains will suck all the rain from
those clouds before it gets to us."

Juan pursed his lips, looked back at the clouds, then remounted.
"You are probably right. The spring rains are late this year."

If they come at all. Clay kept the thought to himself. No need
giving fate ideas. The desert was stingy enough with moisture as it
was.

Clay tapped his heels to the buckskin's sides and moved eastward
toward home, with Juan at his side.

A MILE from the ranch house, Clay knew something was wrong—
terribly wrong.

His chest constricted with panic as though some invisible leather
band—jerked tight—encircled it. The corral and pen beside the
barn were both empty, their gateposts lying on the ground as
though hastily tossed aside. He told himself Martin and Augusto
had taken the mares and foals out to pasture, but that did not
explain the gateposts.

Chickens idly strolled before house and barn, pecking and
scratching at the ground. It was not unusual for the chickens to
escape their pen—it had happened dozens of times. What was unusual was not seeing Elizabeth and Sarah chasing the culprits back
behind the wire enclosure. The hens were his wife's private domain; she was mighty proud of the eggs they laid year around.

Although it was not unusual to ride upon the ranch and not see
anyone walking around, it was unusual for this time of day, with
sundown but an hour away. There were too many evening chores to
be done. No one should be idle.

Nor should the kitchen be abandoned at this hour. Supper was
too close at hand. Elizabeth should be busy preparing the evening
meal. Yet, no smoke came from the stone chimney atop the kitchen
building.

Clay's legs wrenched high. He slammed his spurs into the buckskin's sides. The horse lunged forward with a winded snort. Its long legs stretched out to dig hooves into the sandy soil. The animal covered a full eighth of a mile before Juan reacted and spurred his own mount after Clay.

The worst of a thousand imagined fears tightened that invisible belt strapped about Clay's chest, drawing so taut that he could barely suck down a breath when he reined the buckskin to a halt before the barn. Augusto lay sprawled on his back before the open door. A single feathered arrow jutted from the center of his chest—a shaft that had ended his life when it drove directly into his heart.

"Elizabeth! Elizabeth!" Panic squeezed Clay's voice to a high-pitched cry as he swung to the ground. He wrenched the Winchester from the saddle holster and cocked it. "Martin! Sarah!"

Clay saw why his son did not answer. Martin lay by the wide-open front door to the house. Clay did not have to examine his unmoving body to know the fifteen-year-old boy was dead. The three arrows shafting from his body were all he had to see.

Leveling his rifle before him, Clay moved toward the house.

"Wait!" Juan backed on his reins to bring the brown mare to an abrupt halt amid flying dust and sand. He glanced at Augusto and Martin then came out of his saddle with rifle cocked and ready. "Don't do it, my friend. Let me go inside."

Clay ignored his companion while he stalked straight toward the ranch house, stepped over the body of his son, and went through the door.

Knowing what he would find inside did nothing to prepare him for the impact of seeing the dead bodies of his wife and daughter, each with throat slashed from ear to ear. Blackened blood pooled around their heads as they lay on the floor.

"No!" Clay backstepped, forcing himself to move before his legs buckled under him. "No! No! No!"

Outside was no escape from the vision seared into his brain. Dead—his family was dead! His rubbery legs went out from under him; he collapsed to his knees on the ground. The heat pressed around him like a smothering blanket. His stomach lurched then churned to upheave violently. He doubled over, emptying himself onto the sand.

Seven

"I MUST GO, my friend. It will be dark soon." Juan double-checked the knotted ropes that held Augusto's body, wrapped in white sheets, tied behind the mare's saddle. "I must see about María."

"They're Apache arrows." Clay did not look at the Mexican, but stared at the four arrows pulled from Augusto's and Martin's bodies. "Lipan arrows—you can tell by the markings."

"I know that." Juan reached out his hand to rest gently on Clay's shoulder.

"I'm going after them, Juan." Clay turned to stare directly into his neighbor's eyes. "I have to go after them. There's no other way, not after what they did."

Juan pursed his lips and nodded. "Do you not think that I know that? This is my cousin I must take home and bury. He was like a brother to me. We grew up together—have always been together."

Juan paused as though searching for more words as he drew a deep breath. "I will go with you. But now I must ride to my home and see about María and the others. I will return tomorrow with fresh horses, after I have buried Augusto properly."

Clay said nothing, but watched Juan mount the mare, rein her head about, and ride to his home. The rancher was not certain how long he stood there, but Juan was no more than a dark speck in the distance when Clay's eyes gradually turned to the ranch house.

His stomach churned again at the thought of what he must do. He gulped down a series of breaths and exhaled them until the queasy rumbling subsided. There was no way he could avoid what he dreaded with all his soul. No man, no matter how strong—and

Clay felt as though every bone in his body was shattered and every muscle frayed—could face the task easily.

Inside, his family waited for the final attentions of a husband and a father. Juan had helped him lift each to their beds and cover their bodies with sheets. That was not enough. They must be given a final resting place, and there was no one else to do what must be done.

Clay closed his eyes, his body shuddering. He steeled himself to hold back the flood of tears. The tears did not come. This was not the time for weeping and mourning. His family needed him one last time, then . . .

It was the "then" that focused clearly in his mind when he turned and walked into the barn to retrieve hammer, nails, and shovel before he entered a house he once had considered home, but which now seemed to rise like an alien structure about him.

Clay went to the back wall of the main room and lowered himself to the wooden floor. He used hammer and hunting knife to loosen the first board. The others he needed came up easily after that. Wood, milled lumber, was rare in desert country. The floor provided the flatboards required for three coffins.

It was far too easy to imagine what had occurred here. It played over and over in his mind while he nailed the boards into simple rectangular boxes. Crow-Who-Flies-Far and his Lipans had not been satisfied with the steers Clay had given them. They wanted horses, and they had come back to get them.

They had not come back the night after their visit to the ranch, he realized. The Apaches had waited to make sure Clay and his family felt safe and secure, thinking the Lipans had crossed back into the New Mexico Territory and rejoined their band. Perhaps they had taken the steers back to their camp, or they may have waited in the mountains until they felt it was right for the raid.

He was sure that they had struck this morning with the rising sun. Unlike Comanches, Apaches preferred to fight in the light of day, unless they were certain they could kill an enemy at night without endangering themselves. Although not universal among Apache bands, the belief of many was that a warrior's spirit would be trapped in this world if he were slain at night. So they waited for daybreak to fight.

Fight doesn't describe what happened here. Clay cursed aloud. Augusto fell first, if he read the signs correctly. The Lipans took him as he stepped from the barn, probably intent on relieving himself after a night's sleep. One notched and waiting arrow was all it took.

In all likelihood, Augusto cried out before he died. That brought Martin running from the house. Clay's mind-eyes saw the arrows as they struck his son. Because he darted from the house, the first bit into his right thigh. It did not kill, but it brought him down. The second arrow drove into his left shoulder as he hefted his carbine. The small rifle had dropped from his hands as pain knifed through his body. When the third arrow shafted into his chest, Martin died.

Then the Lipans swarmed through the open door to the house. Still in their nightdresses, Elizabeth and Sarah had died quickly. He shuddered at the thought: *And mercifully*—if such a brutal death ever could be merciful.

It was at that point the Lipans realized something was wrong, something they had not anticipated. Clay Thorton himself was not to be found. Nor were they certain where the rancher had gone.

That he was missing had frightened, perhaps even panicked, the braves. Clay read that from the house's interior. It was not ransacked. Nothing was missing, not even food. A strange thing for starving Apaches to leave behind—unless they feared something or someone.

Clay knew that someone was himself. They were afraid he would suddenly ride upon them. Although only one man, he had a reputation among these mountain Apaches, and that would have doubled their fear.

The Lipans had abandoned all the spoils of their bloody raid, except for the horses they had returned to the ranch to steal. These and only these they took, fleeing west and then north, back across the New Mexico border.

That's where I'll find them, Clay thought, his jaw setting in a firm, hard line. He realized the Lipans knew he would come, and they would be waiting. That knowledge might work in his favor.

These were not the strong Lipans of his youth. They were a weak, dying band. Knowing he was following would eat at their minds. They would never be sure when he would be standing outside their wickiups, never sure when he might be hiding in the underbrush ready to pick them off one at a time. Knowledge like that made men, even Lipan Apaches, nervous. Nervous men were prone to making mistakes.

Whether Crow-Who-Flies-Far and his braves feared his coming or welcomed it did not matter to Clay. Neither their bullets nor their war lances and arrows could harm him more than seeing what had been done to his family. Today the Lipans had killed the man who was Clayton Thorton just as surely as if they had driven an arrow into his chest. For the first time in his life, he fully understood the name the Apaches had given him as a boy. A man who was already dead inside fears not death.

As THE SUN, a bright angry yellow in color, broke above the eastern horizon, Clay gently lowered Sarah's coffin into the ground. He used the shovel to fill the grave, then covered the mounded dirt with rock, as he had with both Elizabeth and Martin. He stepped back and eyed the task he had completed during the night.

He had placed Elizabeth beside their infant son Jonathan, hoping she now held in her arms the child she had known for far too short a period in life. At his wife's side he left space for a future grave—his own. Whether his final resting place would be at Elizabeth's side was doubtful in his mind.

In truth, he did not expect to return from the New Mexico Territory. He was sure of only one thing: he intended to send as many of the Lipans to hell as possible before he was finally cut down. Perhaps the vacant plot of ground represented wishful thinking. He did not know, or much care, at the moment.

There, beside the spot he left for himself, he had placed Martin and Sarah. Again his chest tightened, and he found it hard to breathe. A man was not supposed to outlive his own children. That was not the way of things. Children were meant to bring forth other children—grandchildren who sat on their grandfather's lap and listened to his stories of how life used to be.

Clay closed his eyes, trying to blot out the future memory of his children's children and their children. The Lipans had robbed more than one man of his family. They destroyed a whole line of Thortons meant to populate the years to come. Only one Thorton remained on the earth, and except for a flesh-and-blood body that continued to perform the actions expected of it, he was dead.

He turned from the three freshly dug graves and lifted the Bible he had placed atop his mother's grave. Clay had never heard the words a preacher read to send a soul on its way to its maker. What he read aloud was the story of Jesus feeding the multitudes with the fishes and the loaves of bread. Those had been Elizabeth's favorite passages. She had told him many times that more than anything else in the Good Book it spoke to her of the bounty awaiting those who believed. And Elizabeth had believed. He silently prayed she and their children now reaped that bounty and all memory of the sufferings they endured in this life was washed from their minds.

The thin pages of the Bible fluttered in the first stirring of a morning breeze. Clay let the book close. His gaze returned to the graves that lay at the crest of the rounded hill a quarter of a mile from the ranch house. These sandy heaps of dirt and rock represented the only family he had ever known. In his own way, he loved each of them, even the mother he had never known.

Turning his back on the rising sun, he walked to the barn. Determination quickened his strides. He ignored the nagging weariness of his body, pushed to the edge of exhaustion by the long ride from El Paso and his night's work.

His original evaluation of what had occurred during the attack was wrong, he thought when he reached the barn. Crow-Who-Flies-Far and his braves took more in their raid than his horses. They had stripped Augusto of his rifle and pistol. Gone, too, was Martin's old army carbine along with the Sharps that hung on the wall of the ranch house's main room.

Their haste in fleeing the ranch became apparent again when Clay opened a wooden chest shoved into a corner of the tack room. He tugged open the lid and gave a nod of approval. The lead and powder he kept within were untouched.

From the keg of powder he filled a homemade leather powder bag that held four times the powder as the metal flask Colt sold boxed with its pistols. He checked another leather pouch he pulled from the chest. It brimmed with lead slugs to be melted and molded into bullets. A small, scarred wooden box he lifted contained a bullet mold, a box of Bley Brothers percussion caps, and the paper required to make the ammunition for the Colt .44 six-shooter he carried.

From the bottom of the chest he lifted a shiny new wooden box. He had intended this as a gift for his son on his sixteenth birthday. Clay flipped the lid. Inside lay a polished, ornately engraved, ivory-gripped Colt .44 that matched the one he carried.

Martin will grin from ear to—

Clay struggled to push aside the image of his son's face. The only facial expressions he would now see were ones of horror when he emptied the weapon's chambers into the bodies of Apache braves.

Extracting the pistol from its velvet-lined case, he broke it open and loaded the six chambers of the cylinder with prefabricated paper cartridges that came boxed with the handgun. He did the same with the spare cylinder he had purchased for his son. The remaining three boxes of ready-made cartridges, each containing six loads, were dropped in the saddlebags he took from the wall, along with four boxes of cartridges for his .44-caliber, lever-action Winchester.

He stood and stuffed the second Colt beneath his holster belt. Two pistols with extra loaded cylinders for each, and seventeen cartridges in the Winchester totaled forty-one rounds. A man could not carry more and hope to move with any speed.

Before leaving the tack room, the rancher pulled four empty canteens from a peg in the wall. When filled, these would hold twice the water he usually carried for long rides. It was a simple precaution. He headed into unknown territory where water was certain to be scarce.

Outside he saddled the buckskin and secured half a sack of oats behind the saddle. He wished for a packhorse, but the Lipans had robbed him of that luxury. He would make do with the gelding.

He led the buckskin from the barn and tied its reins to a hitching post outside the house. From a pantry inside the kitchen, he finished filling his saddlebags with measures of flour, soda, cornmeal, dried beans, and two sacks of jerked beef. He cast a longing eye at a line of jars containing canned wild plums, but left them on the shelf to gather dust. The jars were too bulky for the saddlebags. He carried only essentials for the ride.

Adding the stuffed saddlebags to the buckskin's burden, Clay repressed an urge to walk inside the house for one final look. Instead, he took the gelding's reins and led the horse to the creek that flowed fifty yards behind the house. While he filled the four canteens, he let the horse have its head to drink all the water it wanted. The animal would be denied that simple pleasure in the days ahead, unless Clay accidentally stumbled onto a watering hole.

Canteens filled, Clay cupped a hand and dipped it into the clear water that ran from the mountains. He drank far beyond the point needed to quench his thirst, filling his belly with the cool water.

When he could hold no more, he splashed water over his face and neck, then stood to loop the canteens' straps over the saddle horn.

He slipped the braided reins over the buckskin's head, placed his left foot in the stirrup, and climbed into the saddle. He edged the gelding around so that he could scan the southern horizon. He did not expect to see the dust of an approaching rider, nor did he.

It was just as well. Juan Morales was a friend, a good friend, if not the best Clay had ever had in his life. He did not want the Mexican at his side when he came upon Crow-Who-Flies-Far's camp. Juan still had a family, a reason to live. It was not right for such a man to die beside one who no longer lived.

Slight pressure on the reins brought the gelding's head around until the animal faced west. Clay's spurs lightly tapped the buckskin's sides. The horse's pace held no urgency, nor did its rider push it to greater speed. The mountains ahead were no place for haste, only caution.

Eight

A SLENDER WISP of dust caught Clay's eye the second morning away from the ranch. It rose not ahead of him amid the rocky hills that skirted the New Mexico side of the Guadalupe Mountains, but over his shoulder.

He drew the buckskin to an easy halt, shifted his weight in the saddle, and peered back. Had Crow-Who-Flies-Far left some braves behind in the mountains? He did not have to second-guess the purpose of an Indian rear guard. Its task would be singular: follow Clay and wait for the moment it could take him.

The rancher studied the rising dust while the morning breeze whipped at the slender finger. If Apaches were following him—Clay seriously doubted the dust came from a white man casually out to explore the Guadalupes—the old war chief's rear guard could be no more than one or two riders.

One or two Lipans eliminated here meant fewer to deal with when he finally located Crow-Who-Flies-Far's camp. Clay wasted no time weighing the possibilities. The advantages were obvious. He had surprise on his side here, something he expected would be lost to him as he approached the Lipan camp.

Jumbled boulders twice the height of a man, dislodged from the mountain faces, provided easy cover. Clay maneuvered the gelding into a wide crack between two of the boulders, looming at least half the size of his ranch house. Dismounting, he tied the horse's reins to a heavy rock to prevent the animal from straying. He took the Winchester from the saddle holster and eased back among the rocks.

A hundred yards from the buckskin, he found the boulder he

sought. Its gravity-guided fall from the mountains left its face cracked and pitted, providing handholds and toeholds that accommodated the rancher's climb to its top. There he lay belly down on the sun-heated stone. Then he waited.

Five minutes grew to ten, ten to thirty, and that doubled by his pocket watch before he heard the clack of hooves on stone. Clay cocked the Winchester, injecting a cartridge into its chamber, and snugly nestled the rifle's stock into the hollow of his right shoulder. The Indians had followed him at a distance of four or five miles, he estimated while he sighted down the barrel and aimed at the point his pursuers would round a humpbacked hill sprinkled with creosote bushes.

The distance was farther back than Clay would have trailed a man he sought to kill, but the tangled skein of an Apache's mind often evaded those who attempted to unravel it. Clay was not here to delve into the inner workings of an Indian's brain; he came to repay those who had murdered his wife and children. Lead would be the coin of that transaction.

The sound of hooves neared. Clay's right forefinger curled around the rifle's trigger to rest there lightly. The blazed head of a strawberry roan came into view first. The rancher shifted the rifle's barrel upward, elevating the muzzle to chest height of the horse's rider.

His finger began to squeeze, then pulled away from the trigger. A shaky breath hissed through clenched teeth. There were two horses, as he had guessed, but only one rider. The second animal was a packhorse in lead. The rider was Juan Morales.

Without rising to expose himself, Clay called out, "Have you gone *loco*? You trying to get me to put a bullet in you?"

Juan's head jerked around. The rifle he held across his lap swung from side to side as he attempted to cover half the ground around him in a single sweeping motion. "Clay? Clay, my friend, is that you?"

"Damned right it's me. If I'd been one of Crow-Who-Flies-Far's braves, you'd be buzzard bait by now." The rancher pushed to his feet. "Up here, above you."

The Mexican's head lifted. A nervous smile of relief spread across his brown face. "I knew I gained ground on you, but I did not realize you were this close."

Clay shook his head with disbelief as he started down the boulder. "I gave you credit for more sense than to come after me."

"You did not have a horse to carry your pack." Juan pointed to the horse behind the roan and the canvas-covered load it carried. "And it is as I said, Augusto was of my family. His murder must be avenged."

Clay gave his head another shake. He had offered his friend the opportunity to change his mind when he had ridden west without him. Juan was a grown man; he had made his choice.

"What are you doing?" Clay brought the buckskin from between the boulders.

Juan stood beside the pack animal, pulling items from beneath the canvas. "I am going to cook breakfast." The Mexican tilted his head to the twisted branches of a dead juniper ten feet behind him. "The wood is old and dry. It will make little smoke. The smoke it makes will be carried away by the wind."

"We ain't got time to be eating." The rancher glared at his friend. "Food ain't what brought me way out here."

"I have not had a real meal since I left María. Neither have you. Remember, I have been at your heels and I have seen no camp-fire." Juan pointed to the juniper. "Get the wood. Men cannot do what we must do if they are half-starving."

For the space of three heartbeats Clay considered telling Juan what he could do with his hot meal. Then the rancher's stomach growled loudly. Tough jerky gnawed while in the saddle and washed down with tepid sips of water did little more than keep a man going. It did not provide him with strength.

Clay gathered the wood and started a small fire. Juan put the small flames to good use. Within a half hour the Mexican handed his friend a tin plate piled with fried bacon and biscuits. A cup of steaming coffee accompanied the meal.

"Did you study the tracks around your house and barn?" Juan asked between alternating bites of bacon and biscuit.

"Yeah." The hot coffee rolled into Clay's stomach, quelling the demanding growls. "Why?"

"So did I. Do you not find it strange there was only one set of moccasin tracks to be found?" Juan lifted questioning eyebrows.

Clay stared at his companion while he popped a strip of bacon into his mouth. "Unusual, but the way I figure it, Crow-Who-Flies-

Far's bucks got sloppy. One of 'em had to go back for something after they had brushed away their tracks. I didn't make much of it."

"*Sí*, that is the way I read the tracks, too."

The rancher caught the hesitancy in his companion's voice, as though the Mexican were uncertain of their mutual conclusion. Perhaps he pondered the same thought that had crossed Clay's mind when he first saw the one pair of moccasin prints in the sand. It was a thought that led nowhere; Apaches did not raid alone. They bolstered their courage with the bravado of other warriors. A raid meant nothing unless other eyes witnessed their bravery.

"Those moccasin tracks don't mean nothing. It's where those hoofprints are headed that we got to worry about." Clay jerked a thumb toward the trail of the stolen horses he had followed from the ranch. "Finish up your food, we're wasting valuable daylight sitting here."

"*Sí.*" Juan glanced at his companion, shrugged, and returned to his meal.

THE CRYSTAL TRICKLE of water oozing from the crack in the rock was a seep—water from rains higher in the mountains whose course was mischanneled to the surface as the moisture worked through the soil seeking the water table deep below the two men's feet. The tiny rivulet rolled down the face of the rock to spill onto the earth for three muddy feet before it was sucked away by the thirsty sand.

"It is cool and sweet." Juan smiled when he pulled his head away from the trickle. "We were lucky to find this."

Clay did not argue their small stroke of fortune. He leaned forward, pressed his lips to the stone, and sucked in the water while it flowed from the rock. Mouthful after mouthful he gulped down, savoring the coolness of the water as it rolled down his throat. It would have been a piece of heaven to strip away his clothes and bathe in a tub of water this cool. For the moment the rancher contented himself with drinking its sweetness.

"We should give the horses their fill," Juan said when Clay abandoned the seep. "There is no way to know when we will find more water."

"Use the water in the canteens first," Clay directed. "You want to do the watering or refilling?"

"I will water the horses." Juan took his hat from his head, filled the inverted crown with water, which he stuck beneath his roan's muzzle, then tossed the rancher the empty canteen.

Clay pressed the open mouth of the canteen into the trickle. He glanced about, once more struck by their fortune. If he had not noticed the strange coloration in the rock and ridden to investigate, they would have passed by the needed water. He could only guess at the number of similar seeps they had missed.

The Apaches, he was sure, knew the location of every seep in the Guadalupe range. Men spoke in supernatural awe of the Comanches and their knowledge of every depression in the plains that might hold water after rain. Apaches, if anything, knew the mountains and deserts even better. It was a dry land; men did not live without knowledge of every drop of water there was to be found.

Clay put no supernatural weight to the Indians' ability. It was simply a matter of survival. The desert and its mountains had been the Apaches' home for hundreds of years. They knew this land, that was all there was to it—no magic, no medicine, no guiding hands of spirits.

"We should consider making a camp here tonight," Juan suggested when Clay corked the last of the refilled canteens.

After swallowing two more mouthfuls of water sucked straight from the rock, the rancher looked at the western sky. "We got at least two hours before sundown. We'll make use of them. No telling when a wind might come up and blow away the tracks."

Juan offered no protest, but allowed himself the luxury of another drink before mounting. He wrapped the packhorse's rope lead around the saddle horn and turned the roan northward. The horse had not completed the two steps required to make the turn when the Mexican tugged back on the reins. "We have company ahead."

Clay pivoted. A sandy hill supporting a handful of spiny yuccas blocked a clear view of the north, but he saw the thin white cloud that caught his friend's attention.

"Smoke or dust?" Clay swung astride the buckskin.

"Dust—a lot of it," Juan replied, his eyes narrowing. "It was not there when we stopped. I looked to the north before I dismounted."

"Then that means whoever it is, is coming this way." Clay nudged the gelding's sides as he slipped the Winchester from its holster. "Let's go take a look."

Juan cocked his fifteen-shot Henry and moved out at his friend's side.

Halfway up the hill, Clay halted, dismounted, and handed the Mexican the buckskin's reins. On foot and finally on his belly, he crested the hill. His lips set in a thin, grim line as he surveyed the scene below. He pulled back. Half-running, half-sliding, he reached Juan and remounted.

"It's Crow-Who-Flies-Far and two braves," Clay said. "They got my mares and foals. They're heading this way."

Deep lines creased the Mexican's brow. "This way? That does not make sense. Why would they ride this way? The tracks we follow go north."

Clay waved away the questions. Half the things an Apache did made no sense. This was not the time to try to decipher the Lipans' reasoning. "I want to take 'em straight on. No ambush. I want them to know who it is that's sending their souls to hell."

Juan unlooped the pack animal's rope from the saddle horn and let it drop to the ground. "We ride over the hill and straight down on them."

"Now." Clay dug his spurs into the gelding's side.

The horse clambered up the hill, sand and rock flying from its hooves, while Juan's roan kept pace at the buckskin's side. Together the animals brought their riders to the crest of the hill and started down the other side in a run for the three mounted Indians a quarter of a mile to the north.

Halfway down the hill, Juan called, "Wait! Clay, wait! Something is wrong!"

The rancher ignored his companion. His spurs once more bit at the buckskin's sides as he urged the horse on.

"They are not fighting," Juan called over the rush of the wind. "Look, they do not want to fight."

Still Clay refused to acknowledge the Mexican. Juan did not understand why the Lipans stopped and sat frozen before the charge. They faced Fears-Not-Death. Clay Thorton rode to spill blood in payment for the three precious lives they had taken from him. He imagined the trembling death songs that quavered from the Apaches' lips.

"No!" Juan shouted. "Stop, my friend! There is something wrong!"

"Son-of-a-bitch!" Clay cursed at the top of his lungs when he saw Juan wrench back on his reins, bringing the roan to a sliding halt.

If he had to take on the three Lipans by himself, then so be it. He let the braided reins fall to the buckskin's neck. Sitting straight in the saddle, he hefted the Winchester to his shoulder and aimed.

What? Clay blinked as he sighted down the barrel. *What in the hell is this?*

He wanted his first shot to take Crow-Who-Flies-Far. The old war chief no longer sat atop his pony's back. The Indian dismounted. With empty hands extended before him, the Lipan leader walked toward the man who charged down on him.

If that was the way Crow-Who-Flies-Far wanted to meet his death, Clay was willing to oblige him. He lowered the rifle's barrel to aim on the Apache's exposed chest. He mentally gauged the shot and the next two, which would cut down the mounted braves behind the ancient chief.

Why doesn't he run? Doubt furrowed Clay's brow. Why didn't the aged war chief draw his knife and at least go through the motions of fighting? Crow-Who-Flies-Far was no coward or crazy man. Something was wrong.

The words echoed in Clay's brain—the same words Juan had shouted. Niggling doubt wiggled through the rancher's mind. This was no ploy, no ruse. The chief expected to die. There was no fear in his dark eyes, only acceptance. This was not the way it was supposed to be.

"Damn!" The single syllable tore from Clay's twisted lips in a tortured cry.

He lowered the Winchester and snatched the loose reins from the buckskin's broad neck. He yanked back. Twenty feet from the Lipan Apache, the gelding threw out its legs, dug hooves into sand, and slid to a shaky halt.

Nine

IF RELIEF for an unexpected reprise from death passed over Crow-Who-Flies-Far's face, it was a fleeting shadow that Clay missed. The Apache's expression appeared unchanged when he lowered his hands and stared up at the man with the muzzle of a Winchester pointed directly at his nose.

"You have come, as I told my people you would," the old chief began. He looked back at the braves with the stolen horses. "We hoped to reach your lodge before you came searching for us. We sought to return your horses."

"Return . . ."

The question died a confused sputter on Clay's lips. He heard Juan approaching behind him, but did not risk a glance over a shoulder. He kept Crow-Who-Flies-Far dead in his sights while he watched the remaining two braves with his peripheral vision. If one of the three made a wrong move, they would all die.

"The braves of my camp did not raid your land, Fears-Not-Death," Crow-Who-Flies-Far continued. "It was the one who is one of the People in name alone that did this deed."

"Coyote Man?" Clay recalled the adopted Kiowa and the trouble the brave had tried to start over the horses at the ranch.

"It was him," the Apache leader answered. "He acted alone, telling none in my camp of his plans."

"Then those moccasin tracks did not lie." Juan edged back the brim of his hat and looked at his companion. "It was only one man who hit your ranch."

"Only one brave," Crow-Who-Flies-Far repeated. "It is not our way to attack those who have aided the People."

The barrel of his rifle dipped, but Clay kept his finger on the trigger. Seconds ago everything seemed so clear. Now confusion muddied his thinking. Was the Apache up to some new trick?

"Pronghorn-Eater named his adopted son well." Crow-Who-Flies-Far's dark eyes never left Clay's. "Like his namesake, Coyote Man is a sly trickster who aided the People with one hand while he tried to betray them with the other."

Speaking more words than Clay had ever heard an Apache say at one time, the war chief explained that the remnants of his band sought to avoid the blue-coated buffalo soldiers. Those left behind prepared for the trek north to Fort Stanton, where they would join the Mescalero chief José La Paz and his band.

"There is no fight left in my people." Sadness colored the Apache's voice. "We only wish to live. If it means digging in the earth to be left alone, then we shall plant fields and tend cattle like the white man."

Although the three major Mescalero chiefs, Cadete, Roman, and Santana, and their bands still roamed free, Clay had read in a Santa Fe newspaper about the minor chief La Paz who had come to Fort Stanton in February. The article said the Indians already tilled fields.

The rancher lowered his rifle. Perhaps this was the beginning of the long-sought peace with the Apache bands. At least there was hope. The Society of Friends had taken up the reins of every Indian agency in the country last summer.

"I was to rejoin my people for the long journey north after I returned these ponies to your lodge," Crow-Who-Flies-Far concluded. "The meat you traded to us will not last long. We must move quickly before the cries of our children grow loud again."

"What of Coyote Man?" The tears of Lipan offspring were of no concern to Clay, not after the tears of his own children had been stilled forever.

Crow-Who-Flies-Far's eyes lowered. Whether in shame or to avoid Clay's gaze, the rancher was not sure. The chief told of how the Kiowa had left the camp the very night the Lipans had returned with the steers.

"When the sun rose yesterday, he came back to us." The ancient Apache once more looked at Clay. "He boasted loud and long of his deeds, how he had taken the ponies from your corrals and barn.

We knew you would come or lead the long-knives to us. That is why we bring the ponies back to you."

Clay did not doubt their reason for returning the horses. Crow-Who-Flies-Far had correctly judged the consequences of the Kiowa's action. Clay also noticed that the Lipan made no mention of Elizabeth and the children's murders, although he was certain Coyote Man had also bragged of his bloody deeds. How else would the old chief have known that Clay still lived and sought revenge?

"Where is the Kiowa coward now?" Clay pressed.

Crow-Who-Flies-Far lifted a hand to the south. "He shamed our people and was driven from our wickiups. He left riding the mare with the blue spots on her hindquarters. The colt followed behind them. Even Pronghorn-Eater disowned him as a son."

Juan spat in disgust beside Clay. "We are too late. The whoreson has gotten away from us."

"He hasn't gotten away, not yet. It'll just take a mite longer to get to him. He's only a day ahead of us." Clay slipped the rifle back into the saddle holster and glanced over a shoulder to the south.

Apaches lived off the desert when other men died, but they were too exposed in the open wastes. They needed mountains to conceal their camps, to escape those who pursued them. The mountains and the knowledge of treacherous twists and turns were the Apaches' greatest strengths. How many times had the army chased a band for days only to lose them when they reached the shelter of a mountain range? Since the days of the early Spanish, the Apaches had evaded those seeking retribution.

Coyote Man was no Apache; he was Kiowa. The plains were his home. He was like a fish out of water alone in this harsh country, Clay thought. Unless, he found others to aid him. Those others would be Apache or perhaps a passing band of raiding Comanches.

Clay looked back at the Lipan chief. "Your way is right. I accept your words. Return my horses to my home. For this you may select another two steers to feed your children. You also may choose two ponies for your braves. These must be from the horses that pasture with the cattle. They must be geldings and not mares or stallions."

Crow-Who-Flies-Far's eyes brightened. "Fears-Not-Death is generous."

"To those who would be his friend and aid him," Clay answered. "To those who would harm him, I offer only death."

"That is as it should be," the old Lipan said with an approving nod. "We shall return the ponies to your home. We go now."

Clay did not wait to watch Crow-Who-Flies-Far rejoin the two braves. He reined the buckskin around and rode toward the hill where Juan had left the packhorse. Daylight remained, and while the sun rode above the horizon miles could be covered.

"Where do we now go?" Juan edged the strawberry roan beside his friend.

"South," was all the rancher answered. His mind was occupied by the terrain that lay ahead. The Hueco Mountains stood between the Guadalupes and El Paso. If Coyote Man found no refuge there, he would have to turn either southeast, seeking the Mescalero chief Gómez, who often ventured into the Davis Mountains, or westward deeper into New Mexico Territory.

Clay did not intend for him to do either. The Kiowa was only a day ahead. A determined man could easily cut that distance by riding hard and resting little. That was Clay Thorton's simple plan. There was nothing else to be done.

Ten

THE SUN GRADUALLY SANK toward the western horizon. Clay Thorton and Juan Morales had lost count of the sunsets they had witnessed since beginning their search for the elusive Kiowa who bore the Apache name Coyote Man. Nor did either pay attention to the setting sun that set a line of high clouds ablaze with brilliant reds and fiery golden oranges. The New Mexican town ahead of them held their eyes.

By Texas standards, with bustling cities such as Jefferson, Austin, Corpus Christi, and even El Paso, a hard day's ride south along the Rio Grande, Los Cruces was no more than a village of whitewashed adobe mud buildings. In the sparsely settled New Mexico Territory it was a major center.

Clay held no liking for the town, although he had never stepped foot in it before. All towns irritated him. Apaches did not live in the relative security of a town.

"It looks friendly enough here." Juan returned the waves of five children who stopped chasing a rusty barrel hoop long enough to greet the two dusty riders that entered their town. "And look at all the gardens. Plenty of water here."

"That's the Rio Grande right over there." Clay jerked a thumb over his shoulder. "What did you expect?"

Juan ignored his companion's sarcasm, preferring to smile at three black-dressed women carrying baskets on their heads. "Smell those tortillas! I will stuff myself tonight. It might be a lifetime before we have real food in our bellies again."

"That's what you said last night in El Paso."

The Mexican shrugged off the comment, as had become his

habit whenever they rode into a town. In their months together Juan quickly learned to accept the rancher's dark moods whenever they came upon a settlement of more than three houses.

Clay determined to see his friend well-fed tonight to make up for his own sour attitude. The feeling that they wasted time here was inescapable. Nor would they have visited Los Cruces were it not for the army captain in Fort Fillmore downriver. The officer mentioned talking with a wagon master in Los Cruces who had sighted an Apache mounted astride an Appaloosa last week. That man, Delbert Cole, ran a string of road wagons between El Paso and Santa Fe. Cole headquartered in Los Cruces.

Clay's lips drew back in hard lines as he sucked in a breath. Were it not for the stolen Appaloosa, he would have admitted defeat when he and Juan had journeyed to Fort Davis. A spotted-rumped horse was an oddity in this country, one that caught the eye of every man who saw it. Such a horse had been seen ridden by a brave who traveled with the Mescalero chief Gómez.

So it was that Clay and Juan signed up to serve a stint as trackers for the 25th Infantry under the immediate command of Lieutenant John L. Bullis. The two had ridden with Bullis's Seminole scouts. Finding such scouts so far from the Indian Nations never ceased to surprise the rancher. During the War Between the States the Kickapoos fled the United States into Mexico, taking Seminole slaves with them. After the war, when they returned, many Seminoles signed on with the army.

Through the spring and summer Clay and Juan remained with Bullis until an extended campaign against the Mescaleros led back to the Guadalupe Mountains. There a brief fight resulted in the capture of eight squaws. They told of a Kiowa, now called by the Apache name Coyote Man, who rode a horse that came from Indians in the northern forests. Coyote Man escaped with Gómez by crossing the Guadalupes. The squaws believed Gómez intended to head west and join forces with either Santana or Cadete.

When Bullis decided the Mescaleros now belonged to the army forces in New Mexico and turned back toward Fort Davis, Clay and Juan collected their pay and parted company with the lieutenant the Seminoles dubbed the Whirlwind, because of the officer's never-lagging endurance in the field.

As September slipped into the chilly mornings of October, Clay and Juan spent two days with Juan's family. It was time enough for

the Mexican to assure his wife that he was still alive; though his
irritation with his mother-in-law, whose brief visit had stretched into
months, flamed anew.

Clay learned that Ernesto and Manuel cared for his stock as well
as seeing to the needs of the stage line. He gave them all the money
collected from the stage, and a fourth of the money brought by the
Dunton trail drive. The remaining three quarters and the money
that came from the sale of four horses, he placed in the cubbyhole
beneath the floor of the bedroom of his home. The brief minute
needed to stash the money was all the time he spent on his ranch.
The memories waiting for him there were too painful to face while
Coyote Man still lived.

On their third morning at the Morales ranch, the two men
mounted fresh horses and road west to El Paso. Fort Bliss provided
the latest updates on Gómez's movements into the San Andres
Mountains north of Los Cruces. Clay and Juan's intention to ride to
Fort Selden and again sign on as trackers changed when the captain at Fort Fillmore mentioned Delbert Cole's sighting of an Appaloosa.

"Cole's office." Juan tilted his head to a white shingle painted
with black letters which hung over the door of a building ahead of
them. It read:

COLE'S OVERLAND TRANSPORTATION—WE HAUL ANYTHING THAT WILL FIT IN A
WAGON.

Clay grunted when they stopped in front of the office and found
another sign, in the window. It simply read: *Closed Until Morning.*

"It appears Mr. Cole keeps banker's hours." Clay peered up and
down the dusty street. Dusk was rapidly becoming night. Los Cruces
would soon be asleep. "Looks like we'd better find us a place to
spend the night."

"There is a *cantina.*" Juan pointed to the left. "We could stop
there and inquire about this Mr. Cole."

"Cole can wait until morning," Clay said. "But we might be able
to rustle up some grub and a few drinks in the *cantina.*"

Juan offered no complaints when his companion reined toward
the bright light that spilled onto the street from the *cantina's*
opened doors.

DELBERT COLE stood no more than five feet six and appeared to have
a rough time tipping the scales at over a hundred pounds. The

slightly-built man did not fit Clay's image of a wagon master. But it was not wagons he had come to discuss with the man, who handed them mugs of steaming coffee poured from a black pot atop a pot-bellied stove.

Cole took a tentative sip from his mug and settled behind a scarred desk littered with papers. "That cuts the chill, doesn't it?" Cole's pleased smile revealed a dark gap where he had lost one of his front teeth. "Now how may I help you, gentlemen? I got wagons leaving out of El Paso or here in Los Cruces at least once a week. Sometimes more often, if the damned redskins ain't raising hell. Hard to keep drivers when they're raidin'."

Clay held the mug with both hands, letting its warmth ease the morning chill from his hands. "Mr. Cole, Juan and I aren't here about shipping cargo."

Cole's eyes narrowed as he peered through the steam rising from the coffee. "If you two men are here looking for work, you've come to the wrong place. Times ain't that easy, what with the money problems this country had last year. I'm afraid there ain't much in this whole town. El Paso's the place you should be asking."

Clay covered an amused smile by sipping from his cup. Cole's attitude changed in the blink of an eye. How easily the "gentlemen" became simply "men" when Cole realized there was no chance of profit from this conversation.

"We haven't come looking for work either." Clay watched Cole's eyes narrow even more. "We just need the answers to a couple of questions about the Indian brave you spotted last week riding an Appaloosa mare.

The relief that washed across Cole's face left Clay pondering what less-than-legal activities the man participated in to evoke such a strong reaction. If Clay had to wager, he would put his money on rotgut whiskey. A few jugs of moonshine spiced with red pepper for kick and boot polish for color would be a cheap insurance policy to ensure Cole's wagons made it safely through Apache territory to Santa Fe.

Apparently noticing the rancher's interest in his reaction, he took a swallow of coffee and shuffled through the papers atop his desk. "Friends, I'm a busy man. I haven't time for—"

"Captain Kitree at Fort Fillmore told us about you seeing the brave and horse." Juan cut the wagon master off and pressed for the answers for which they had come. "All we want is to know where and when you saw the Kiowa brave."

Weary exasperation seeped into Cole's voice when he finally answered. "First of all it weren't no Kiowa. The brave was Apache—Mescalero."

"His name is Coyote Man, a Kiowa adopted by the Apaches," Clay said. "We just want to know where you saw him."

"I wouldn't know about his name, but he was with a band of about twenty Mescaleros around Columbus on the border. I was bringing three wagons loaded with cornmeal up from Palomas down in Chihuahua. I ain't sure what side of the border they was on. There ain't no Rio Grande to mark the boundary in that country, just rock and sand for the most part. The mountains kinda spill over into Mexico, you know."

Cole explained he saw the Apache camp tucked back into a canyon. "There must've been water back up in there, 'cause I saw them Indians workin' in the fields they'd planted. Looked to be corn and beans they were growing."

The brave and the Appaloosa stood near the mouth of the canyon, the man explained. "He was just sitting there on that blue-spotted horse watching the wagons as we rolled by. Kept an eye on us, but didn't give us no trouble. And I didn't stop to discuss the weather with him. I don't get no closer to any redskin than I have to, especially a Mescalero. Not with Santana stirring up trouble again."

Clay nodded. The New Mexican Mescalero bands, who had been quiet since the first of the year, abruptly began raiding again at the beginning of October. The El Paso newspaper had been sprinkled with reports of Apache depredations. "Did you happen to notice a colt with the same markings?"

Cole shook his head. "Just the brave on his pony. Wouldn't have noticed him, except for the way he just sat there and eyed my wagons."

Thanking the wagon master for the coffee and the information, Clay and Juan walked onto the streets of Los Cruces. The town appeared as sleepy during the day as it did at night.

As he mounted, Juan asked, "And now, my friend?"

"We find us some grain for the horses and some directions on how to get to this Columbus," Clay answered. "We aren't going to find Coyote Man here."

"SMOKE!" Juan poked a finger to the right. "See it?"

Clay did. Like a gauzy haze of the palest blue, it hung beyond a long, spiny ridge of rock that jutted from the mountains for two miles. The smoke's pale hue indicated whoever lit the fire was burning dry wood. In this country that meant those tending the flames could find only dry wood, or they sought to conceal themselves.

"Do we take a look?" Juan asked.

"We take a very careful look. If it's Apaches, they'll be having breakfast just about now," the rancher said. "They might not take kindly to having visitors."

Clay tried not to give the smoke too much importance. However, there was no way for him to avoid the possibility this could be the Mescalero band they sought and Coyote Man might be stepping from a wickiup to stretch his arms and legs to greet the new day.

The location's right, the rancher told himself as he reined to the spine of rock. Two men in Columbus last night mentioned seeing Apache sign south of the town in Mexico. Whether Juan and he had crossed into Chihuahua, Clay was not sure. As Delbert Cole said in Los Cruces, there was no Rio Grande to delineate the border here.

Reaching the line of rock, the two ranchers dismounted and peered up the jumbled wall. Here and there corridors in the stone led in and up through the boulders.

"I make it two, maybe three, hundred feet to the top." Clay craned his neck back to gaze at the weathered boulders perched high above their heads.

"At least two hundred," Juan answered. "I guess we just start climbing."

"There aren't any road signs pointing the way."

Twice they started into the rock and climbed upward for less than twenty-five yards only to discover the way blocked by impassable talus. Their third avenue led beneath an arch formed by two collapsed boulders leaning against each other. On the other side lay a foot-worn path. They followed the meandering trail upward in easy strides.

"Pay dirt." Clay nodded below after moving across the hundred-yard-wide crest of the ridge to peer into the sheltered canyon below. "That has to be the Mescalero camp Cole saw."

Located by a glistening water seep that ran from the side of the mountain dead-ending the box canyon were a dozen wickiups, oven-shaped structures made from brush woven over a frame of branches. Squaws busied themselves around a community fire at the center of the camp while a half dozen braves sat waiting for the meal that boiled in a black kettle hung above the flames. Apache children did as all children; they played, chasing each other around the camp. Beyond the cluster of wickiups were fields. Five acres or more of cultivated crops, Clay estimated.

"I do not see Martin's mare among the ponies." Juan tilted his head to twenty Indian ponies grazing on the sparse grass west of the Apache village.

Neither did Clay, but he was not ready to call the camp a bust. It fit Delbert Cole's description. "Coyote Man could be out hunting."

Doubt shadowed Juan's eyes when he looked at his friend, but he said, "He might be hunting."

Clay realized the probability the Kiowa hunted was small, especially since the camp members gathered about the cooking fire. An empty belly was the only thing that made an Indian brave rise early for the hunt. The bubbling kettle below said the Mescaleros were not starving.

"Do we wait here, or ride in?" Juan returned to scanning the small camp below them. "They appear to be diggers rather than warriors."

"With Apaches, looks can be deceiving." Clay was not certain how to proceed. He wanted to ride into the camp and question the Indians about Coyote Man. Even Mescaleros who tilled the soil were not that far removed from their cousins raiding western Texas, New Mexico, and the Arizona Territory. A hate for white men was a constant among Apache bands.

He drew a heavy breath and released it in a gust. "I reckon we ride in, taking it slow and careful like. The only thing we'll accomplish sitting up here is to bake our brains."

He edged from the rim and started back along the twisting and turning footpath. He did not savor the idea of riding among the Mescaleros. Yet, he and Juan could not stay perched atop the rocky ridge. Sooner or later they would be discovered. Their intentions would be damned hard to explain. The direct approach offered less chance of misunderstanding. Besides, the Apaches had not attacked Delbert Cole's wagons. That pointed to more interest in their fields than scalps.

The thought still floated in Clay's mind when three copper-skinned braves leaped from behind boulders ten feet away from him. All three leveled rifles at the rancher.

"Take cover!"

Clay pivoted, prepared to dive behind the nearest rocks large enough to shelter him. His abrupt twist came to an equally abrupt halt that almost sent him to the ground. There was nowhere to run. Three more Apaches stood behind Juan. The muzzles of their rifles were lifted and ready.

The Winchester Clay clutched in his hand was useless, as was Juan's Henry. In the time it took to raise the weapons and cock them, two men could die in a crossfire of Apache bullets. Clay did the only thing he could, he cursed under his breath as a brave stepped forward, wrenched the rifle from his hand, and yanked the Colt free of its holster. The brave tossed the weapons to his companions, then relieved Juan of his weapons.

Something hard and unyielding slammed into the side of Clay's head. He groaned in pain and reeled, staggering as his knees quaked, then collapsed. Somewhere behind him, he heard Juan moan. The Mexican, clutching at the back of his head, stumbled into Clay's side.

As Juan fell to his knees, he spoke—rapid-fire Spanish. Clay's dazed brain caught only one in four words, barely enough for him to comprehend his friend's plea for their lives, telling the braves why they were there.

"On your feet," a voice that was not Juan's barked. "Your words are spoken with the tongue of a snake."

Before Clay recognized the command was directed at him or what was wanted, a moccasined foot lashed out, burying itself in his side. He tried to hold back the surprised moan that burst from his lips, but could not. His display of pain seemed to please the braves; four more times brutal kicks drove into his ribs while he rolled on the ground in a futile attempt to escape the punishment.

Then there were rough hands and arms dragging him to his feet and another moccasin planted against his tail, shoving him forward. When he moved too slowly up the path to suit one of the braves, he received a rifle butt against the side of the face to help him along. The biting metallic taste of blood filled his mouth.

Nor was he the only focal point of the braves' torment as he and Juan were thrust, shoved, and kicked up the footpath and hastened along another path that wound toward the Apache camp. Again and again a well-placed rifle muzzle jabbed into the Mexican's lower back, driving for the kidneys. Twice Clay saw a brave slap a rifle barrel against the side of Juan's head, nearly knocking the stout Mexican to his knees once more.

That was what Clay saw. The rest of the time, he fought to keep his eyes focused as unseen braves delighted in trying to crack his skull with their own rifle barrels. Each time he stumbled and fought to keep his footing, the Mescaleros whooped and laughed with obvious pleasure.

How he managed to stay on his feet all the way to the floor of the canyon, Clay did not know. Once in the camp there was no chance of maintaining a steady stance. Braves and squaws swarmed forward. He saw Juan go down beneath a wave of battering fists a heartbeat before that human wave broke over him. He offered no resistance against the swirling blackness that opened and swallowed him. If this were death, he accepted it to escape the unrelenting punishment of the fists that pelted his body.

CLAY THORTON groaned as light penetrated the blackness, and he floated upward. He groaned again when his eyes opened to peer blankly at a cloudless sky above him. Death proved to be a jester that left him to suffer the throbbing agony.

He swallowed down three breaths, igniting fiery pain in his chest. *Cracked ribs,* he told himself as he fought above the tormenting knives twisting deep inside him. Where the Apaches had gone, he did not know. They had left him alone, and he had to take advantage of that. He forced his aching muscles to move, to sit up.

And found his body completely immobile. Naked, he lay on his back, tied spread-eagle between four stakes driven solidly into the ground. Rawhide cords bound his wrists and ankles. Three feet to his left Juan lay stretched in the same painful position.

The Mexican's head rolled to the side. A sound that vaguely imitated a grunt and a laugh came from Juan's bleeding lips. "You look like hell, my friend."

Clay tried to roll his eyes and winced. The sockets hurt too much for movement. "You don't look too good yourself, *amigo.*"

The rancher did not lie. Juan's left eye was a mere swollen slit. Blood oozed from a half dozen scraps and cuts on the rest of his face. His arms, torso, and legs were a quilt work of purpling bruises.

Clay did not want to imagine what he looked like—what he felt was bad enough.

"Are you all right?" The question sounded ridiculous, but it was the only thing that came to Clay's mind. "Anything broken?"

"I feel bad all over more than anywhere else," the Mexican replied dryly. "But I do not think my bones are broken, except, maybe, for a rib or five."

Clay blinked against the harsh sun above. It did not help. Nor did closing his eyes eliminate the searing light. The interior of his eyelids seemed to glow red-hot like iron heated in a forge.

"That does no good." Juan's voice came weakly. "Turning your head from side to side gives relief to one eye at a time."

The rancher tried his friend's suggestion. He could not decide if the pain ignited in his neck from the simple act of turning his head was worth the brief respite from the sun.

"What do you think they will do with us?" the Mexican asked.

Clay caught himself before he shook his head. "I don't know."

He lied. Like his companion, he knew exactly what the Mescalero band intended to do with them. Male captives in Apache hands received only one treatment—torture. The form that would take was the sole decision the braves of the band had to make.

Which must be what's taking them so long, Clay reflected. He had heard all the reports and tales of captives who died at Apache hands. None of the recountings was pleasant to hear. The thought of facing such an end held even less appeal.

"I guess there is nothing we can do except wait," Juan said.

"I reckon you're right," Clay replied, steeling himself for the sound of approaching Mescaleros, who could come at any moment.

The whooping cries of the Apaches did not ring out. Clay's confused uncertainty transformed into cold realization. Staked naked beneath the broiling sun was to be their way of dying. Slow and hard that death would come as the elements gradually leeched the life from their bodies with each passing moment.

Gritting his teeth to fight past the agony that fired anew with each movement of his body, he struggled against the rawhide cords binding him between the stakes. His actions proved worse than futile. All he succeeded in accomplishing was to tear his flesh until blood trickled from the open wounds.

Exhaustion washed over him when at last the darkness of the night settled over the desert. With the night came the cold, as the sand and the air rapidly lost the heat it had stored during the day. Teeth a-chatter and gooseflesh rippling over his nakedness in a feeble defense against the cold, Clay closed his eyes. After hours that crept by like lifetimes, sleep enclosed him in its protective arms.

Eleven

A BREAKING WAVE crashed over Clay, wrenching him from a sleep that precariously bordered on unconsciousness. He gasped then gulped, trying to find the water and draw it into his parched throat. There was none; the wave receded as rapidly as it rolled in.

"This one is alive." The voice spoke in Spanish. "See if the other one still lives."

"Sí, patrón," another voice answered, followed by the sound of splashing water and the sputtered awakening of Juan Morales.

Clay forced his swollen eyes open. The blurred shadow that loomed above him gradually focused into the image of a man—not Mescalero, but Mexican.

"You and your companion are lucky." The man pushed back a white sombrero and smiled through a neatly trimmed snow-white beard. "When I heard my friends had taken two captives I expected to find you dead, or at least your flesh flayed from your bodies."

Clay's dazed mind failed to find the humor this man apparently saw in their situation. Nor did his brain fully comprehend how this stranger could be dressed so finely in his white suit with its delicate embroidered designs in gold thread while he lay naked between four stakes.

"I suppose it has been so long since my friends have taken captives that they have forgotten what used to come without thought. You see, Winter Bear and his people have lived on my *ranchero* for the past ten years. They are almost civilized *indios.*" The man flashed a brilliant smile, then added, "Almost."

With a decided relish he described the great quantities of *tiswan,* the Apache version of moonshine made from fermented corn sprouts, the village braves consumed in their attempt to decide a fitting demise for their captives. "So unaccustomed are they to having captives to play with, they have yet to reach the decision. In truth, their minds are confused. They are unsure whether the braves should be given the honor of disposing of you, or you should be placed in the care of the squaws."

The dandified Mexican squatted on his heels and stared down at Clay. That smile hung on his lips as he suggested, "If I were in your position, I would pray to the Holy Virgin for the braves. Apache squaws exceed the appetite of their mates when it come to the blood thirst."

The man stroked a hand over his white beard and stared around him as though pondering. The smile returned to his face when he looked at Clay again. "There is another solution to your obvious predicament. As I mentioned, Winter Bear and his people have lived on the lands of Raúl DeOro for ten years. We are close friends. This band would never harm those who are my friends. I am willing to extend the hand of friendship to you and your companion—if the price is right."

Clay tried to explain DeOro's father's matrimonial relationship with a female dog, but his lips and throat were too swollen to form the five syllables required for the task. Incoherent sounds awkwardly fell from his lips.

Raúl DeOro's smile widened. "I see my proposition interests you." He glanced up and waved an impatient hand. "Luis, this man wishes to speak with me, but his throat is parched. Give him a drink."

A second Mexican, a *vaquero* by his clothing, knelt beside DeOro and pressed the mouth of an open canteen to Clay's lips. Gratefully the rancher drank, long and slow. He felt the swelling in his lips, tongue, and throat receding.

"Ah, is that not better, señor—" DeOro's smile vanished long enough for a question to form on his face. "I am afraid my friend Winter Bear made no mention of your name, señor."

"Thorton, Clay Thorton." The rancher managed to give his head a painful tilt toward Juan. "You might give my friend some water, too."

DeOro nodded to the *vaquero* Luis, who moved to Juan with the canteen. When DeOro's gaze returned to Clay he said, "I am a simple businessman, Señor Thorton. Shall you and I do business?"

"You son-of-a-bitch!" Clay let the venom spew in his words. "They'll hang you for this!"

"Perhaps that would be the case in your country." DeOro's damnable smile once more curled his lips. "But this is Mexico—my country. And this is my land, Señor Thorton. If you and your friend should die, no one will ever question it. Besides, is it too much to ask that you give me a reason to save your lives?"

Clay swallowed the curses that worked their way up his throat. Like it or not, Raúl DeOro was not a man to anger, not while he held their lives in his hands. "What do you want? What money we have is in our saddlebags. We've got our rifles, pistols, horses, and saddles. Pick what you want, or all of it."

"You have only a few American dollars." DeOro hefted two lightly weighted money pouches that he had already taken from the saddlebags. "I have no need of your pistols and rifles. As to saddles and horses—"

A frown crossed the Mexican's face as he peered questioningly at Clay. "You said that your name is Thorton, Clay Thorton?"

The rancher nodded.

"I have heard of a man with such a name from an old friend in El Paso—Hernando Díaz," DeOro said.

Before he could continue, Clay spoke up. "I know Señor Díaz. He has bought horses from me."

DeOro's smile spread to a pleased grin. "Then perhaps there is a common coin by which we may do business, Señor Thorton. I have admired those magnificently trained horses he purchased from you. I would accept one in trade for the lives of you and your friend."

The proposition did not require a second thought; horses were of no use to dead men. Clay nodded acceptance.

"Luis, cut them free and help them to the wagon." DeOro stood and motioned to his *vaquero*. "I will ride ahead to the *hacienda* and see that rooms are prepared for them."

IF CLAY'S FIRST IMPRESSION of Raúl DeOro placed the Mexican a notch or two lower than something that had crawled out from beneath a rock, DeOro did everything in his command to erase that image during the next four days at his spacious *hacienda*. The man's treatment of the two ranchers went far beyond mere hospitality. Clay and Juan were treated as honored guests.

First DeOro appointed two women each to care for his guests. Juan and Clay found themselves being bathed from head to toe and then each of their cuts, scraps, and bruises carefully tended. Before they were tucked into beds with crisp, ironed sheets, every inch of their bodies was coated with the soothing juice of aloe vera plants, a balm repeated twice a day to ease the pain of their sun-blistered skin.

When their fevered sleep passed and they could walk, DeOro brought them to his table and fed them on red meat and wine to "give strength to the blood." Although he appeared to be a man who hungered for conversation, he graciously allowed his guests to return to their beds when their healing bodies demanded further sleep.

The third morning Clay awoke to find his clothing, cleaned and pressed, folded in a chair beside his bed. With a minimum of aches and pains to be expected after the treatment at Apache hands, he rose and dressed. His two nurses, who sat in chairs in the hall outside his room, led him to a large veranda overlooking DeOro's *ranchero*. Raúl DeOro, himself, sat at a wrought-iron table, drinking coffee from a silver cup while he watched five men loading two roadwagons.

"Señor Thorton!" DeOro stood and waved an arm to an empty chair across the table from him. "Please be seated and join me for breakfast. I eat late in the morning, after I have made my rounds of the *ranchero.*"

Clay accepted the seat. DeOro's expression was perplexing. His smile, which had appeared so cold and calculating three days ago, now brimmed with genuine warmth, as though the man were delighted to have company during the meal. Clay's attempts to pigeonhole him were interrupted when a rotund woman placed a silver plate in front of him. It contained three fried eggs atop an island of refried beans that floated in a sea of tomato and chile sauce. He did not wait for DeOro to signal him to begin; he lifted an elegantly patterned fork and dug in.

"Except for the need of a shave, you appear to have successfully escaped the grave, Señor Thorton." DeOro politely thanked the woman when she brought him a plate similar to Clay's.

"Bought myself from the grave," Clay corrected, between forkfuls of beans and eggs.

DeOro chuckled with amusement. He swept an arm out toward

the land surrounding the *hacienda*. "It is a terrible land in which men like you and I have chosen to build their lives. For as far as your eyes can see, and beyond that, the cattle you can find will bear my brand. Many men with guns ride south and try to take the cattle from me. I thought you and Señor Morales to be such men."

"That's why you forced us to buy our own lives?" Clay eyed the man across the table.

"I am sorry about the arrangements I forced upon you. I did not know who you were then." DeOro shrugged and beamed another one of his warm smiles.

"Sorry enough to forget about that horse I promised you?" Clay asked as the woman refilled his coffee cup.

"Not that sorry. I admire your work with horses. I will be proud to own a horse you have trained." DeOro's smile faded. "It is as I said, my friend. I am a businessman. You and I struck a deal. I stood by my part. I expect you to do the same."

The man's tone was friendly, but his words held an undercurrent of something dark that hinted Raúl DeOro would not look favorably on anyone who reneged on a business deal. While Clay stayed in DeOro's home, he preferred that the man viewed him in a favorable light. "I promised you a horse. You'll get it."

The answer seemed to satisfy DeOro; his attention returned to his breakfast.

"The cattle business must be a mite better here in Mexico than it is in Texas." Clay tapped his fork against the silver plate. "This is mighty fancy eating wear."

Again an amused laugh pushed from his host's throat. "If I depended on cattle or the crops grown on my land, I would still be just another *peón* breaking his back for some *patrón*. This land is too poor to support one man, let alone all those who look to me for the food on their tables."

Clay's brow knitted. "If not cattle, then what?"

DeOro nodded to the wagons. "I am what some men would call a merchant." He paused, his gaze shifting back to Clay. "Others, especially those in your Texas, might call me by other names."

If DeOro expected the rancher to let the matter drop there, he misjudged his guest. Clay asked, "Names? Such as?"

"Comanchero," DeOro replied simply.

Contempt washed over Clay's face; he made no attempt to disguise his disgust. To a Texan, a *comanchero* was the lowest form of life that crawled on its belly through the dirt. These men traded with the Comanches!

Raúl DeOro appeared unaffected by his guest's reaction. However, his words came in defense: "Your expression condemns me, my friend. Am I any different than those men who manufacture the pistols and rifles? They know the weapons they make find their way into Indian hands. Yet, they do not close down their factories. No, they increase the number of weapons they produce."

He paused briefly as though giving Clay the opportunity to answer. When the rancher did not, he continued, "What of the respectable Texas merchants who bring in the rifles and ammunition that I buy from them? Surely you do not believe they are ignorant, that they have no glimmering of what I do. They do not refuse to sell me those weapons. The only question they ask is, do I have the money to meet their price?"

"But you sell to Comanches," was all Clay could say.

DeOro's eyebrows lifted, and he leaned closer to the table. "The Americans who moved into the lands you call New Mexico sold guns and whiskey to the Apache bands. They still do. Your government does nothing to stop them, although the Apaches have long raided my people." He shrugged. "Weapons are not all I bring to the plains tribes. Those wagons are being filled with coffee, sugar, tobacco, and flour. Like us, Comanches have a taste for such things."

Clay shook his head, then took another drink of coffee. There was logic in what DeOro said, but he could not escape the feeling that a twisted snake lay coiled at the heart of that logic.

"WHAT STILL ESCAPES ME is why you travel this country? Do you look for stock for your own *rancheros*?" DeOro asked Clay and Juan the fourth morning of their stay in his *hacienda*.

The man showed them his stables. The finely groomed horseflesh left Clay pondering whether the Mexican would be disappointed when he viewed Clay's own horses, so the question took him by surprise. "What?"

"What brought you to Mexico, to my land?" DeOro asked again.

"A Kiowa brave called Coyote Man, who disguises himself as a Mescalero or a Lipan," Clay answered, and explained why they searched for the Indian. "He rides a blue Appaloosa mare. And there's a colt, a weanling by now, that had the mare's markings.

They belonged to my son. If you ever saw them, there'd be no way to mistake them."

"I know the horses, my friend—the colt especially well. He is in this very stable." DeOro led the two down a line of stalls, stopping at the end and pointing inside. "See. Is this not the colt you mentioned?"

Clay's mouth gaped when he looked inside. The colt was Martin's. It had grown and filled out during the long months, but it was Martin's. Without hesitancy the rancher said, "It's the colt."

DeOro nibbled at his bottom lip for a moment while he studied the young Appaloosa. "When I bought this colt, I did not know its history. An animal such as this, that belonged to a dead son, is held dear by a man. I would not want to keep the colt from you. But the price I paid was high. The colt's beauty is unusual."

Clay listened when DeOro suggested that he would return the colt on the condition that he receive the first Appaloosa the colt sired, be it filly or colt. The strange mixture of steel-hard cold and warm human compassion that was this man named Raúl DeOro once again struck the rancher. There was complexity within DeOro that Clay realized he would never fully understand, even if he could know the man for a lifetime. In one instant he found himself liking DeOro, accepting the man as a friend; in the next moment he found himself repulsed by DeOro and his life.

"It's a deal." Clay stuck out a hand, which DeOro took and shook.

"It is good." DeOro gazed back at the colt. "It is easy for a man to fall in love with such a beautiful animal."

The unexpected horse-trading session completed, Clay's thoughts returned to the reason that brought him to Mexico. "You said you bought the colt from Coyote Man?"

"No, from a brave who won the colt from the Kiowa in a wager." DeOro told of a band of ten braves who suddenly appeared at Winter Bear's camp two weeks ago. They stayed in the village for three days before riding north. "It was a wager such as Indians often make—who can do what better than another. This time it involved bows and arrows. Coyote Man lost."

"Where did these braves go, Señor DeOro?" Juan asked.

"North, seeking Santana," DeOro replied, while they walked from the stable. "That is what Winter Bear said. I do not think this

Coyote Man was with them. He left a day before the Mescalero braves."

Deep creases lined Clay's brow. "Any idea where he might be headed?"

"North also," DeOro answered. "But I would guess he rides farther than the Apache bands."

"To the plains?" Clay pressed.

DeOro nodded in affirmation. "To rejoin his own people."

Clay drew a deep breath and looked at Juan. They had wasted enough time here, and Coyote Man was getting farther away with each passing day. "I reckon we should be heading north, too. We appreciate your hospitality, but the time has come to say our farewells."

"I understand. I will have my men saddle your horses and have supplies prepared for your journey. However, I suggest you delay your departure until tomorrow morning." DeOro motioned to his waiting wagons. "I leave tomorrow for my *hacienda* in Santa Fe. There is safety in numbers where we ride, and you are welcome to accompany me. It would be an excellent time for us to make a side trip to your *ranchero*. I still have to collect the horse you owe me."

The expression on Juan's face said that he was more than willing to travel with the man. That side trip would give him the opportunity to be with his family again. The time required to return to the Guadalupe Mountains also would give Clay the chance to examine fully the idea that germinated in his mind.

Clay accepted DeOro's offer. "You got yourself extra company for the ride," he said.

Twelve

CLAY STRIPPED AWAY his trail-soiled clothes, all the way down to his socks, and tossed them into a corner of the bedroom. He stepped to a bucket of steaming water and lifted the bar of soap that floated within. Then he scrubbed. Beginning with his hair, which felt as though it carried enough dirt to be tilled as a cotton patch, he worked down his body inch by inch.

His attention focused beyond the bedroom window. Outside, Raúl DeOro worked a sorrel filly in a wide circle on the end of a long rope attached to the animal's halter. It would have been better for the horse and man to get to know each with saddle and bridle, but there was no time for that. Raúl intended to send the filly, his payment for freeing Clay and Juan from Winter Bear's stakes, back to Mexico with one of his men. The horse would have to wait for the man's full attention until early December, Raúl's scheduled return from Texas's high plains.

From the broad grin half-hidden beneath the Mexican's white beard, Clay concluded the man was satisfied with the filly. The rancher's earlier concerns that Raúl might feel cheated in the trade proved groundless.

Of course, Clay admitted, Raúl still had Martin's Appaloosa colt on his ranch. Above all, Raúl DeOro was a practical man. Before leaving Mexico, Raúl bluntly pointed out the very real possibility that Clay might not return from his search of the Llano Estacado, and convinced Clay to leave the colt in case worse came to worst.

"I am a fair man," Raúl said, "but I will not be cheated out of owning such a magnificently marked horse."

Clay had agreed, in part because Raúl's point held a validity the rancher did not like to consider, and in part because Raúl said he would think about Clay's proposal to let the two ranchers accompany him and his wagons onto the Staked Plains. Two nights ago, when they had reached the top of Guadalupe Pass, before Juan rode to his home, Raúl agreed to take them with him, saying he would not be able to live with the guilt of letting them ride alone and getting themselves scalped within a day.

"But you, Clay, must not look so much like a Texan," Raúl had said. "There is nothing the Comanches hate as much as they do a Texan. Even with my protection, it will be difficult to convince the bands of the Antelope-Eaters that it is safe to have a white man in their camps."

That Clay agreed was why he stood naked and began to dress in the Mexican *vaquero*-cut clothing laid out on the bed. The waist-cut jacket with its fancy braid and the flaring legs of the pants were not to Clay's taste, but the disguise was worth a try. Adding to it, Clay decided not to shave. A thick beard would help hide his features—although the beard would not conceal the pale blue of his eyes.

The rancher kept his gaze from wandering around the ranch house while he finished dressing in the new attire, complete with black sombrero atop his head. Far too many memories lay within the ranch house's walls for him to linger here long.

In the months since the search for Coyote Man had begun, he had confined the memories of Elizabeth, Sarah, and Martin to the shadows far within his mind. He tried to keep them there, away from his thoughts, and succeeded, except during long nights when they worked free to torment him with vivid recollections of the life and love that once had been his.

Clay caught himself. He felt doors opening in his mind. He slammed them shut before the memories could escape. Danger lurked here on the ranch—too many things that might act as a key to those locked doors. To avoid them he had chosen to sleep outside with Raúl and his men for two nights. Pain permeated the ranch house. A man gained nothing by recalling the ghosts of the past. The future held a single vision of a lone Kiowa—Coyote Man. Better, Clay told himself, to focus on the task that lay ahead. His resolve must remain unbending until he saw the brave receive full measure for his murderous raid.

Clay skeptically lifted an eyebrow when he examined himself in a full-length mirror mounted on the back of the bedroom door. He definitely did not look like Clay Thorton, but he doubted that he looked like any Mexican he had ever seen. Perhaps Raúl's idea was not as good as it first sounded.

At the foot of the bed, Clay knelt and lifted a board from the floor. Beneath sat a box, which he opened to extract a heavy-weighted leather pouch. He tugged open the drawstrings and emptied the contents atop the bed. One by one he lifted the gold coins, tallying them while he returned each ten-dollar and twenty-dollar piece to the pouch. The twenty-five coins totaled five hundred dollars—his and Elizabeth's life savings. Once the amount brought pride. Now the weight held in one hand seemed insignificant.

It was not, he tried to convince himself. The money would keep him alive long enough to find Coyote Man.

Closing the empty box and replacing the board in the floor, Clay securely tucked the pouch under his belt. With brisk, hasty strides he walked outside and closed the door on the gathering memories behind him.

"What have we here?" Raúl allowed the sorrel filly to slow to a walk. "What have you done with my friend who went into the house but minutes ago?"

Clay attempted a weak smile. "I don't look that much different."

Raúl shrugged. "Perhaps it is true what they say about clothes making a man. You are changed. I doubt many would recognize you as Clay Thorton."

"Will these clothes be enough to hoodwink the Comanches?" Clay asked skeptically. "It's the Antelope-Eaters we have to worry about."

Raúl tilted his head toward his men, who stood by wagons watching their *patrón* work the filly. "Luis has suggested our deception might have a stronger foundation if your Spanish was improved. Your accent is that of a Texan."

"I *am* a Texan," Clay said, thinking that a sufficient answer.

"We will have you talking like a Mexican before we reach the Llano Estacado. I have decided that none may speak to you except in Spanish," Raúl replied with a smile. "You must do the same, that is, if you wish my men or me to answer you."

"Next you'll want me to be grunting like a Comach." Raúl's plan presented a new wrinkle that Clay did not expect or particularly like.

Raúl grinned. "Ah! An excellent idea! I will assign Luis to tutor you in the Comanche tongue while we ride north."

"Wait a minute, Raúl. I wasn't serious about speaking Comach," Clay protested.

"But I was, my friend." Raúl's smile evaporated. "Your presence endangers more than yourself. Speaking Comanche, no matter how little, will enhance your charade. Comanches will not suspect a man who knows their tongue of being a *Tejano.*"

Clay shook his head. "I don't know."

"I do." The finality in Raúl's voice said there was no room for argument.

Clay let the matter drop. The Mexican was right. He needed anything he could get to help him. If that meant speaking Comanche, then he would do it.

One of Raúl's men led a pinto from the barn and mounted the horse. Raúl led the sorrel filly to the rider, wishing them God's speed on their journey to the *hacienda.* The rider thanked his *patrón,* then reined toward Guadalupe Pass.

"Our friend Juan Morales should be here by now, should he not?" Raúl turned back to Clay.

The rancher arched his eyebrows and shrugged. "He and María might be taking extra-long to say their good-byes." Clay turned and pointed to the south. "I shouldn't think it will take him much longer before he comes riding right over—"

As though he waited for his friend's signal, Juan topped the rise to which Clay pointed. In an easy gallop he rode to the waiting men. A frown shadowed the Mexican's face when he halted the roan he sat astride.

Juan did not dismount, but leaned an arm on the saddle's broad horn. "I am sorry about being so late. Matters have weighed heavily on my mind all night."

"Is there a problem at home?" Clay walked to his friend and looked up at him. "Anything wrong with María or your children?"

"There is much wrong. They want—" Juan hesitated. He drew a less than steady breath and glanced around nervously.

"What is it, Juan?" Clay pressed his friend.

"María and my children want a husband and a father," Juan answered. "They need me to be with them. We are a family."

Clay glanced away, trying to ignore the hollowness that expanded within him. He knew what was coming. He was surprised it had not happened before now.

"I cannot ride with you any longer, my friend." Juan spoke softly, but without shame. "I have hunted for my cousin's killer for more than six months. No man can ask more of me. I have a family and a ranch I must attend."

Clay nodded. He had grown used to Juan, and riding on without him would be hard, but he was sincere when he said, "I don't ask any more of you. Your place is with your family."

"Clay, if it were not for—"

The rancher stopped him before he went further. "There's no need to explain. I understand. I really do."

A hint of a smile touched Juan's lips in relief. "I will tend your stock for you until you return. I will care for them as though they were my own."

"You'd better," Clay answered. " 'Cause they'll be a quarter yours."

"No, my friend, I could not accept that." Juan shook his head.

"You can and you will. Whatever you make off the stock is a quarter yours. I'll have it no other way." Clay stuck an open hand up to his friend.

Juan's mouth opened as though to argue, then closed. He took the proffered hand and shook it. "May I make us both rich men."

Clay smiled. "Now get on out of here. It's a long way to Santa Fe, and we ain't getting any closer standing here chewing the fat with you."

"God's speed, my friend." Juan eased the roan's head around and rode toward his ranch.

Clay watched him depart for a few seconds, then walked into the barn to saddle a mount for the ride to Santa Fe.

Thirteen

FOREWARNINGS, of which there had been many, left Clay ill-prepared for the desolation of the Llano Estacado. Unlike the plains stretching west from Fort Worth to the arid lands of far West Texas, the prairie lay unbroken by hogback, butte, ridge, or rolling hump of a hill to give the rancher's eyes relief from the interminal flatness. In all directions ran miles upon miles of nothing but miles upon miles.

In spite of himself, a constant urge to glance over a shoulder beset him. It dominated his thoughts the way the nagging ache of a tooth robs a man of concentration. Accustomed to rocky crags and miniature mountains of talus strewn at the foot of the Guadalupes, he found no escape from the haunting feeling of vulnerability. The prairie offered no place in which to hide should Indian attack come. The thought that he would be able to see approaching braves far in the distance provided no comfort. Comanche eyes also would be able to find him.

The unsettling sensation also played on the minds of Raúl DeOro and the ten men who accompanied his three wagons. Clay saw the uncertain glances that swept across the Staked Plains. Like Clay, they searched for something, and that something simply was not there.

For the first three days on the high plains, Clay rode close to his three packhorses, purchased and loaded with trade goods in Santa Fe. He occupied himself with checking and rechecking the ropes that held their canvas-covered burdens. It offered little relief from the vast openness, and left him feeling like a fool. Knots tied in rope could be inspected only so often.

The lush grass told of by those men he had met who had ridden upon the Llano Estacado was nowhere to be seen. The first freezes of autumn came to this land weeks ago. Frost-brittled husks of buffalo grass undulated in the wind, which never seemed to die, like waves on an ocean. The dull, monotonous brown of the dead prairie leeched at his spirit until the only strength he seemed able to muster was that required to keep him in the saddle during the long days.

The small band crossed sign daily. More often than not, the trampled grass indicated the passage of the pronghorn antelopes that inhabited the Staked Plains. When the prints of unshod Indian ponies were discovered in the sandy soil, they were old, partially erased by wind and rain.

"Patience, my friend," Raúl answered Clay's dubious expression. "This is the way it has always been. We will not find the Comanches, but they will find us when they want to be found."

Although Raúl's words and smile contained a lightness, the Mexican's face held concern. The quicker the Antelope-Eaters were found, the faster Raúl could make his trades and return west to Santa Fe. Even Clay understood this land was no place for a man when a blue norther swept down, carrying ice and snow in its dark, churning clouds.

On the seventh day of their incursion into the flatlands, Comanches found them. Two braves sat astride ponies a hundred yards from the traders' camp when the morning sun broke. Clay had not heard their approach, but Raúl told him they had been there through the night. He also assured the rancher that the braves were known to him.

After filling the two Comanches' bellies with hot tortillas and numerous cups of steaming coffee, laden with at least four spoonfuls of sugar, the braves announced they would lead the traders to their camp.

That village lay but a mile from where Raúl had ordered his men to spend the night. The smells and sights of the camp were not surprising to Clay. Not even the twenty conical shapes of the tipis appeared unusual. Many Texas Apaches, Lipan and Mescalero alike, had adopted the portable stretched-leather tents of the plains Indians.

What did widen the rancher's eyes was the camp's location. It lay in a canyon that sliced into the prairie. He estimated at least five

hundred feet stretched from canyon floor to prairie above. So well
concealed by the dead grass was the canyon that Clay was mere feet
from its edge before he noticed it. How many similar gullies and
ravines had they ridden by in the past week and failed to see?

An uneasy shiver trembled along Clay's spine. The Llano Estacado held a sinister aspect he had not expected. As easily as
Apaches hid within the mountains, Comanches concealed themselves in the open vastness of the Staked Plains.

If any brave, squaw, or child suspected him of being anything
more than the Mexican he appeared to be, Clay did not discern it
on their hairless faces—plucked smooth of even eyebrows. Nor did
he do anything that might draw attention to himself. He stayed
close to the wagons and packhorses, watching, listening, and learning.

The hours of tutelage by the persistent *vaquero* Luis paid off. Clay
discovered he mentally stumbled over only a few of the Antelope-
Eaters' words. Those, he found, he could decipher by the sign language the Comanches used to complement their spoken words.

During the day-long palaver, Clay worked up the courage to use
his newfound knowledge but once. While Luis bartered with a
brave carrying three buffalo robes who sought tobacco and coffee,
Clay asked about Comanche horses with spotted rumps.

"None of the People rides such ponies." The brave appeared to
notice nothing strange about the rancher's accent. "There is one
among the People to the south who rides a mare with spots as blue
as thunderclouds on her hindquarters."

The Comanche's face twisted with disgust. "This one is a Kiowa
who wears the clothing of the Apaches. Only a Kiowa brave would
ride a mare. Such a pony is not for a brave of the People, but for
their women and children."

Clay concealed his excitement. Although the mare offered no
interest to Comanche braves, who rode geldings, her distinct markings had caught their attention. As Raúl predicted, Coyote Man *had*
traveled north seeking other plains bands. The Kiowa now camped
with Comanches south of this small canyon. He was near!

As the sun settled toward the western horizon, Raúl concluded
his trading with the small band and ordered the wagons back onto
the plains. They traveled five miles before camping for the night.

Invisible as the Comanches had been for the first week on the
Llano Estacado, the next three days proved them to be almost as

numerous as the blades of grass that carpeted their lands. Five different bands, none as large as the first encountered, allowed the *comancheros* into their villages.

Each incident struck at the very roots of Clay's beliefs about Indians. Men, Mexican or white, did not ride into an Apache village without facing the very real possibility he would not ride out again. Yet, the Comanches displayed no signs of hostility to these strangers who invaded their lands.

The rancher was hard-pressed to find man, woman, or child who appeared to have any interest in the traders other than procuring a share of the luxuries their wagons brought to the high plains. Though the Comanches were fierce and bloody when on a raid, in their camps they were squat-bodied men who looked strangely out of place without a horse beneath them. Their interest centered on eating, napping, and amusing the children.

The many scalps that hung from tipis and war lances belied the tranquil image. These were Comanches, once a weak nation who had been driven from the game-rich Rocky Mountains by other tribes. Here on the barren plains they would have died slowly had it not been for Spanish explorers and the horses the Comanches stole from them. For nearly three hundred years the sturdy mustang and the Comanche had been one.

The Dog-God, Clay learned from Luis, was the name the Comanches gave the horse. With their newfound god, they became nomads, following the great herds of buffalo. What the horse did not provide, the buffalo did. From hide to bone, the Comanches used every inch of the massive, shaggy beasts.

The mobility of the horse also made the Comanche a raider. The depredations his ancestors suffered at the hands of other tribes, he returned tenfold. He spread his bands from Colorado to Texas and eastward into Kansas. He ruled the plains. Even the U.S. Army officers Clay had ridden with called Comanches the finest light cavalry in the world.

The history of Comanche and horse proved that. The Comanche had kept Spaniard, Mexican, Frenchman, Englishman, and American out of his lands. He, more than Kiowa, Sioux, Apache, or Cheyenne, had prevented the settlement of a continent by the pale-skinned Europeans who sought to claim it as their own.

In spite of the solace the Comanche braves found in their camps and families, Clay never forgot that bloody history. He was the foreigner here. A mistake, no matter how insignificant, could spark anger that could result in his scalp dangling from a war lance. So he did as Raúl and Luis directed, and learned.

"Our time here will soon reach its conclusion." Raúl saddled his mount on the eleventh day of their trek. "By this evening we will reach a great canyon called Palo Duro. There many bands of the Antelope-Eaters joined for the winter."

"I'll find Coyote Man there," Clay told his friend. "I've talked with several braves these last days. A lot of them have seen the Kiowa and the Appaloosa."

"I know. I have asked after Coyote Man, too." Raúl gave the saddle's cinch a final tightening tug and turned to Clay. "I know you wish to repay this brave for what he has done to you. But I must warn you, where we go today is not the place in which to do it."

Clay's eyes narrowed, uncertain what the Mexican was trying to tell him.

"I cannot allow it, my friend. Not while my men and I are with you," Raúl continued.

"My fight ain't with you and your men, or even the Comanches." Clay still was not sure what Raúl tried to say. "I just want Coyote Man."

"If he is among the Comanche bands, you may do with him as you wish, but only after I have taken my men safely from the canyon." Raúl stared into Clay's eyes. "My concern is not for myself or even these men with me. The profit we make on these journeys is not just for ourselves. The money goes to feed and care for all on my land. That is more than fifty families."

"I know that," Clay answered. "I saw what you were doing in Mexico."

"Then know that I will not allow you to interfere." No smile touched Raúl's lips. His voice came cold and hard. "I will draw my pistol and put a bullet into your head, my friend, before I will allow you to destroy what I do for my people. Do you understand?"

Clay bit at his lower lip and nodded. "Understood."

"If the Kiowa is in the Comanches' camp, all I ask is that you wait until I have taken my wagons a three days' journey from the canyon before you go after him," Raúl said. "You may ride away with us and then go back, or you may remain in the camp with your packhorses and goods. I do not care. I only wish three days' start before you act."

It would be hard—damned hard—to hold himself in check once he found the Kiowa, Clay admitted, but Raúl was right. He had no desire to harm these men who befriended him. "I agree."

The smile returned to Raúl's bearded face. "That is good, because it would grieve me deeply to kill one who I have come to respect as a friend."

"I don't reckon it would make me none too happy either." Clay tried to make light of the comment. Yet, there was no question in his mind that the Mexican was capable of killing him if Raúl felt the rancher endangered his reason for being deep in Comanche territory.

"It is time we were going." Raúl mounted and signaled to those who followed to do the same.

True to Raúl's expectations, the wagons rolled to a halt at the edge of an immense canyon ripped into the flat grasslands. Nor were they alone. Three miles from Palo Duro, ten mounted braves rode out of nowhere to escort them to the Antelope-Eaters' winter camp. The Comanche's mysterious appearance from out of thin air, Clay learned from Luis, was accomplished with the aid of a slight depression in the ground. No more than an eroded buffalo wallow, the hole and high grass provided enough cover to hide the riders.

Raúl greeted the escort with a handful of cigars and a jug of whiskey, the first produced during their time upon the Staked Plains. The Mexican waved away the concern he saw in Clay's expression. "I bring only enough whiskey to brighten their spirits, not to make them drunk. Were whiskey all I carried, there still would not be enough to do that. There are far too many of them. You will see."

Clay did. There was no disguising his sharp intake of breath when he first gazed over the rim of Palo Duro Canyon. Village fell short of describing the scene below. This was a Comanche city!

A full three hundred tipis sprawled for miles across the red floor of the canyon eight hundred feet below. Fingers of greasy smoke rose from as many fires. Comanches—everywhere the rancher looked were braves, squaws, and children moving amid the city of stretched-leather cones. From his vantage point on the rim, they looked like swarming ants busily preparing for a winter that would soon sweep down from the north.

And the horses! The herd that grazed along the banks of a

muddy red stream that ran through the canyon numbered well over a thousand. There, too, mingled among the ponies were beeves— long-horned cattle taken in raids against ranchers whose herds encroached upon the plains the Comanches considered their sole domain.

"I told you there were many!" Raúl grinned at Clay as the Mexican halted the wagons at the head of a collapsed canyon wall. "It is too steep to safely take the wagons down. We will stop here and unhitch the teams. Tonight we take whiskey and tobacco below as a sign of our friendship. Tomorrow we will load the horses with packs and begin trading."

CLAY KEPT CLOSE to his companions, wandering through the village only when they ventured forth from the spot they chose from which to conduct the trading. And trading there was. It came at a furious pace as each of the Comanches, brave and squaw, sought to come away with at least one item from the wagons, be it tobacco or a yard of gaudily colored ribbon. The leisurely haggling, which Clay had come to expect from the visits to the other Comanche villages, was abandoned here, replaced by the Indians' frenzy for coffee and sugar.

"You would make yourself a small fortune if you brought down your own packhorses," Luis suggested, as he accepted two longhorn steers for a steel hunting knife.

"I will wait." Clay shook his head. His hesitancy stemmed from the fact that no brave or squaw he talked with knew of either Coyote Man or the Appaloosa mare. "I don't think I've come far enough."

Luis shrugged and began bargaining over a bolt of red cloth with a brave whose excited squaw stood at his side. However, Raúl glanced at the rancher. "One comes who will know of your Kiowa."

The Mexican tilted his head toward a muscular brave who strode toward the piles of goods spread around the traders. Although no taller than Clay, the broad-faced, handsome Comanche appeared to tower like a giant among the Indians who stepped aside and opened a path before him. His tight-braided hair hung over his shoulders and dangled below his chest. His dark eyes were as steady as his confident strides.

"He is called Quanah," Raúl whispered.

Clay's gaze shot to his friend. "Quanah Parker?" He watched the Mexican nod.

All Texas knew Quanah Parker and feared the half-breed son of Cynthia Ann Parker, a woman taken in a Comanche raid on a Central Texas settlement. Few full-blooded Comanches were as effective as Quanah in uniting the scattered bands of plains Indians in their fight against the white man's westward movement.

Whatever Clay thought such a man would look like, this brave did not fit the image. Quanah's movements, his bearing, radiated pride. *Regal,* the rancher thought, realizing the word perfectly fit the half-breed.

"He will seek me out," Raúl said beneath his breath. "Let me do all the talking. I will find out about your Kiowa."

Clay offered no argument, but watched Quanah Parker while he casually examined the various items brought from the wagons. He eventually worked his way to Raúl. His wants were simple—coffee and tobacco, enough to last until the spring thaws.

The rancher listened carefully as Raúl and the brave bargained. Others in the camp might be willing to set aside the Comanche custom of haggling, but not Quanah Parker. It was the Comanche way, and, in spite of the white blood coursing through his veins, Quanah was Comanche. Try as he did, Clay found no trace of the woman who had given him birth in the brave's appearance or mannerisms.

Only when Raúl and Quanah agreed on a price of six buffalo robes for the coffee and tobacco did the Mexican mention the Appaloosa mare. "In my own land, I have seen the Kiowa brave who rides her and have admired the mare. I would bargain for her, if the brave is interested in trading."

"There was one, a Kiowa, who rode such a horse," Quanah answered. "He took great pride in the pony, although it was but a mare. He no longer is with us. He has ridden to join his own people."

Raúl did not press the matter further, nor did Clay urge him to do so. His mind wandered to the northeast and the Kiowa bands that rode the plains there.

"ARE YOU CERTAIN of this, my friend?" Raúl watched while Clay tightened the ropes on his packhorses.

"There's no other way that I can see." Satisfied with the knots, he turned to face the Mexican. "I've got to go after him."

"I will not tell you the plan is wise, nor will I stand against you. What you do is what you must do." Raúl reached atop a stack of buffalo hides piled in a wagon. He pulled down two and handed them to the rancher. "You will need these. Winter comes quickly. They will help warm you."

Clay knew what he did would be considered insane by most men, but there was no other way. He had learned from Raúl and the others; now he intended to put that knowledge to use.

"Where will you go, Señor Clay?" This from Luis who stood beside Raúl.

"Fort Sill in the Indian Nations to begin with," Clay answered. "Then wherever need be, if that's what it takes."

The thought of traveling east of the Red River on his own brought no comfort, but Clay could no longer remain with Raúl. The Mexican prepared to swing west, back to Santa Fe. Coyote Man was somewhere in the east.

Clay took Raúl's hand and shook it. "I'll be riding down your way to get my colt one of these days. Take good care of him until I do."

"I will do that, Clay Thorton. I will do that."

Mounting, Clay reined toward the northeast and the Red River. He tried not to think about the sadness he had heard in Raúl's voice, the sadness of a man who mourned a lost friend.

Fourteen

"SCOOT OVER, CLAY. Make some room for me. It's cold out here."

Clay, from the warmth of two down comforters, smiled up at his shivering wife. "I feel mighty cozy right like I am."

Elizabeth leaned to the bed and gently kissed his lips. There was a playful seductiveness in her voice when she suggested, "I think I know a way to make it a mite more cozy."

The rancher required no further coaxing to accept what his wife suggested as a means to hold off the chill of the winter night. He tossed back the comforters, opening a space for—

Icy air lashed across Clay's body. He bolted upright. His eyes blinked and focused. A cold sweat that turned to ice prickled over his body.

A dream. He drew a steadying breath. He had been dreaming and, while lost in that dream, tossed aside the buffalo robes. He swallowed hard and closed his eyes as he hugged the hides to his body. He had not known dreams could be so cruel, taunting him with glimpses of a life that could never be his again.

The icy pinpricks still nicked at Clay's face. He grumbled a curse. Snowflakes gusted in flurries with each breath of the bitter February winter. He yanked his hat low and pulled the buffalo robes higher so that only a small strip of flesh on his cheeks remained exposed to the freezing blasts. He then settled back to the hard ground, wanting sleep, but dreading the memories that awoke as dreams each night for the past months.

"Thorton!" a voice called to him. "If you're awake, you might as well get up. Sun's risin', and we got coffee boilin'."

Clay rolled to a side beneath the heavy robes, cracked an eye and peered to his left. Two soldiers clutching blankets to shoulders and chest stood by the wind-whipped flames of a fire, warming themselves.

"The coffee, she is hotter than the freezing ground." A private named DiIulio lifted a steaming tin cup, took a sip, smacked his lips, then grinned beneath a shaggy mustache aglisten with ice. "She warms the belly, if not the soul."

DiIulio represented a new wave of men entering the U.S. Army—Italian immigrants. Like the blacks after the Civil War, and the Irish before them, the Italians newly arrived to the nation, finding themselves on the lowest rung of the social ladder, gravitated to military service when no jobs were to be found in the eastern cities.

"I'm too stiff to get up, even for coffee." Clay groaned when a half dozen aches in his back protested as he rolled over again. "I've got time for another forty winks."

"Not that much time," said Corporal Jack Pageant, DiIulio's companion by the fire. "Reveille will be soundin' in ten minutes or so. And Captain Stowers was lookin' for you last night. Said he had some information for you."

"Looking for me?" Clay gave another inward groan as he sat up and stared at the two soldiers, who had apparently been assigned to guard the horses during the early morning hours. The various nations who populated the Indian Territory delighted in liberating army mounts whenever the opportunity to do so presented itself. Raids on the stock would increase as spring grew closer and the plains tribes left the territory to return to the prairies. "He say what he had in mind?"

Pageant shook his head. "Nope. Just mentioned he wanted to talk with you."

Abandoning the hope for sleep, Clay shoved to his feet. With robes still wrapped around him, he moved to the fire and squatted to fill a cup from a pan of boiling coffee.

"Why did you not sleep in a tent?" DiIulio asked as the rancher sipped the scalding brew.

"Got in late. Didn't want to disturb the hardworking troops of this nation's army while trying to find an empty tent." Clay warmed his hands with heat radiating from the tin cup. "There's little-enough pleasure for a man stuck here at Fort Sill, except sleep."

Pageant and DiIulio nodded solemnly. Clay hid an amused smile.

He had yet to meet a man in uniform without complaints about his post.

"Any luck with them Cheyenne?" Pageant asked.

"Another wild-goose chase." Clay said nothing else; the less he elaborated the better. It made it easy to live his lie.

For the army at Fort Sill and the other army posts he had visited in the Indian Nations, Clay Thorton was a Texas rancher in search of a four-year-old daughter taken captive by Kiowas. The lie allowed him freedom of movement through the territory. The U.S. Army frowned on men searching for braves they intended to kill.

That he kept three packhorses laden with trade goods had not brought one lifted eyebrow. After all, a man needed goods with which to barter, even if the item he bartered for was information. Indians, no matter what their tribe, loosened their tongues when gifts were offered. That was the one thing Clay had learned during his months within the Indian Territory.

That, however, was about all he had learned. During December, January, and now into February, he had visited Indian camp after Indian camp—thirty in all. Comanche, Cheyenne, Kiowa, Wichita, Osage, Kansa, many tribes he had never heard of until reaching the Nations, all were visited on rumors and threads of rumors about a blue-spotted Appaloosa mare.

He had found nothing but more rumors and frayed threads. The mare and the Kiowa who rode her remained elusive.

A bugle sounded reveille in the distance. The notes, barely audible above the wind's howl, soon were taken up by other company buglers throughout the fort. To Clay the sound was like a grating echo that refused to die.

He stood and glanced at the pale glow in the east that barely illuminated the low clouds blanketing the sky. He grimaced. For a week the unbroken clouds had slid by overhead, moving to the northeast. With them had come intermittent snow, sleet, and freezing rain. For a man raised in the arid wastes, the damnable cold felt as hellish as the summer sun in the Chihuahua Desert.

Clay drained the coffee cup and placed it beside the fire. "Best look up Captain Stowers before he gets away from me for the day."

"Good luck," Pageant offered with sincerity. "I hope the captain's got something that'll lead to your girl."

The corporal's genuine concern brought a pang of shame to

Clay's breast. It passed quickly. He could live with guilt and his deception as long as it brought him to Coyote Man.

Thanking the soldier, Clay clutched the robes tightly, turned, and started toward Stowers's tent. Ice-coated grass shattered and crunched like broken glass beneath his boots. Clods of dirt, ripped from the ground by horses' hooves, felt like jagged stones under his feet.

Outside the tent, he called, "Captain Stowers? Clay Thorton here. Understand you've been looking for me."

"Be right out, Mr. Thorton."

Clay heard a rustle of cloth within the tent, then a man no more than thirty years old pushed aside the tent's flap and stepped out. He shivered and slapped his hands to the arms of his blue woolen coat. "A bit of hot breakfast might take the edge off the morning. Will you join me in the officers' mess, Mr. Thorton?"

Clay accepted the offer and within fifteen minutes sat before a plate of fried eggs, ham, biscuits, and red-eye gravy. He allowed the officer to sample a bite of the breakfast before questioning, "Why were you asking after me?"

"A couple of reasons." Stowers paused to pop a portion of ham into his mouth. "First, I was wondering if you noticed any horses carrying army brands in Two Birds's camp?"

The captain referred to the Comanche village Clay had ridden to visit three days ago. He had an unspoken agreement with Stowers; he kept his eyes peeled for stolen mounts, and the officer questioned newly-arrived Indians about the Appaloosa mare.

"I saw a brown gelding and a bay mare in Two Birds's *remuda*," Clay answered. "Could have been more. Didn't get a good look at the ponies."

"I'll send a patrol out to pay Two Birds a visit." Stowers shook his head; his lips pursed tautly in disgust. "The government never should have placed these heathens in the hands of the Quakers. Matters will not be set straight until the Indians are returned to the control of the army. The Friends are too damned lenient. They have no understanding of these savages. They think they are dealing with men versed in Christian ways. Sometimes I'm not certain Indians are even men. Their ways mimic animals more often than not."

Clay said nothing. He understood the captain's frustration. The winter brought band upon band of Indians in from the plains, all desiring government beef to feed them through the harsh winter. Many even appeared ready to accept the white man's ways, listening attentively as the Quakers lectured on farming methods.

With the first thaws of spring the "reservation Indians" returned to their old ways. They slipped from the Indian Territory, often riding the backs of stolen army horses. Through spring, summer, and fall they hunted the buffalo and raided farms and ranches. Then with winter's ice and snow, they crept back to the Indian Territory to accept handouts of government beef.

It did not take a man with a West Point education like Stowers to realize the Indians took advantage of the situation, Clay thought. Unlike Stowers, the rancher placed little faith in the army's ability to contain Indians on reservations. The army had been given ample opportunity to prove itself and had failed.

During the long months' search for Coyote Man, Clay had also learned something that seemed to evade Stowers. Indians were not animals. They were flesh-and-blood men who lived and died, leaving children and grandchildren to carry on in their ways. They were no different from white men or brown men.

It was the ways that were different. The Indians were like the cavemen Clay read about in the newspaper articles concerning the controversy that surrounded the English scientist Charles Darwin. They had lived their day and now faced a tide of Americans who felt it their destiny to claim this country from the shores of the Atlantic to the shores of the Pacific Ocean.

The simple truth—there was no way of stopping the Americans or the machines and factories they brought with them. That fact lay beyond the grasp of the Indian. Like the buffalo that had sustained them for centuries, they were dying. The only question in Clay's mind was: would that death be quick and clean, or would it be a lingering agony?

He knew which he preferred, but the choice was not his. It lay in the hands of politicians in Washington who had never heard a Comanche war cry or faced an Apache determined to free a man of his scalp.

"You speak Kiowa, don't you, Mr. Thorton?" Captain Stowers's voice wedged into Clay's reflections.

"Some." Clay speared a bite of biscuit with a fork and slopped it in egg yoke. "Mostly I use Comanche and sign. All the bands seem to know a bit of Comach. Enough for me to get by."

Stowers let his gaze rove around the officers' mess a moment. He lifted a hand and signaled to someone across the room. The captain's attention returned to Clay. "A ragtag band of fifteen Kiowas came dragging into the fort yesterday. They were more dead than alive by their looks. Mostly squaws, children, and a couple of old men."

Stowers paused when a lieutenant approached the table and saluted. Clay finished the last of his breakfast, paying little attention to the exchange. He lit a morning cigar as the captain dismissed the man.

"As I was saying, these Kiowas aren't much to look at," Stowers picked up where he left off, "but I think you might want to talk with their chief, an old bastard calling himself Hundred Horses. Although I'd say it's been many a year since he's seen even two horses."

Clay exhaled a stream of blue smoke. The cigars available at the fort were a better grade than those found in El Paso or Santa Fe. The smokes represented the only pleasure he had discovered while in the Indian Territory. "Any particular reason this Hundred Horses caught your attention?"

Stowers pulled a pipe and tobacco pouch from a coat pocket and packed its bowl. "He made no mention of your daughter, but I think he's seen the mare you've been looking for."

Clay made no attempt to hide his interest. "When can I talk to him?"

"Soon as I finish my morning coffee," Stowers replied.

THE HOLDING AREA to which Stowers brought Clay was little more than a stock pen crowded with thirty Indians. From the beadwork on their clothing, the rancher noticed they were all Kiowas. This represented an improvement in the fort's administration. In the past the army paid no attention to their wards' tribes, caring little that they mixed tribes with long-standing blood fueds. The results were often disastrous—for the Indians, not the army, who saw the dead as fewer Indians to worry about.

"This group will be taken to a Kiowa camp on the Cache this afternoon," the captain explained while he motioned for two guards to open the pen.

Clay's gaze moved over the faces that turned to him when he followed the officer into the holding area. The Kiowas gathered here would become true "reservation Indians," he thought. The majority were too old to return to the plains. They would live out their remaining days as wards of the United States Government.

The captain found Hundred Horses bundled in a buffalo robe by a small fire. At his side sat three squaws with faces as leathery and wrinkled as that of Hundred Horses. All four gnawed at twists of jerked beef. The meal became a major task, since all four ancient Kiowas displayed more gaps in their mouths than teeth.

Clay settled cross-legged to the ground across the fire from Hundred Horses. He passed two small paper- and twine-wrapped bundles to the old Kiowa. Hundred Horses lifted each to his nose and inhaled deeply. He smiled when his nostrils filled with the scent of coffee and tobacco.

"It is said that the honored chief Hundred Horses can help me find my daughter," Clay spoke in Comanche. The surprise he saw in the Kiowa's tired eyes said the chief understood. "She was taken from me by a Kiowa brave adopted by Lipan Apaches and given the name Coyote Man. This brave now rides a horse, also stolen from me. It is a mare with blue spots covering her rump."

Hundred Horses nodded knowingly. Clay had learned never to expect a direct answer from an Indian, no matter what his tribe. Nor did Hundred Horses provide one.

Thirty minutes passed while the rancher listened to miseries the small Kiowa band had faced during the summer and fall. Having lost their young braves to larger bands and the lust for blood raids, Hundred Horses and the squaws who looked to him to provide food for their kettles slowly died.

"It was the time when the leaves change their color that Rides-A-Mare came into our village," Hundred Horses finally said. "He was a Kiowa, although he wore some clothing of the Apaches. He spoke of his many brave deeds and how he had slyly saved himself from torture at the hands of Apaches by saving one of their great war chiefs from being torn apart by a mad coyote. He said this chief had given him the name Coyote Man."

Rides-A-Mare? Clay's heart raced, and he cursed inwardly. Had Coyote Man evaded him simply by using this latest name?

His fears were laid to rest when Hundred Horses added, "Rides-A-Mare is a great hunter, but there are many bellies to feed in our band. His rifle and bow could not find the game needed for our cooking fires. It was hunger that drove us to the fort of the long-knives. Rides-A-Mare refused to come with us. For as many risings of the sun as there are fingers on my right hand, he has been gone from our band. He rides for the land of the *Tejanos* to the river the *Tejanos* call the Brazos.''

Thanking the old chief with a cigar, Clay rose and looked at Captain Stowers. ''Seems I've been wasting my time here in the Nations. The brave I'm looking for has never been here. He's down in Texas.''

''Then you'll be leaving us, Mr. Thorton?'' the officer asked.

''Just as soon as I can get my goods packed,'' Clay answered, holding back the string of profanities poised on his tongue. He had wasted the whole winter. Coyote Man never came near Fort Sill!

Fifteen

FIFTEEN TIPIS formed the Comanche camp. Within ten of those conical tents lived braves of warrior age, and they were suspicious of the white man dressed in Mexican clothing who rode into their village beside the muddy water of the Brazos River.

Clay's wariness tripled when he sensed the Comanches' distrust. The stunted forest that covered the mountains, ridges, and hogbacks of the Cross Timbers was not the open plains of the Llano Estacado. No longer could Comanche bands call it their home. Fifteen miles from this wide bend in the river, Clay had passed a farm with plowed fields. White settlers edged into this area of Texas during the 1850s. With each passing year they encroached farther into the Cross Timbers with its wealth of pecan trees, oaks, and game.

The rancher kept Winchester and Colt holstered while he dismounted and spread the goods carried by one packhorse on the ground. The bounty of flour, cornmeal, sugar, coffee, and dried leaves of tobacco more than interested the Indians. However, the dozen honed-steel hunting knives presented a temptation that could not be ignored. One by one they came forward with hides and buffalo robes ready to trade and share the coffee he boiled over a small fire.

The seventh brave who sat in front of him carried the name Sees-Like-The-Owl, and he spoke of a Kiowa brave who had ridden with them for a month. That brave rode an Appaloosa mare from which the Kiowa derived his name Rides-A-Mare.

"Rides-A-Mare felt the breath of the time of high grasses," Sees-Like-The-Owl said after concluding fifteen minutes of haggling for a hunting knife. "With the full moon, he rode north to join his people. Though a brave may be welcomed in the camps of others, his heart longs to be among those of his own blood."

Something twisted and knotted deep within Clay. He felt the strength flow from him. A full moon had lit the night sky two weeks ago. Again, he was too late to find the Kiowa he sought. Coyote Man, or Rides-A-Mare as he was now called, had ridden north.

A full year! The thought repeated itself in Clay's mind as he finished his trading, packed his goods, and rode northward. From April to April, he had trailed the elusive brave from Mexico to the Indian Territory and halfway back again. In those long months, he had never glimpsed the brave.

Perhaps Juan was right. Maybe it's time for me—

Clay shook his head, freeing himself of the thought before it fully formed. He urged his mount forward. He had yet to accomplish what he started a year ago. Until he finished that task he could not consider returning to the ranch. If Rides-A-Mare rode north, so would he. Sooner or later the trail would run out for the Kiowa, and Clay would be there waiting to repay a debt.

SPRING RAINS swelled the usually tame Red River to a torrent of foaming water. Branches and saplings ripped from the river's banks, propelled by the raging current, shot atop the water like deadly missiles.

"Ten cents, one thin dime, is all I'm asking." An unshaven man in muddy boots and pants looked up at Clay. The man's eyes lay shadowed by the brim of a hat that sported three rips in its crown. "A dime each for you and your horses."

Clay's gaze shifted from the man to the raft tied to the bank of the river. "The price seems a mite steep just to take a man fifty yards across some water."

"I reckon that all depends on how bad a man wants to get across that water." The man chuckled, apparently amused by the thought. "Now the house over yonder on that hill is mine. Once I get across, I'm goin' into that house and have me my supper. I ain't comin' back across until tomorrow morning. It makes me no never-mind whether you try to swim them horses across or you sit here 'til the morning. The decision's up to you. But you'd best make up your mind. I got three men already waitin' on the raft."

Clay felt the stares of the men standing beside their horses on the raft. He did not like being held over a barrel, but he had little choice. To try to swim the river bordered on insanity. Nor did he believe the Red River would soon subside. Black thunderheads moved in from the northwest, promising another gully-washer by sundown.

"A dime apiece for me and the horses," Clay repeated the man's price.

"A dime apiece for man or beast." The ferryman grinned up at the rancher.

"Pay the man, stranger, if you're comin'!" one of the men on the raft shouted. "Me and the boys here'd like to make camp 'fore that storm catches up with us."

Giving in to the inevitable, Clay reached inside his shirt and withdrew a money pouch a-jingle with coins. From the corner of an eye he noticed the three riders' undivided attention centered on the heavily-weighted pouch while he unknotted the drawstring to extract a fifty-cent piece, which he handed to the ferryman.

"I owe you a dime." The man dug deeply into a pocket to produce the change, which he dropped into Clay's waiting palm. "Now get yourself and them packhorses aboard. My supper's gettin' cold."

Clay dismounted and led the horses onto the raft. The three riders' gazes followed the money pouch back inside his shirt.

"Have to agree with you 'bout the price of the fare, friend." This from a man who introduced himself as Jake Neal. He tilted his head toward the ferryman, who began to pull the raft forward via a rope strung across the river. "Reckon ol' Willis there knew a good thing when he saw it. His price is usually a nickel a head."

"Supply and demand." Clay stroked the neck of a packhorse that pawed at the raft while it bobbed atop the churning water.

"We're up to Fort Sill to take a look at some stolen cattle the army took off the Indians. Comanches hit us hard the middle of March. Might be we can get some of our steers back," a man who did not offer a name said. "You headed thataway? Welcome to ride 'long with us, if you are."

"Arkansas. I'm headed for Arkansas." Neither of the men had the look of ranchers. They appeared no different from the nameless drifters that moved through San Antonio and Fort Worth looking for a cattle drive or work as ranch hands. "Got family in Arkansas."

"From the looks of them heavy packs, you're pullin' up stakes and givin' up on Texas," Jake Neal commented, while he eyed the packhorses.

"Just visitin' family." Clay eased back, as he continued to stroke the horse's neck, so that the pack animal stood between him and the three riders. The men's concern for his money pouch and goods exceeded neighborly interest.

"Must be presents you got all packed away on them horses?" The third man, who had remained silent until this moment, cast a shy smile at his companions.

Clay gave a noncommittal tilt of his head and released a soft sigh when the raft bumped into the northern bank.

"You can bring your horses off now." The ferryman leaped to the ground and securely lashed the raft to two posts. "She ain't gonna drift on you."

Clay waited until the three men took their horses from the ferry, mounted, and slowly rode toward Fort Sill. He felt their eyes on him, glancing back over their shoulders, as he brought his mount and the packhorses from the raft. Keeping the three at the corner of an eye, he climbed into the saddle, and reined eastward.

His original intention was to ride directly to Fort Sill and then move northward into Kiowa Territory. The riders and their interest in his goods demanded a slight alteration to that plan. A lone man offered easy pickings for three men who decided to relieve him of his pack animals and money poke.

For an hour he kept the late-afternoon sun directly at his back. When the sun lay two fingers from the horizon, he swung his horse northward. *Two days,* he told himself. He would ride north and then edge westward to pick up the trail to the fort. That way he would avoid running into the riders.

In spite of repeatedly twisting around in the saddle and searching the terrain behind him, the sensation he was followed still beset him when he halted beside a nameless creek. The clear water and tender lengths of spring grass eliminated the need to grain the animals that night. He dismounted, unloaded the packhorses, and unsaddled his mount. After tethering the animals' forelegs, he gathered branches from winter-barren bushes beside the creek and started a small campfire.

While he quickly prepared bacon, beans, and coffee, he probed the dusk that settled around him. The land lay open in all directions, rolling grasslands with short, choppy hills. The few stunted junipers sprinkling the prairie provided little to conceal three riders, or even three men on foot.

When they come, it will be with the night. The thought that the men would not come never entered Clay's mind, which was occupied with an array of scenarios by which he would meet the attack. A dozen plans were examined and discarded as he ate a plate of beans and bacon, then washed the supper down with a cup of black coffee.

The ruse he selected was so old and overused that it found its way into the purple prose of almost every nickel pulp magazine he read. Although almost certain that Jake Neal and his two companions would never be fooled by the trick, it was the only thing that offered him a chance at surprise. Surprise, even a small one, might make the difference against three guns.

The two tarps from the packs, rolled and covered with buffalo robes, did not look like a sleeping man beside the fire to him. Nor did placing his hat atop the mound, so that it imitated being drawn down over sleeping eyes, improve the situation. He told himself that the illusion fell short of the desired effects because he stood close to the heap of tarp and hide. At a distance the view would be different. At least, he prayed it would.

After throwing another armload of branches atop the fire, he settled to the ground beside the decoy bundle. He lay there for a few minutes, then rolled to his stomach and belly-crawled into the night with his Winchester clutched in his right hand. He stopped when he reached a copse of bushes twenty-five yards away. Working behind their skeletal forms, he hunkered there and waited, rifle cocked and ready.

The moonless darkness gave no hint of any movement around him. Nor did he hear anything except an occasional coyote that howled its lonely cry. The stars overhead marked the time. Two hours passed, leaving Clay with the undeniable feeling of being a total fool. Jake Neal and his two friends had not followed him. Instead of shivering in the cold behind some skinny, leafless bushes, he could be warm by the fire and fast asleep.

The creak of saddle leather, groaning beneath the weight of a man sounded to the right. He sucked in a quick breath and held it. Thirty feet away, a shadow moved in the darkness. Repressing the urge to swing his rifle around and fire on the rider, he remained motionless. His gaze followed the man as he eased toward the campfire.

The others? His eyes darted from side to side. He saw them now. From three different directions they converged on the camp. Clay exhaled and drew in another breath. The three men dismounted. Seconds remained until they discovered his trick. Clay cautiously pushed to his feet and lifted the Winchester.

"Damn!" Jake Neal reached the bundle of robes and tarps. He lashed out with a booted foot, scattering Clay's ruse. "The whoreson ain't here! The bastard's expecting us!"

"The bastard's right behind you." Clay managed to find his voice and shout, "Drop your guns. First the rifles, then undo the gunbelts and toss them aside."

"You can go to hell!" Jake Neal spun around.

The yellow-and-blue flame that spat from the man's rifle barrel pointed fifteen degrees to Clay's left. Blinded by the campfire's light, Neal had no idea where the rancher was. Three times he sent bullets into the darkness.

Clay knew exactly where his targets stood. He squeezed off a carefully aimed shot. Lead hammered into the center of Neal's chest. The man's body jerked, feet flying from beneath him as he hurled back and dropped to the ground twitching.

Using the blossom of flame that burst from the Winchester's muzzle to home on, the two standing men swung their rifles around and opened fire.

Clay dropped to the ground. His reaction came a split second too slow. A brand of white-hot fire lanced across his left shoulder. He gritted his teeth until his jaw ached to hold back a groan of pain.

The two men each squeezed off three more rounds. Their shots sizzled the air above Clay as they sliced through the night. The reports of those shots covered the metallic clicks when he jacked the Winchester's lever forward and wrenched it back. A spent shell popped from the rifle as another cartridge took its place in the weapon's chamber. The rancher took a bead on one of the silhouetted men and fired.

This time he did not wait to see the result of the shot. He rolled to his left. Pain flared anew when his full weight came down on his left shoulder.

Hollow thuds sounded when two slugs bit into the ground to his right. The man's aim would have been true had the rancher not twisted out of the way. There was no need for the gunman to know that. Clay groaned loudly as he recocked the Winchester.

"Got you! You bloody son-of-a-bitch!" The lone man standing by the fire cocked his own rifle. He relaxed, straightening when he lifted the weapon. "Now I'll make—"

The Winchester's thunder drowned his words. For the second time that night, Clay placed a bullet dead center in his target's chest. The man's rifle flew from his hands as his body jerked and twitched beneath the impact. Then he dropped to the ground.

For minutes Clay lay on the ground watching the three men, their bodies sprawled beside the campfire. Gradually, when his heart stopped its pounding, he found the strength to rise and cock the Winchester. Cautiously he moved forward.

There was no need for caution. The three were dead—two shot in the heart and the third in the head. Clay dragged their bodies from the camp and left them heaped together. In the morning, he would find their horses and throw them over their saddles for the ride to Fort Sill.

He returned to the fire's light and removed his shirt. Bloody and painful though it was, his wound was minor. The bullet had grazed his shoulder, gouging out a small gully of flesh as it went. He washed the wound with creek water and sprinkled it with sulfur powder taken from his saddlebags. Finally, he tied a makeshift bandage around it. Stiffness would plague him for days, but he was a long way from the grave. At the moment, that was all that mattered.

Gathering the scattered tarps and buffalo robes, he covered his trade goods to protect them from rain and dew. Wearily, he stretched on the ground beside the fire and covered himself with the robe. In spite of the throbbing in his shoulder, he soon slept.

Sixteen

HUNTS-THE-HORSE.

Clay Thorton sat on the ground, watching the small band of Kiowas prepare to move their camp of thirteen tipis.

Hunts-The-Horse.

The words of the chief Tall Grass echoed in the rancher's mind, refusing to fade. The words themselves meant nothing; the context in which they were used did. Tall Grass had called Clay by the name Hunts-The-Horse.

Hunts-The-Horse.

"Dammit!" Clay cursed aloud, unable to contain the frustration that welled within his chest, threatening to drown him.

Today was not the first time he had heard the name. Nor was it the second or even the third. Tall Grass was the fifth Kiowa who had called him Hunts-The-Horse.

In Fort Sill, when he first heard the name, he thought it to be no more than Indians giving him a name in their tongue rather than using his Christian one. Nor did it strike him as unusual when he ran into it again when he moved north in search of Rides-A-Mare. The third occasion left him with a sinking sensation in the pit of his stomach.

Here on the Kansas plains, he knew things had taken an unexpected turn for the worse. He had put a lot of ground under him during the winter while he roved from Indian camp to Indian camp. During those months, he and the Appaloosa mare he searched for became known. More well-known than he suspected at the time. The Indians had dubbed him with a name, as was their way—Hunts-The-Horse. Whether they had any glimmering of the reason behind his search, Clay did not know. However, the name ate at him.

Not because he found it insulting, but because it indicated how well-known he was to the Indians. Like some invisible wire stretching from camp to camp, the name telegraphed his identity across the plains. Hunts-The-Horse was known, and that was bad.

It was not fear for his life that brought a cold chill running up his spine. Rides-A-Mare surely had heard of the trader who came into Indian lands looking for a blue-spotted Appaloosa. The brave soon would realize that Hunts-The-Horse hunted the mare he rode.

If he hasn't realized it already!

Clay shuddered as the chill transformed into an icy spike of dread. Coyote Man or Rides-A-Mare, or whatever name he was now called, *did* know he was followed. He had always known!

It was so obvious. Why had Clay failed to see it before? He shook his head. The Kiowa surely had known the rancher would come after him. Clay was certain Crow-Who-Flies-Far had made that clear to the adopted Lipan. The Lipans knew he would come to collect bloody retribution for the murder of his family. Because of that, they had driven Coyote Man from their camp.

Blind! So damned blind! Not wanderlust, but nagging fear kept Rides-A-Mare moving from one Indian band to another. He stayed as long as he judged it safe and then moved on before the man on his trail caught up with him. Weeks, days, even a single day, Rides-A-Mare always seemed to remain just beyond Clay's grasp.

The reason for that was clear, so damned clear now! Far worse, Clay recognized, was the edge Rides-A-Mare held. With the name Hunts-The-Horse, the Kiowa had him and his movements neatly pegged. At the first hint of an approaching Hunts-The-Horse, all the brave had to do was mount and ride hard and long to escape. He could find refuge in a Kiowa, Comanche, or Apache camp. He was free to roam from the Missouri River to the Rocky Mountains, from Mexico to the fringes of the Sioux nations.

The immensity of the region in which Rides-A-Mare might—and could—ride pressed down on Clay like an unseen weight. The string of months that stretched behind him were meaningless. He could not shake the feeling that he began his task anew with each morning, that information gleaned on a previous day meant nothing with the new.

Clay glanced around, his eyes comprehending what had gone

unseen while he had been lost in dark reflection. The Kiowas camp prepared to move on. In a matter of minutes the Indians had broken camp. The alacrity displayed by the plains bands boggled the mind. They were nomads. They claimed one spot of land for a camp one night and by the next night they camped miles away. There was no wonder army patrols had such difficulty in locating the Indians they rode after.

Rides-A-Mare was born of these people. Their speed, their mobility was his. Finding him might be impossible.

Impossible. The word gnawed at him. Yet, there was no way to avoid the obvious. What he attempted was impossible. In a land so expansive he would never find the Kiowa brave.

Clay's head moved from side to side as he pushed from the ground and stared at the departing Kiowas. He denied the obvious. He would find Rides-A-Mare. If it took a lifetime, he would find the brave. *If it takes a lifetime!*

THE SMELLS of Abilene, Kansas, rankled his nose. The overly sweet-smelling astringent splashed on his cheeks and neck by the barber did little to mask the barrage of repugnant odors that assailed his nostrils when he stepped onto the street.

The overwhelming scent of cattle packed into the holding pens of the stockyard was the least objectionable. Far worse were the underlying stinks of rotting garbage and human urine and feces. The last offended more than the olfactory sense. There was something dirty and unclean about it, something that struck at the very foundation of what Americans so proudly call civilization.

Clay told himself he had been too long from the cities and towns of men, that he verged on reverting to the wild. But he could not escape the fact that even an Apache, derided by whites for his uncleanliness and stink, would walk as far as two miles from his wickiup to find a suitable location to evacuate his bowels.

That fastidiousness was sorely lacking in the privies that stood behind each house and building in the town. The lime occasionally dumped down the holes of the one- and two-seaters was the sole concession to the need for hygiene.

The only relief from the malodorous attack the rancher foresaw was that he would be ready to ride from the town by sundown. His morning had been spent trading buffalo robes and hides for a fresh supply of dry goods to fill his packs, as well as securing a small profit.

All that prevented his leaving at this moment was the clothes Raúl DeOro had given him so many months ago. He had taken them to a laundry for cleaning and mending. To kill time while he awaited the completion of those simple tasks, he had purchased a newspaper and visited a barber for a bath, the shearing of the long strands of his hair, and trimming of the rough brush covering his face until it resembled a beard again.

A glance at his pocket watch revealed ninety minutes remained until his clothing would be ready. His gaze moved up and down the street, alighting on a nearby saloon with a gaudily painted sign that proclaimed cold beer and hot meals were to be found inside. Although, he doubted that anything in Abilene could be cold during the sweltering month of August, the prospect of one more real meal before moving out was one he could not pass.

Food prepared by any hands other than his was the only thing he missed about civilization. Even the hotel feather bed he slept in last night—something he had yearned for during the innumerable nights on the hard ground—proved a disappointment. It felt too soft and lumpy to provide any real rest.

Crossing the street, he pushed through the saloon's batwing doors. The half-dozen horses tied to the hitching rail outside ill-prepared him for the crowd packed inside. Cowboys, who had long ago washed the trail dust from their throats left from the long drive from Texas to Kansas, downed whiskey and beer in celebration of their accomplishment. They lined the bar and filled most of the tables. Clay located a vacancy near the back of the saloon and made a beeline for it, signaling a waiter as he went.

Ten minutes later the waiter placed before him a platter spilling over with a fried steak and a mound of boiled potatoes and green beans. The mug of beer, as Clay had suspected, was hot. He did not mind. It tasted like beer, and that was good enough.

"Clay? Clay Thorton?" a voice hailed as he worked halfway through the steak. "Is that you under that face of hair, my friend?"

Clay's head snapped up. He knew that voice as well as his own. "Juan? Juan?" His gaze darted around the saloon.

Juan Morales shoved from the bar and wove through the saloon's patrons toward the rancher's table. A broad grin split his face from ear to ear while a mug of beer in his left hand sloshed foam to the floor with each step he took.

"Juan?" Clay was unsure whether to believe his eyes while he pushed from the table and extended his right hand. "Juan, what the hell are you doing here?"

"I am making you a rich man, my friend." Juan grasped the proffered hand and squeezed it like a vise while pumping Clay's arm. "And I am not hurting my own pocketbook while I am at it."

"Damn!" Clay shook his head in disbelief when Juan settled across the table from him. "You're the last person I expected to see in the middle of Kansas."

"And I was uncertain I would ever lay these eyes on you again." Juan's grin stretched even broader. "Occasionally, I hear stories from the soldiers about you, but I do not know how much weight to give them. The soldiers hear rumors and then add their own details sometimes. Now I can see with my very own eyes that you are still alive. It does my heart good, my friend."

"Still alive"—Clay lifted his beer mug to the Mexican—"and still looking for Rides-A-Mare."

"Rides-A-Mare?" Juan's grin evaporated behind a perplexed expression. "Who is this Rides-A-Mare?"

"The same Kiowa brave Crow-Who-Flies-Far called Coyote Man. It's the name he's using now," Clay explained.

At Juan's insistence, Clay recounted all that had occurred since the rancher left the Guadalupe Mountains with Raúl DeOro and his wagons. Quietly Juan listened, concern lining his face.

"And where is Coyote—Rides-A-Mare now?" he said when his friend concluded.

Clay shrugged, shook his head, and chewed the last bite of potatoes. "Ain't rightly sure. Three days back I was with a small band of Kiowas. They said they had seen a brave riding an Appaloosa mare about a week ago. He was with a large band of Comanches and Kiowas headed west."

"But you are here, not riding after them." Hope sparked in Juan's dark eyes. "Does this mean you have given up the chase and will ride back with me?"

"It means nothing of the sort!" Clay watched Juan wince at the sharpness of his tone. The rancher softened his voice. "It just means I was running low on trade goods and supplies. Abilene was close, so I came in. I'll be riding out this evening."

Juan nodded. "I hoped your mind had changed. Maybe it still will. It has been a good year, my friend." Juan pulled a long, flat wallet from his back pocket and dropped it on the table in front of Clay. "Those are your earnings for the one hundred and fifty head I brought up with Sam Dunton."

Clay opened the wallet and thumbed through the crisp, new greenbacks inside. His brow knitted when he looked back at Juan. "There's over twenty-two hundred dollars here!"

"Two thousand two hundred fifty dollars." Juan smiled. "The packers are buying for the winter. Our steers brought twenty dollars a head."

Clay recounted the money. Even minus Juan's quarter, it amounted to one of the largest sums he had ever held in his hands. He took five twenty-dollar bills from the wallet, stuffed them in a shirt pocket, then handed the wallet back to Juan.

"What is this?" A dubious frown darkened the Mexican's face.

"You keep it for me." Clay drained the last of his beer. "You seem to be doing all right by me, and I ain't got a lot of use for money where I'm heading."

Juan pursed his lips and studied the wallet for several seconds before returning it to a pocket. "I will do that for you, my friend. I will use it to keep your ranch and stock alive. But, it will not be without a cost. A man too stubborn to admit that he is wrong does not leave his home in the hands of others without it costing him. I will do this for the same deal we made when I last saw you."

"A quarter cut?"

Juan nodded.

"You got a deal," Clay answered, while checking his watch. He still had thirty minutes before his laundry would be ready. "Now tell me about María and the kids. And what about Ernesto and Manuel? Is your mother-in-law still at your ranch?"

"Much has changed since you were last at home. First, my mother-in-law now lives in Mexico City. She married a widower from El Paso, and they moved—"

"Ain't you Clay Thorton?" A trail hand, accompanied by two companions, each with a shot glass in their hands, stood by the table. The man's speech was slightly slurred by the alcohol he obviously had been drinking for some time. "I thought I heard this pepper-belly call you Clay Thorton."

Clay lifted a hand to calm Juan when he noticed his friend tense. "The name's Clay Thorton. I don't believe we've met."

"Billy Byrd here usually don't keep the company of your likes, Thorton." This from one of the men behind the cowboy. The man at his side added, "Fact is most decent Christian folks wouldn't keep company with a low-life like you, Thorton."

"That's their right." Clay turned back to Juan. The men were drunk and had burrs under their saddles about something. The best course appeared simply to ignore them. "And María and the kids?"

"I'm talking to you, Thorton." The cowboy called Billy Byrd refused to be ignored. "I'm used to having a man look at me when I talk to him."

Before Clay could answer, one of Byrd's companions pushed beside his friend and jabbed a finger into Clay's arm. "That ain't no man, Billy. I ain't even sure this thing's human."

"It's got the stink of a squaw-loving skunk to me." The third man's face twisted with disgust.

Neither Clay nor Juan spoke, but stared at each other. The rancher found no difficulty in reading his friend's expression. Like him, Juan knew where the cowboys' remarks would inevitably lead.

"We heard about you, Thorton." Billy Byrd spoke after downing his shot. "We heard plenty about you and your Indian-loving ways. How you done gone and turned *Comanchero*. Makes a man wonder what kind of blood you got running beneath your white hide."

Clay held himself back, waiting for the moment he knew would come.

"You done pegged the bastard, Billy. Look at him sitting there with his eyes all hung down like some whipped dog."

"I thought I told you to look at me when I was talking!" Byrd reached down and grabbed Clay's shoulder. He wrenched the rancher around.

Clay's fist snaked out and connected solidly with the cowboy's nose. A surprised grunt burst from Billy Byrd's lips and he dropped like a felled tree—directly atop a table behind him. Mugs and glasses flew high into the air, showering beer and whiskey over three more tables.

In the blink of an eye the saloon's patrons seated at those tables were on their feet. They needed no more than imagined indignities or sheer orneriness to use the opportunity to strike out at the nearest face that turned their way. It took less than another three blinks of an eye for the whole saloon to erupt in an all-out, free-for-all brawl.

Clay took a second to take in the chaotic scene. He did not get the chance for more. One of Byrd's friends doubled his fist and swung right for the rancher's chin. The other trail hand launched himself across the table at Juan.

Clay accepted the only opening the cowboy left him. He ducked. The trail hand's fist whistled through the air above Clay's head. The rancher reacted without thought. When he stood, his right fist slammed into the cowboy's gut.

Wind driven from his body, the trail hand groaned and doubled over. Clay's knee jerked up, plowing into the man's face. The cowboy blinked with surprise as he reeled back and collapsed on the floor, unconscious.

A second later, his friend dropped beside him. Beer soaked his hair and pooled on the saloon's floor.

Clay glanced at Juan, who shrugged while he held the handle of a broken beer mug. "Better his head should ache than my face."

The rancher would have voiced his agreement, except that two men doing their best to throttle the life from each other stumbled into him. Three instead of two spilled onto the table at which Juan still sat.

The unexpected fall did not bother Clay as much as the fact the two men turned their attention from each other to him. It was all he could do to throw up his arms and protect his face from the blows that suddenly rained down.

A solid "clunk" sounded, followed by a second clunk. Both the men rolled off the rancher and crumpled to the floor.

"Your glass was better built than my own." Juan smiled down at his friend, displaying the empty beer mug he had used on the men's heads. "It was also stronger than their heads."

Clay started to rise and immediately ducked when the shattered remnants of a chair sailed at his head from the left. A brief glance assured the rancher that he was not the intended target of the awkward missile. In fact, he could not locate the man who had sent the chair a-flying.

Beside Clay two men rolled atop a table, each flailing the other's face with punishing punch after punch. Beyond them, four cowpunchers squared off like pugilists in the ring, although no prizefight ever sported four contestants who could not discern which of the other men was his opponent. Across the room a minimum of twenty trail hands writhed on the floor. Each man kicked, slugged, and bit with no apparent concern as to who was the recipient of his attack.

Nor did the scene offer much variety as the rancher's gaze completed a circuit of the saloon. Three months of steam and frustration kept under lid during the long trail drive from Texas had entered the saloon looking for a place to explode. Clay's well-applied fist to Billy Byrd's nose served as the spark to ignite the human powder keg.

The resounding report of a pistol snapped Clay's head around. Standing in the saloon's doorway, the batwings swung wide, was a man in a black suit and string tie. Light glinted from the silver star pinned to his chest. He fired two shots into the building's ceiling before the rancher noticed the five shotgun-armed deputies standing behind Abilene's town marshal. The scowl on the lawman's face bespoke of a determination to quickly end the barroom brawl.

Juan tapped Clay on the shoulder. "I think we have overstayed our welcome, my friend. It is time we should go."

When the rancher looked at the Mexican, Juan nodded to a door at the back of the saloon. Clay waved an arm for his fellow Texan to lead the way. Dodging three hurled beer mugs, four whiskey bottles, and a half dozen ill-timed punches, the two slipped through the door into the saloon's storeroom, and then outside via a rear door.

"There is no wisdom in standing here." Juan hastened his companion behind a row of buildings, down an alley, and onto Abilene's main street. When he assured himself that their presence drew no attention from passersby, Juan released a sigh. "I do not think you will be welcome in Abilene this night, Clay Thorton."

"I think you might be right." Clay nodded. He pulled his watch from a pocket and thumbed it open. His laundry had been ready five minutes ago. "It might be best for me to stroll down to the livery stable, get my horses, and ease out of town before that marshal starts asking questions about who threw the first punch."

Juan stared into Clay's eyes. "There's time for you to change your mind. You cannot spend your life searching for the Kiowa. The odds are you will get yourself killed before you find him, my friend. Return to Texas, and I will ride with you this very moment."

Clay's head moved from side to side, rejecting the offer. "I'll be riding home, but not today. I've still got unfinished business to the west." The rancher took his friend's hand and shook it. "Give my best to your family and take care of yourself." With that he turned and walked away.

"This is not like you," Juan called after him. "This is not the Clay Thorton I know."

Clay did not answer. He had laundry and horses to collect before the marshal could find him.

Seventeen

CLAY SQUATTED beside a small fire and stoked it with buffalo chips he pulled from a burlap bag. He held out his hands to the flames and rubbed them in the hope of massaging the aching chill from his fingertips. Gradually warmth spread through fingers and thumbs. He took two more of the patties of dried manure and tossed them onto the fire, before clutching the buffalo robe draped over his shoulders tightly about him.

His gaze lifted from the coffee pan and the small bubbles that formed on its side. Despite the clear sky overhead and a bright noonday sun, the cold seeped all the way to the bone. A north wind howled straight out of Raton Pass and ripped along the Canadian River. Small white-capped waves broke the surface of the narrow river with each bone-chilling gust.

Clay attempted to convince himself to be grateful for plentiful water—something lacking while on the Colorado plains during September and October—and failed. This early November day held a bite that he usually associated with January and February. Winter chomped at the bit, and autumn's weak hands barely held it back.

Not waiting for the pan to come to a complete boil, the rancher poured himself a weak cup of the brew and drank the warmth into his body. He had chosen correctly in turning south for Santa Fe rather than trying for Fort Sill. The black mare and the single bay packhorse were all but played out. He had hated trading his two other horses to trappers, but the deal they cut for his furs and the animals had been too good to pass up. With one pack animal he traveled faster. He would purchase new horses in Santa Fe when he restocked his trade goods.

After that, he was not sure. He had lost trace of Rides-A-Mare two weeks ago. The Kiowa might have turned east to winter in the Indian Nations or ridden south into Apache lands.

Clay pushed aside the decision on which direction to take. He still had to follow the Canadian River through the Sangre de Cristo Mountains to Taos and then move along the Rio Grande to Santa Fe. A week of riding lay ahead of him. Time enough to choose his trail once he reached Santa Fe.

Draining the tin cup, he refilled it with stronger brew and rose to retrieve a strip of jerked beef from the mare's saddlebags. A stride from the horse he stopped. Two riders rode toward him from the east across the grasslands that swept from the river to Laughlin Peak.

Jerky forgotten, Clay backstepped to the fire and retrieved his rifle from the ground. He cocked the Winchester and silently wished he had taken the time to cross the Canadian before stopping to rest the horses. With water between him and the riders, his position would have been far more secure. All he could do was wait, hope for the best, and prepare for the worse.

Three hundred yards from the camp the riders drew their mounts to a halt. In spite of the buffalo robes they hugged about themselves, their sombreros, saddles, and bridles marked the two men as Mexican. As did the border Spanish one of the riders called out, "May we ride into your camp?"

Clay's head cocked to one side. The voice was vaguely familiar, but he could not place it. "That depends on what you intend on doing when you get here."

"Just talk, my friend Clay Thorton," the rider answered. "I only wish to visit with a man I thought to be dead."

Clay squinted. The voice and the snowy white beard covering the man's face belonged to . . . "Raúl! Raúl DeOro! And Luis!"

"*Sí!*" the Mexican *Comanchero* answered. "Luis and I have been riding hard all this morning hoping to find you."

Clay waved the two men in while he dug two more cups from the pack and got the jerky from the saddlebags. He handed his friends steaming cups when they dismounted. "It ain't much, but the jerky ain't tainted and the coffee's hot. Warm yourselves by the fire."

"*Muchísimas gracias.*" Raúl sat on his heels by the fire and motioned Luis to do the same.

While the two men busied themselves with coffee and jerky, Clay added three more buffalo chips to the fire. "I'm not complaining about the company, but you said you were looking for me. How'd'ya know I was here?"

"Two days ago we camped with a band of Comanches on the Purgatoire," Raúl said. "They told me of a white man who dressed and spoke like a Mexican. He had come to their camp a day before us, looking for a Kiowa brave riding an Appaloosa mare. That man could be no one else than my friend Clay Thorton, I told myself. So I came in search of you."

"But what brings you here?" Clay drank from his own cup.

"What always brings me into the Comanchería," Raúl replied. "My wagons are behind us. Luis and I left them this morning at the base of Raton Pass."

"We had searched for you all this morning," Luis added. "We would have turned back were it not for the smoke from your fire."

"Well, I'm damned glad to see you." Clay grinned. "Doubly glad for company on the ride into Santa Fe. You are headed for Santa Fe, aren't you?"

"*Sí,*" Luis said, with a nod.

"But you might not wish to travel west with us, my friend." Raúl stared at the rancher. "I have seen the brave you seek, the one the Comanches call Rides-A-Mare and the Apaches called Coyote Man."

Clay's temples pounded. "You've seen him?"

Raúl bit at his lower lip and tilted his head in the affirmative. "Three weeks ago near Horse Creek."

Clay knew nothing of the creek, nor did Raúl's description help place its location. Neither had the rancher heard of the Comanche chief Double Wing in whose camp the Mexican had seen Rides-A-Mare.

"I saw him ride from the camp, my friend," Raúl explained. "Double Wing and his band asked that he leave the camp and never return."

"They drove him out?" Clay asked, uncertain he understood.

"While showing all the hospitality Comanches display for guests in their camp, they did just that," Raúl replied as he refilled his cup from the pan. "This Kiowa is a bad one. He is reckless—wild and dangerous. His own people fear him. That fear is something the Comanches have learned to respect."

Clay frowned. "Fear him?"

"Both the Kiowas and Comanches say he is a brave with great medicine," Raúl answered. "His courage is great. He leads many raids, but those raids cost too many lives. The Comanches believe his medicine is both good and bad. He is like a double-edged knife to them. He cuts both enemy and friend."

The rancher recalled Crow-Who-Flies-Far describing the Kiowa in similar terms. The old chief had said the brave helped the Lipans with one hand while hurting them with the other, or something to that effect.

"He has become an outcast among the Kiowa and Comanche bands," Raúl continued. "While the Americans Sheridan and Mac-Kenzie lead soldiers deep into the plains, a brave so reckless cannot be trusted. He is friendless on the grasslands."

"Then he moves south!" Clay's gaze shifted to the southern horizon. "Rides-A-Mare intends to become the Apache Coyote Man again."

"There is no other refuge for him but among the Apaches," Raúl confirmed Clay's speculation. "Double Wing said the Kiowa indicated he would join old friends in the Guadalupe Mountains."

Clay's chest tightened, and his heart doubled its tempo. Those friends had to be Crow-Who-Flies-Far's band. Clay was certain of that.

"I reckon you were right about me not heading for Santa Fe." Clay traced the southern route he would take along the Canadian and its tributaries and then down the Pecos to Fort Sumner. Still following the Pecos's banks, he would eventually reach the Rio Hondo. Heading east along that river would bring him to Lincoln and Fort Stanton, where Crow-Who-Flies-Far said he intended to take his band of Lipans.

"There is more, my friend," Raúl said. "The Kiowa knows that you follow him."

Clay nodded. "I figured that out last spring. It didn't take much for me to realize that's why he was moving about so much—trying to stay ahead of me."

Raúl shook his head when he placed his empty cup aside. "You misjudge this brave. He moves because he finds himself unwelcome in each camp he comes upon. He fears you not, but delights in the chase he has led you on for more than a year."

Clay stared at Raúl as his words penetrated his mind. He had been a fool. Rides-A-Mare was Kiowa; the Apache fright of a white man they called Fears-Not-Death meant nothing to him. The long months, the endless miles on the trail while Clay chased one slim thread after another had been no more than some enormous joke for the brave.

"You must stay ever alert, Clay Thorton. This brave is dangerous," Raúl warned. "When he wearies of toying with you, he will turn. Then the hunter may become the hunted."

Clay half-listened to the Mexican. His attention shifted to his horses. His plan to buy new animals in Santa Fe was now out of the question. Rides-A-Mare, or Coyote Man, as the Kiowa surely called himself again, was somewhere in the south, not to the west.

The rancher looked back at Raúl and Luis. "Do you think I could interest you in a little horse trading?"

Raúl glanced at his friend's two horses. "It depends—if the price is right."

THE ABANDONED WICKIUP was the first Indian sign Clay had come upon since leaving Tularosa and entering the Sacramento Mountains three days ago. The rancher drew the chestnut gelding he had purchased from Raúl to a halt in front of the oven-shaped structure and dismounted. Except for a ring of stones filled with gray ash from a fire, there were no other inklings that this site had served as an Apache camp.

Tieing the chestnut and packhorse to the limbs of a piñon, Clay poked his head into the brush-covered Indian dwelling. The dirt floor was hard and clean. Better was the absence of insects and snakes. He smiled; the wickiup would provide shelter for the approaching night.

While Clay grained the horses, he did not ponder why the wickiup had been abandoned and the camp vacated by the Indians. He knew. Someone had died in the wickiup and, as was Apache custom, the structure was shunned in fear of evil spirits, ghosts that might possess the living.

After the feed bags were secured to the horses' heads, he loosened the cinches of both animals, but left pack and saddle on their backs. The Sacramentos, like the adjoining Guadalupe range, were Mescalero territory. In spite of a dearth of Indian sign, Clay realized unseen eyes might be observing his movements this very moment. Should trouble break out during the night, all he would have to do is tighten the girths and ride.

Gathering cones, needles, and dead branches from beneath the stunted pines that ringed the clearing in which the vacated camp sat, he placed them in the ash-filled circle of rocks left by the Apaches. He lit a fire and began cooking a supper of biscuits, bacon, and coffee.

Although the possibility of Indian attack was always very real in this land, he gave it little weight. From the fire ash, he judged Apaches had forsaken the campsite three to four days ago. Whoever died had possessed powerful medicine for the band. There was no other reason for the Indians to abandon the whole camp, not with winter so close.

Had the dead Apache been a member of Ishpia's band? Clay wondered while he flipped the bacon with the tip of his hunting knife. He doubted it; that would be too much to hope for—that the first Apache sign he stumbled on was left by the band with which Coyote Man traveled.

The rancher lacked any reason to believe other than the Kiowa rode with the Mescalero Ishpia. At Fort Stanton, Crow-Who-Flies-Far had welcomed him like an old friend. Before Clay had presented the old war chief with gifts of tobacco, sugar, and flour, the Lipan recounted Coyote Man's sudden appearance among the Apaches gathered around the fort. Crow-Who-Flies-Far assured Clay the brave answered to the name Coyote Man again and not Rides-A-Mare, as the plains tribes called him.

The Lipan also told how the Kiowa and twenty young Mescalero braves, following the warrior Ishpia, slipped away from the reservation four nights after Coyote Man's arrival at Fort Stanton. Crow-Who-Flies-Far had heard Ishpia boast he would winter along the Rio Penasco, which, when not a dry bed, flowed out of the Sacramentos, through the northern foothills of the Guadalupes, and eastward into the Pecos.

Clay lifted the lid to a pan, tested the browning biscuits with a fingertip, and judged them cooked when they bounced back. He slipped two from the pan, sliced them open, and sandwiched three slices of bacon in each. The remaining three biscuits, he left in the covered pan beside the fire for his breakfast in the morning. With a cup of coffee sitting beside him, he settled to the ground and ate.

The Penasco flowed directly south of the camp. If he read the lay of the land right, it was no more than twenty miles from his position. *Right down in that valley,* he thought while his gaze traced the slope of the mountains. Farther south he saw the Guadalupes, blazed a brilliant gold by the setting sun. Perhaps a hundred miles separated him from—

He shoved memories of his ranch out of his mind. The Rio Penasco was his destination. Once he reached the river, he had to locate the Mescalero chief Ishpia and the Kiowa brave who rode with his band.

Popping the last bite of biscuit into his mouth, Clay rose. With coffee cup in his left hand, he retrieved the two buffalo robes from the packhorse. Although the sky was clear and the wind still, a chill settled over the land as the sun sank below the western horizon.

Clay crawled into the wickiup, thinking that this was the first time in weeks he would sleep with a roof over his head and there was no cloud in the sky to even hint of rain. The shelter seemed almost a waste.

THE HOWLING WIND grabbed Clay's ears and dragged him up from the dark corridors of sleep. He rolled to his back under the buffalo robes and blinked at the tangled canopy of brush and branches overhead. Several perplexed seconds crawled by before he recognized the roof of the wickiup and recalled the shelter he had found for the night.

It took another ten seconds for him to comprehend that the steam dissipating in the air was not steam, but his breath transformed to clouds of mist by the cold. That was when he noticed the chilled ache of his cheeks and the tip of his nose.

Another yowling gust whined outside. The wickiup shook violently as wind railed against the makeshift structure.

Blinking a dozen times to work the gauzy film of sleep from his eyes, Clay pushed to an elbow and peered at the open entrance to the wickiup. Illuminated by dim morning light, a maelstrom of heavy, moist snowflakes swirled outside, whipped frantically by the wind.

Snow? The rancher's eyes widened, his mind unable to accept immediately the wet, white sheet that covered the ground. *The sky was clear last night—*

The high-pitched neigh of a horse shattered his disbelief. Another whinny came in refrain.

The horses! Something's after them!

Clay thrust the robes aside, snatched up his rifle, and scurried on hands and knees to the wickiup's door. The sharp crack of snapping tree limbs sliced through the wind's howl. The rancher poked his head outside in time to see his mount and packhorse reel and bolt. Dragging broken pine limbs in reins and lead rope, they disappeared into a cedar brake downhill.

Winchester cocked and raised, Clay shoved to his feet outside and quickly took in the area round the wickiup. Nothing—he saw nothing that might have frightened the horses.

It was the wind that scared them, he realized when he peered up through the falling wall of white to the low dark clouds that covered the sky. Somewhere the sun shone above those clouds, but he could not judge where it stood in the sky. It might have just risen, or was hanging mid-sky. The sole thing of which he was certain was that while he slept a blue norther had blown in, bringing what appeared to be the makings of a blizzard with it.

"Damn!" Clay cursed aloud as he ducked back into the wickiup to retrieve a robe, which he threw over his shoulders and wrapped about his chest. He hastened outside again and ran after the horses. He had to find them before they got too far. This was not a land for a man on foot.

Eighteen

WHITE BUFFALO—everywhere! Clay spun around in the knee-deep snow. The white buffalo surrounded him. No matter which way he turned, their great humped bodies stood as they grazed on a feast of ice.

Feast! The thought echoed in his head. He would feast on them, would warm himself in the steam that rose from their innards when he slit open their great bellies.

"Yes." That single syllable spilled from behind his chattering teeth, over his trembling lips, and through his ice-encrusted beard as a puff mist lost in the falling snow.

The warmth to be found inside the shaggy beasts directed his hands and arms more than the gut-twisting hunger. He cocked the Winchester and hefted the rifle to his right shoulder. Sighting down the barrel, he curled a finger around the trigger while he took aim at the nearest buffalo.

Thunder roared above the yowling wind. Lead spat from the muzzle and slammed into the buffalo's shoulder amid a spray of white.

White blood in a white beast! A smile spread across Clay's face when he swung the rifle to the next buffalo and fired, then on to the next, and the next, and the next.

He blinked with incomprehension. His smile drooped to a frown of uncertainty. The buffaloes still stood! It could not be, but it was. Nor did the second round he pumped into their bodies bring them down.

"No." A tremble grew to a shuddering quake as it worked through his body.

Lowering the Winchester, he stumbled through the snow. His left arm stretched out and his fingertips touched the nearest of the buffalo. Horror widened his eyes when his hand sank into the animal's side and struck hard rock.

"No!" He staggered back, fighting the harsh reality that wedged into the cottony fog blanketing his mind.

He saw clearly. The creatures around him were not buffaloes, or creatures at all! He faced boulders—talus from the mountains—covered in the snow that had fallen ceaselessly from the sky for—

His eyes darted from side to side like the eyes of a madman. He could not remember how many days ago he had left the abandoned wickiup in search of his horses. He recalled three nights huddled beside rock or tree to escape the damnable wind. Had there been more? Or did he imagine those nights?

Tears rolled from his eyes, stinging his cheeks as they turned to ice. The fever that burned in his body and mind denied his brain something as simple as a clear thought.

The horses—he remembered the horses. They were important; he was certain of that. Although he could not recall why.

He turned away from the snow-covered boulders and began walking. Something told him, if he found the horses, everything would be all right. He had to find the horses.

His right foot caught on a rock hidden beneath the snow. Arms flailing to maintain his balance, he swayed, then fell face down in the freezing white blanket.

He had to get up and find the horses. He tried to move; his body refused. He would go after the horses, he told himself as he allowed his eyes to close, just as soon as he rested. All he needed was a little sleep to get his strength back.

"You've got to keep the covers on."

An angel hovered over Clay. On each of her sides stood a cherub. He nodded while the angel tucked the covers beneath his chin. He tried to thank her, but the darkness sucked him back into the yawning pit.

The voice was soft and soothing. It did not demand that he open his eyes.

"See if you can keep down a few spoonfuls of this broth," the voice said. "Then you can sleep again."

Clay's lips parted to let the rich broth slide down his throat into his stomach. Then he slept.

"MOMMA." The voice belonged to a young girl.

Sarah? A haze covered Clay's eyes; he saw nothing more than blurred light moving amid shadows. He tried to call his daughter's name, but his mouth and tongue were too dry and swollen to move.

"Here, drink this water."

A woman he could not see placed a cup to his lips. He gratefully swallowed the cool water. He felt a moist cloth bathe his brow.

"The fever's trying to break," the woman said. "Keep resting. Sleep's the best way to fight it."

"Yes," Clay managed to murmur before he slipped back to sleep.

CLAY'S EYES opened to stare at a ceiling of twisted cedar post beams and adobe brick. He did not recognize the ceiling or the stone wall to his left. Nor did the bed in which he lay feel familiar.

The crack of burning logs and a glowing warmth drew his attention to the right. A young woman, as beautiful as the angel who came to him in his fever dream, sat in a rocking chair in front of an open hearth. Her graceful hands worked with needle and thread as she darned what appeared to be a pair of socks.

The rancher tried to lift his head from the feather pillow, but lacked the strength. Nor could he push his words past the dryness in his throat and mouth. He worked his tongue and cheeks to produce enough moisture in his mouth to form the word "Water."

The woman, raven-black hair cascading down to her waist, turned to him. A smile touched her lips and aquamarine eyes as she put aside her mending and rose from the chair to bring a water pitcher and cup to the bed.

"You're awake again." Her voice was gentle and soothing, like the angel in his dreams. "I thought you would sleep through the night."

Clay drained the cup she placed to his lips, then asked for more of the cool water. She obliged, laying a palm to his forehead while he drank.

"There's still some fever," she said with another smile, "but it's nothing compared to the fire that was burning inside you for the past six days."

"Six days?" Clay blinked up at her.

She nodded. "Ben heard your shots and found you laying in the snow. He thought you were dead." She placed the cup and pitcher on the floor. "I mashed some potatoes from our supper and kept them for you. Do you feel strong enough to eat something?"

The mention of food brought the realization he was ravenous. "A bear, horse, or cow would do nicely."

"You are feeling better, aren't you?" Her smile widened, then she crossed to a rough-hewn table and picked up a bowl and spoon.

Clay's gaze moved around the single-room house as she returned to the bed and sat on its edge. The dwelling was small with a single door and window. Whoever had constructed it had done a good job with stone and adobe mortar. Clay felt no draft, though he heard the wind whistling outside.

"Can you sit up?" she asked.

He tried and failed. She displayed no concern, but he felt like a helpless babe as she spoon-fed him mashed potatoes laced with rich beef gravy.

"You mentioned a Ben," he said after several satisfying bites. "Your husband?"

"Son."

He followed a tilt of her head to the opposite side of the room. There a young boy and girl slept in beds pushed head to head into a corner of the house.

"My daughter's name is Mary," she said. "Mary just turned five and Benjamin is seven—although he always adds a 'half' to his age."

While Clay swallowed another spoonful of potatoes, his gaze continued around the one-room house. He found no other bed, except the double one in which he lay. "I'm in your bed. I should be—"

She cut him short by pressing another mouthful of potatoes to his lips. "There's more than enough room for me beside Mary. I'm comfortable there."

Clay wanted to protest; he could not. It took all his strength to handle the food the young woman ladled from the bowl. When she scraped out the last bit and placed it in his mouth, he closed his eyes, swallowed, and sighed.

"I feel better, a lot better." His words slurred as he felt himself drifting back into sleep. Just before he slipped into the darkness, he realized he had not asked the woman her name.

· · ·

A BLAST OF COLD AIR and the slam of a closing door awoke Clay to the smell and sound of bubbling oatmeal. A boy—Benjamin, he remembered—stood by the door holding a steaming wooden bucket.

His mother lifted a smoke-blackened pot from the hearth and carried it to the table. She looked at her son. "The morning milk isn't doing us any good over there. Bring it here so I can put it on your breakfast."

The boy complied, but not without protest. "Ma, you know I don't like oatmeal. I like eggs."

Clay silently agreed with the boy. The rancher preferred sliced cold cornmeal mush for breakfast if it came down to "druthers." Oatmeal had a slimy texture and always left his mouth coated for what seemed like hours.

"You know the hens aren't laying. The oatmeal's hot and will fill your stomach." The woman ladled out three bowls of the hot cereal and added a dipper of fresh milk to them. She called her daughter —Mary, Clay was pleased to recall—who played on her bed with a rag doll.

"Morning," Clay said, while the young woman helped her children into their chairs. His voice was weak and shaky; he barely recognized it as his own.

The young woman looked up and smiled. "Good morning, Mr.—"

"Thorton, Clay Thorton."

"Mr. Thorton," she confirmed with a nod. "I've hot oatmeal for breakfast, if you'd like some. I think it will help build your strength."

Clay could think of a few hundred things he would rather put in his mouth, including the Comanche delicacy of honey-dipped grasshoppers. However, he lied, "That sounds fine."

The woman picked up the bowl of oatmeal meant for herself and took a step toward the recovering rancher when Mary called out, "Momma, I can feed the sick man." The girl scampered from the table and ran to her mother's side, with arms lifted for the bowl. "I can. I feed Thelma Ruth all the time." She looked at the rag doll left on the chair.

The woman shook her head. "I don't think you—"

"Give her a try," Clay suggested. "I don't mind. You've got your own breakfast to eat."

"I don't think that's a good idea, Mr. Thorton. I've seen my daughter serve tea to her doll. Half of it usually ends up spilled on Thelma Ruth's lap," the woman replied.

"I'm willing to risk that," Clay said. "Besides, I feel strong enough to give Mary there some help."

The young mother gave her reluctant consent after the rancher managed to sit halfway up in bed and lift both his arms. She handed the bowl to the girl and looked at Clay. "Don't say I didn't warn you."

With Clay holding the bowl, Mary managed to perch on the side of the bed and spoon the milk and cereal into his mouth. That which dripped found its way into the wild strands of his beard and not his lap. Mary had worked a quarter of the way toward the bottom of the bowl when Clay said, "Mary, I know that your name is Mary, your doll's name is Thelma Ruth, and your brother's is Benjamin. Does your mother have a name?"

"Everybody has a name, silly." Mary directed a spoonful of oatmeal into his mouth. "It's Momma."

The woman at the table laughed. "Although I've taught my daughter her ABCs and to count from one to twenty, I seem to have left some gaping rents in her education. My name is Anna Grant, Mr. Thorton."

Clay nodded. "Pleased to make your acquaintance, Mrs. Grant. I'd also like to add my thank you's for saving my life."

Anna Grant smiled. "We still haven't got you back on your feet, but if you can survive Mary's nursing, Mr. Thorton, I believe you'll make it."

"Can't you do this yourself?" Mary stared at the rancher, apparently bored with the task she had undertaken. "I'm hungry."

Clay took the spoon from the girl. "You run along and eat your own breakfast, young lady. Thank you for helping me. I think I can manage this myself."

"Good." Mary scooted from the bed and ran to her place at the table.

"I was camped on a mountainside above Rio Penasco when the blizzard hit," Clay said between bites of cereal. "My horses broke free. I chased after them and managed to get myself lost. I'm not certain how long I was out there. The fever hit me quick and hard.

"The Penasco? That's twenty-five, maybe thirty miles north of this ranch," Anna said. "You wandered a piece while lost. The snow lasted four days. Ben found you the evening of the third day. I think you had pneumonia, or close to it, Mr. Thorton. To be honest, I was afraid you wouldn't make it. I've never seen a fever like the one that was burning inside you. The worst is past, but it'll take some time for you to gather your strength.''

Clay placed the empty bowl on the floor beside the bed. He closed his eyes. Three days lost and seven in the bed fighting the fever made ten days and at least twenty-five miles from the Rio Penasco. He prayed the Mescalero Ishpia and his band had not fled the mountains before the snows.

"CAN YOU DO CIPHERING, Mr. Thorton?" Ben looked up from the book opened before him atop the table.

"My pa taught me to add and subtract and my multiplication through twelves," Clay answered from the bed. He then boasted, "I can even do a bit of dividing.''

A smile lit the boy's face. "Think you can give me a hint or two with these figures?"

During his two conscious days in the Grant home, Clay discovered Anna Grant was as strict about her children's book learning as Elizabeth had been. Today, before she left the house, dressed in a man's trousers and shirt with rifle on her shoulder, she placed Ben and Mary at the table with their day's lessons. For Mary that consisted of printing her ABCs ten times. Ben's task was arithmetic.

"I might be able to help," Clay said. "Let me take a look.''

"Good." Relief washed over Ben's face. "I've been working on this division for two weeks and can't get the hang of it. Ma gets awful mad at me sometimes.''

Dread suffused the rancher. He boasted too quickly. Dividing, especially when it involved fractions, was not his long suit. He accepted Ben's book and scanned a column of simple division problems. He could solve these. "Which one's got you stumped?''

"All of them," the seven-year-old boy admitted with downcast eyes.

"Mmmmm. Maybe you aren't looking at this the right way. You know your multiplication?" Clay asked.

"Through the twelves, like you." The boy brushed a stray strand of hair as black as his mother's from his forehead.

"Then you know the answer to every one of these. You just don't know it yet." Clay pointed to the first problem. "Two goes into ten how many times?"

Ben shook his head. "I don't know."

Clay recalled Martin having a similar difficulty with division until he had showed his son a little trick. "Then tell me what times two gives you ten."

"Five," Ben replied without hesitancy.

"That's your answer to this problem."

Ben stared at the book for a moment, then looked at Clay. "You mean this is backwards multiplying?"

Clay gave his head an affirmative tilt. "Starting off it is. Try this one—four goes into eight how many times?"

"Two," Ben answered tentatively, as he tested the backward multiplication.

He beamed proudly when Clay said, "That's right. Now this one here."

By the time Anna returned with two rabbits to skin for the supper stew, Ben was prepared to work his way through the day's assignment for his mother. When he concluded, he added, "Mr. Thorton showed me how it's done."

Anna cast a skeptical eye at the stranger. "You didn't give him the answers, did you?"

"That wouldn't have done the boy any good," Clay replied. "I just showed him a different way to look at them figures."

"I'm not sure I want to know what that way is, Mr. Thorton," Anna said, while she cleaned the rabbits, "but since Ben appears to know his answers, I thank you."

"Can Mr. Thorton help me with printing my numbers tomorrow?" Mary asked her mother.

"Mr. Thorton would be glad to, young lady," the rancher answered. "That is, if you'll start calling him Clay and not Mr. Thorton."

Mary grinned with obvious delight.

ANNA GRANT quietly straightened the disarrayed blankets without disturbing her sleeping children. She then sank into the rocker in front of the hearth, watching the flames.

"You have a son and a daughter to be proud of," Clay said softly while he sat in the bed.

Anna looked at him and smiled. "And you have a surprising way with children, Mr. Thorton. From your appear—" Embarrassment left her stumbling over the rest of her sentence.

Clay finished it for her. "From my appearance, someone might get the idea I was raised wild in the mountains." He ran a hand over his shaggy beard. "When a man's traveled as much as I have for almost two years, he sometimes forgets that he ever made an acquaintance with a razor."

He glanced back at the sleeping Ben and Mary. "They remind me of my children when they were younger."

"You have children?" Surprise colored the woman's voice.

"Had—a son and a daughter," Clay replied. "They were killed along with their mother by a Kiowa brave called Coyote Man. He's why I've been traveling."

"One can't escape sorrow by running from it, Mr. Thorton," Anna said softly.

"I ain't running. I'm looking for that brave." The cold edge to his voice sounded out of place to him within the cozy warmth of the small house. "I heard he was riding with Apaches somewhere along the Rio Penasco."

Silence hung heavy in the house for several moments. When Anna spoke, her voice came as little more than a whisper. "I know what it is like to lose someone that you love, Mr. Thorton. My husband Amos was taken from me . . . almost a year ago now."

Clay studied the gentle lines of the young woman's face while she stared at the flames that licked over the pine logs on the hearth. He felt a kinship with her, sensed the pain within her. Until this moment Anna Grant had made no mention of a husband, nor had the rancher asked.

"I met Amos during the last years of the war. He was a captain, and, in his blue uniform, the most handsome man I had ever seen." She recounted how they had married shortly after they met. "After the war, Amos was assigned to Austin and then San Antonio."

Fort Davis and Fort Bliss became homes to the growing Grant family as the officer was given assignments farther and farther west. His final post was a brief stint at Fort Selden, north of Las Cruces, along the Rio Grande.

"He was on patrol when he discovered this land," Anna said. "He was so excited as he described it—'green like the Garden of Eden amid the rocks and sand of the desert.'"

Two years ago Amos Grant resigned his commission and brought his family to the Sacramento Mountains, determined to build a life.

His vision was realistic, uncolored by desires to carve out a cattle empire. He wanted a simple, good life for his wife, children, and himself.

"I think he would have provided us that, had God given him the time." Anna described how he was gathering stone for a barn when he uncovered four rattlesnakes. "He never had a chance. There were six bites on his arms and four on his legs."

Anna's eyes closed. Clay found himself wanting to reach out and place a reassuring hand on her shoulder. The reaction surprised him and left him frustrated. He barely had the strength to sit up in bed. He tried to find words of comfort, but as it had been throughout his life, the right words were not there. The best he could utter was an inadequate "I'm sorry."

Anna turned to him. A weak smile lifted the corners of her mouth. "So am I, Mr. Thorton. So am I."

THOUGH HE TRIED TO DENY IT, a week on his back in the bed demanded he accept the truth. Clay Thorton had almost died in the blizzard. After that week, he managed to stand and walk, although only for short distances, usually to sit outside in Anna's rocker on sunny days.

In spite of wishing to repay a measure of the kindness this young woman and her children gave him, all he could do was watch as Anna went about her chores. Few men he knew held the conviction and determination she displayed in her effort to keep alive the dream she had shared with her husband. Nor was she lacking in ability. A ranch, no matter how small, required more than one pair of hands to keep it from falling apart. Ben did his best to help his mother, but he was still a child.

Though admiring the young woman, Clay could not escape the harsh reality—Anna Grant's ranch was falling apart and would soon come tumbling down around her ears. The barn Amos Grant started had begun to crumble. Anna had constructed a lean-to against its walls to shelter her two horses and single milk cow. Like the roof on her home, the lean-to did next to nothing to keep out the rain when it stormed.

Clay focused on the roof when his fourth week on the Grant ranch started. While Anna tended her small herd, he found a ladder, repaired it, and carefully climbed atop the house. Working until his strength played out, he took two days to patch or fill the dozen holes he discovered.

Work was a medicine for him, that and the feeling of accomplishment upon completing the simple task. Although he hated to admit it, he had been too long from real work, work that a man does with his hands.

With Ben's help, he started the job Amos Grant had left incomplete. The young boy gathered the flat rocks, careful to flip them over first with a long pine branch and check for coiled snakes. Clay mixed the adobe mortar and placed each of the stones atop the growing walls. At the end of the rancher's sixth week, Ben and Clay completed the barn's roof and proudly led Anna into the new structure to display their handiwork.

Nor did their efforts go unrewarded. "It's beautiful. I think it's bigger than Amos imagined!"

She gave her son an enthusiastic hug and a smacking kiss on his cheek. For an instant her arms opened for Clay, then they dropped awkwardly to her sides. She stuck out a hand and shook his. "Thank you, Clay. I never expected this. Clay, you don't know how much this means to me."

With a grin beaming on her face, she examined every inch of the five stalls and tack room, before announcing, "I am so excited, I almost forgot our supper! Tonight we'll have steak and potatoes to celebrate. And I've got some dried apricots for fried pies." She looked at the rancher. "That's your favorite, isn't it, Clay?"

"Especially the apricot fried pies," he agreed with a nod.

"They're Ben's favorite, too. You both deserve a reward." She turned and hastened toward the house, pausing to glance back at the barn a dozen times.

Clay patted Ben's back. "I think we've gone and done ourselves proud today, boy."

"Yeah," the seven-year-old agreed. "Ma don't make fried pies except on extra-special occasions. We'd better get into the house. We don't want Mary eating more than her fair share. It was you and me who finished the barn."

"Go on. I'll be along in a bit."

Clay watched the boy run to the house. He then turned three hundred and sixty degrees, admiring the barn. The structure was good and solid. Although, he admitted, he was as pleased with Anna's reaction as much as with the barn itself.

He found himself wondering what it would have felt like had the woman not caught herself and hugged him. He shook his head and smiled. It was enough that she called him "Clay." After all, it was the first time in five weeks that she had dropped the very proper "Mr. Thorton."

Before Clay left the barn to join the others, he filled a bucket with water and found a bar of saddle soap. The soap was not meant to lather a man's face, nor was the sharpened blade of a hunting knife a fit razor. Yet, they were all he had to scrape the beard from his face and neck.

Nineteen

"CLAY!" Anna hailed him as he led a saddled brown mare Ben called Dusty from the barn.

Clay stopped and watched the young woman walk from the house. She wore a yellow gingham dress that appeared as bright as the spring sun that hung over the mountains in the east. The rancher, accustomed to seeing her in work clothing when she went about her chores, found himself struck by how feminine and delicate Anna Grant truly was.

"Seeing you all prettied up like that, it's not hard to see why I thought you were an angel come to take me up when I had the fever." He thought he detected a slight blush of red spread on her cheeks.

"All compliments like that and a hard day's work will get you around here is a hot supper come night," she said.

"Fair enough trade." He smiled, his gaze lingering on the beauty of her face.

Then his eyes abruptly darted away to stare at the ground. Guilt constricted his chest.

"Are you certain you feel up to riding out by yourself today?" Anna asked, doubt lining her face.

"I've been in the saddle for the past two weeks and haven't fallen on my backside yet. I don't think a man can feel any fitter than I do," he assured her.

"You certain? I can be ready to go with you in ten minutes," she pressed. "I worry about you going out without me."

Her concern touched something within him that blossomed with warmth. "I'm sure. You've patched me up and healed me. Besides, somebody's got to stay here. That cow looks like she's liable to drop her calf any second. Milk cows are scarce enough in this country. You need to tend the one you have."

She acquiesced with a tilt of her head, then handed Clay a small bundle in a knotted napkin. "Some biscuits and ham left from breakfast, in case you get hungry."

"I think I'll start spreading the compliments thick as molasses," he joked, while he placed the napkin in a saddlebag. "You never fix food when we ride together."

"Just want to make sure you keep up your strength," she answered lightly. Her smile told him she was pleased he noticed the extra touch.

"I'll be back before late afternoon. You and Ben keep a close eye on that cow. This is her first calf. She might need a hand," Clay instructed as he stepped into a stirrup and rose into the saddle.

"And you head back quicker, if you suddenly feel yourself weakening," she ordered.

"I'll be fine." He waved back at her when he nudged the mare into an easy lope. "Watch the cow!"

The guilt and the tightness in his chest returned as he reined his mount to the pasture where Anna's twenty-five-head herd grazed on spring grass. The roots of that sensation eluded him.

Or do they?

Although he denied it to himself time and again, the truth was, he found himself liking it here more than a man should. He was comfortable. In the two months since the blizzard, he discovered with each passing day he viewed Anna and her children more like family than strangers who had saved his life. He enjoyed their company. He found a peace here that had not been his for two years. Anna, Ben, and Mary needed him, appreciated him, even—

His mind stumbled over the thought that formed within it—*loved him.*

He attempted to shove it away, bury it. He could not. The warmth that suffused him refused to be locked out. With Ben and Mary, he held no doubt. They were children open with their feelings and admiration. He returned both.

Anna was another matter. Yet, he sensed she felt something neither she nor he put into words. He saw it in her eyes, heard it in her voice, reveled in the way her fingertips lingered when they accidentally touched. More than any of those, he felt it in her concern. She worried about him—a care that had long ago crossed the border of simple friendship.

His own feelings? He nibbled at his lower lip. He still had a debt to collect. There was no time for all the feelings that awoke within him whenever Anna was near or when she smiled at him. Denying those feelings, he realized he had stayed on the Grant ranch for weeks beyond the point he had grown strong enough to ride on. His gut knotted. He betrayed the wife and children who had once been his.

At the same time, he betrayed Anna. Although he rode with her and helped tend the herd, he found excuse upon weak excuse to ride alone into some canyon or over a ridge. His real reason had nothing to do with cattle. He searched for Apache sign.

Four times he found traces of Indians passing. The brief trails went on for no more than fifty yards and then vanished. Never were they enough to lead him to a Mescalero camp or provide any proof the signs belonged to Ishpia's band.

Clay touched his heels to the mare's side to nudge her into a gallop. The past tore at him while the future tugged him in a different direction. He could not be true to both. They demanded too much of him for that.

He topped a rise speckled with blooming prickly pear cactus. Below, Anna's stock grazed on green grass that lined the banks of a nameless creek. During the night the herd had grown by three. Spindly-legged calves that wobbled at their mothers' sides while trying to get at milk-swollen udders did not bring a smile to his lips.

He reined the mare down the low hill to examine each of the calves. The hairs at the back of his neck prickled as though trying to stand on end. Without stopping the mare, he let his gaze move over the terrain around him. He saw nothing to alert him, but could not shake the sensation unseen eyes studied his every move.

Today was not the first time he had felt those eyes. Three times last week he had been certain he had been watched. Not wishing to alarm Anna, he had searched the rocks and brush on the pretense of looking for stillborn calves. He found nothing, not so much as a moccasin print in the sand.

As his gaze made another circuit of the land, he remembered Raúl DeOro's warning—the hunter may become the hunted.

·   ·   ·

"ARE YOU CERTAIN this is what you want?" Anna finally broke the silence that had filled the house after Clay made his request. Her gaze remained on the hearth.

Clay drew in a breath and slowly exhaled. He wanted to tell her everything, about his feelings for her and the children. After the plans he described, that would not be fair. The least she deserved from him was honesty. "I'm not certain about anything."

"Why, then? Why do you want to leave?"

He saw her body stiffen as though her mind snagged some stray thought. Her head turned, and her eyes met his.

"It's the Indian, isn't it? You want to go after him, don't you?"

"It's not a matter of want." He pursed his lips and sucked in another breath. He mentioned Coyote Man once during his stay on the ranch. That had been almost two months ago, yet, Anna remembered. "It's a matter of what I *have to do*. He killed my wife and children. A man can't let that happen without doing all he can to put it right."

"Put it right?" She was incredulous. "Killing another man is going to bring your family back? Revenge will reverse time and give you the life you had? Clay, think what . . ."

He had feared this. She did not understand. She had been spared seeing a family butchered by the renegade Kiowa; he had not. Coyote Man had to pay for what he had done. The sole currency Clay would accept was the Indian's life.

". . . Was I wrong? Have I misjudged everything?"

Her questions brought him back to what she was saying. "What?"

She reached out and took his hand in hers. "Have I read you wrong? Have I been seeing what I want to see, believing that you feel what I feel?"

He tried to answer, but the words in his mind balked when they reached his mouth. How did she feel? He knew what he hoped, but she never had said anything.

"I thought you cared for us. I know I can see love in you when you're with Ben and Mary. A man can't hide something like that. I felt—hoped"—her eyes shifted away from him—"that you felt the same for me—the way I feel for you."

"I do," he answered. The ease of those words surprised him. His hand squeezed hers, and he leaned forward to lightly kiss her lips. "I do."

"Then why do you want to leave us?" Her tone said she held no comprehension of what drove him.

He shook his head. "I've already said. I have to do this. Things must be put right."

"All right." Her fingers withdrew from his hand. "If that's the way it has to be, then that's the way it will be. You can have the loan of a horse."

"I'll be back this side of a week," he said. "I just have to ride to my ranch. I need two, maybe three horses for what I have to do."

She stared at the fire again. "Then you'll be gone again, searching for the Indian."

"I won't be gone forever," he insisted, feeling her slip away from him. "I'll be back. I promise you that. I'll be back after I've found Coyote Man."

Her body trembled. "When will that be, reckoning this Indian doesn't kill you? A week? A month? A year? Maybe another two years? That's how long you've been looking for him, isn't it?"

He did not give her an answer. Two years spent trailing the Kiowa had taught him there were no guarantees.

"Clay, you saw this place before you came. As much as I refused to accept it, I was fighting a losing battle. Everything was falling apart a piece at a time. I couldn't keep up with it, no matter how hard I worked," she said. "I can't say we'll be here when you decide to return. Those are my children sleeping over there. If I can't make a life for them and myself here, I'll have to go somewhere else."

Clay understood her meaning; he still had no answers for her. Leaving was a risk he had to take.

Anna looked back at him. "Will you say good-bye to Ben and Mary before you leave?"

He had intended to head south hours before daylight. However, he amended his plans. "I'll wait to say good-bye."

"Good. It would hurt them to wake up and find you gone." She nodded her approval. "Now, you'd better get some sleep. You've got a long ride ahead of you tomorrow."

He bent to kiss her lips again, but she turned away. Without another word, he walked outside toward the barn and his bed in the tack room. Halfway to the structure, he stopped. His head tilted to one side and then the other. Night sounds touched his ears, nothing more. He just was worried about leaving Anna and her children alone, he told himself. Yet, he could not shake the distinct sensation that he was being watched.

Twenty

CLAY walked through the empty rooms of his ranch house. The ghosts he had come to confront were not there. The only things meeting his eyes were abandoned rooms that once brimmed with human life and love.

He read the signs of the house's present residents in the thick dust that covered everything. Mice tracks crisscrossed in all directions, as numerous as the cobwebs that attached themselves to the ceilings, walls, and every piece of furniture in the house.

He saw water stains on the floor in a half-dozen places. Two years without care left the roof in bad shape, he realized when he walked outside, closing the door behind him.

The house's exterior fared no better during that time. Rain, wind, and sand had conspired to leave mere flakes of dirty paint on the once brightly whitewashed walls. Here and there portions of the adobe mortar had crumbled away to reveal the house's stacked flat rock structure. The elements had carved a toehold in the house; with enough time, they would eat away all the adobe and begin to work on the stone itself.

Another two years?

Anna's question echoed in his mind.

The nicker of a horse drew the rancher's attention to the corral near the barn. Anna's mare Dusty and the two geldings Clay had brought from pasture stood waiting for the return ride into the New Mexico Territory.

His gaze moved over the barn. It, too, showed signs of neglect. Although, he also saw where Juan Morales and his two cousins had repaired crumbled adobe. They had not applied a fresh coat of whitewash to the structure in the two years he had been gone.

Nor have I. He did not condemn his friends. They cared for his stock. That was the deal he had made with Juan. He could not expect more. Juan, Ernesto, and Manuel had their hands full maintaining the Morales spread. They could not be expected to see after his house and barn, too.

The memories that had remained buried for the day he had been on the ranch flooded his mind in a torrent. His gaze shifted between the barn and house repeatedly. He and Elizabeth had gathered and placed each stone for the structures. More than a need for shelter directed them. They worked with love. They built a home for themselves and the family they wanted to bring into the world. This had been their future.

Now, it stood cold and empty. Another year or two and it would fall to ruin.

Coyote Man! Clay cursed the Kiowa who had caused this. He also recognized the lie in the heart of his curses. The brave had killed the rancher's family, but he had not neglected the ranch and the dream Elizabeth and Clay had shared.

Clay Thorton—his shoulders bent under the weight of his acceptance—was the man responsible for that. He alone had to leave the ranch and hunt down Coyote Man.

An eye for an eye, retribution, justice, putting things right—all the reasons Clay used to justify two years' riding throughout the plains—fell away while he walked to a small hill a quarter of a mile from the house. He knew, when he knelt by the six graves atop the crest, there was only one reason for his actions—revenge. That and that alone had driven him. He searched for Coyote Man to satisfy his need to spill blood. Revenge was for the living; it meant nothing to the dead.

The spring rains had been good this year. The proliferation of weeds that poked through the rocks covering each grave told him that. Carefully he pulled the weeds and tossed them aside.

While still on his knees he moved to the simple wooden cross he had placed at the head of Elizabeth's grave. It had toppled. He set it back in the ground and supported it with a ring of rocks about its base.

Heated shame suffused him as he studied the cross. It bore no name, no birth date, date of death, or simple words to commemorate the person who lay at rest here. The crosses like those marking Martin's and Sarah's graves were no more than the common courtesy he would have given a total stranger. Two years had gone by since their deaths, and he had yet to mark their final resting places with proper stones.

Two years. Tears welled in his eyes. He fought to hold them back. The effort was in vain.

Hotly they streamed down his cheeks, burning. Two years of unmourned sorrow released itself in shuddering sobs that racked his body. Unashamed, he wept for his family, for himself.

CLAY CAREFULLY PACKED half the canned goods still shelved in the kitchen. He cradled every jar in a nest of dried grass, then covered it with more grass. He imagined Mary's and Ben's faces when he placed the canned fruits on the table. Like all children, they had a sweet tooth and would relish these treats.

He left the rest of the jars of fruits and pickled vegetables that Elizabeth had so diligently preserved for her family. If all went as he planned, those jars would soon have a use. He felt no guilt as he selected the jars. He could almost feel Elizabeth's presence around him and her approval. He would breathe new life into this ranch they had built. She would like that.

Of course, that depended on Anna. If what she had said their last night together was a true indication of her feelings, then he had no worries.

The clack of hooves on stone drew Clay's thoughts up short. Setting aside the jars, he grabbed the Winchester leaning against the kitchen door. Levering a cartridge into the chamber, he edged one eye outside. A soft gust of relief escaped his lips.

He shouted to the lone rider who approached the ranch house, "Juan, Juan Morales!"

"Clay, my friend!" Juan slid his own rifle into a saddle holster. "Can that really be you?"

"Can and is." Clay stepped from the kitchen, grinning. "I'd hoped I might see you, but didn't expect it."

Juan swung to the ground to grasp the rancher's extended hand. "I came over to gather a team for the stage due here tonight. Ernesto and Manuel will be along in an hour or so."

"It's damned good to see you, *amigo.*" Clay slapped a palm against the Mexican's back. "Damned good!"

"As it is to see you." Juan's gaze shifted to the kitchen. "You are restocking the larder. You have come home to stay."

"Not yet." Clay shook his head. "But I'm almost back here for good. There's one more thing left for me to do. I have to return that brown mare over yonder to a woman."

"Woman?" Juan's eyebrows lifted with interest.

"It took her and her two children to teach me what you learned after we came back from Mexico," Clay answered. He explained how Anna and her children had found him dying in the snow and nursed him back to life. "I've been with them for more than two months, Juan. They're special people. What's more, they think I am."

Juan grinned from ear to ear. "It will be good to hear children again when I ride here. And it will be good to have you as a neighbor once more."

"I might be getting ahead of myself." Clay held out a hand with fingers splayed wide, as though to stop Juan's speculation. "I still have to ask her the question, and she still has to say yes."

"From what you say, I think she has already given you the answer to that question," Juan replied.

It was Clay's turn to grin. "That's my thinking, too. If so, we'll ride down to El Paso and find us a preacher before we head back here."

Clay paused to pull the money pouch from his shirt. He opened it to reveal fifteen hundred in gold coins and bills. "There's a favor I want to ask of you."

"Anything," Juan said without batting an eye.

"I want you to take what you think it'll take to fix up the house. Go to El Paso for whatever you need. I want this place to be shining when I bring Anna here."

"No need for that money." Juan waved off the offer and winked. "I still have some of your money left from last summer. Besides, I think you might be needing that for other reasons."

Clay tied the money back in its pouch and tucked it in his shirt. "You sure?"

Juan nodded. "I will see to it that this house looks as though it were made only yesterday. I will bring María here. She will keep the little ones busy, as well as Manuel and Ernesto."

"Thank you, my friend," Clay said, then tilted his head toward the jars he had been packing when Juan rode up. "Give me a hand. I was about to saddle up and head back."

With Juan's help, he loaded a bay with the pack and then saddled a buckskin. "I feel like I should stay and help with the stage."

"You will be doing that soon enough." Juan shook his head. "You have business across the border that needs tending."

"Right!" Clay grinned when he swung into the saddle.

"The Kiowa?" Juan asked. "Did you ever find him?"

"No," Clay answered, surprised that he no longer cared that Coyote Man had escaped him. "I never laid an eye on him in two years."

Juan shrugged. "Such is the way of life. We can but accept what it brings us."

Clay stretched an arm down to the Mexican. "I'll be seeing you."

"Vaya con Dios." Juan grasped his hand and shook it.

Reining the buckskin's head around, Clay tapped his heels to the horse's sides. In an easy lope he rode westward toward the young woman and two children who waited for him.

Twenty-one

THREE PLUMES of gray smoke drifted into the sky from the middle of a cedar brake that covered half the sloping side of the mountain. The three fingers, twisted by the afternoon breeze, interwove to form a dark, greasy rope that snaked upward toward the fluffy clouds that drifted across the sky.

Icy needles of apprehension pricked over Clay's body. Anna's ranch lay but ten miles to the north. The rancher eased the Winchester from its saddle holster. Apaches—the smoke came from Indian fires; he did not doubt that.

Ishpia's band? He did not hazard a guess. Spring brought warmth. Young Mescalero bucks were apt to slip away from the government lands around Fort Stanton in the north. Each of the renegades would be looking for a way to make a name for himself. That meant bloody raids. The name of the warrior who led the braves did not matter, the results did. The camp was far too close to the Grant ranch for comfort.

Keeping to the piñons through which he rode, Clay's senses came alive. His eyes moved from side to side, searching for the braves he knew would be posted as guards about the camp. His ears listened for any sound, the merest hint of anything that might alert him to danger.

The whooping battle cries, the charge of attacking Mescaleros he stood ready to face never came. He reached the brake without discovery. Edging his mount into the dense cover of the junipers, he eased to the ground and paused, his head tilting from one side to the other. Still he heard nothing to suggest the Indians were aware of his presence.

Tieing the buckskin and bay to the limbs of a cedar beside Anna's brown mare, Clay pulled the extra, loaded cylinder for the Colt from the saddlebags. He double-checked the loads as he shoved the cylinder into a pocket. He then slipped deeper into the brake, moving one step at a time, with eyes and ears alert.

The Apache camp stood a half mile from where he left the three horses. Crouched behind the bushy limbs of the cedars, he studied the mixture of tipis and wickiups that crowded the uneven clearing at the center of the brake. He made a quick count of the Indian dwellings—twenty in all.

What he did not see were ponies. The *remuda* that usually grazed beside a village was missing. Perplexed, his gaze moved to the squaws, braves, and children who moved within the camp. Although he saw a sprinkling of young women, obviously the mothers of the children, most of the adults sported hair more gray than black. These were old men and women. Where were the young braves?

Clay repressed the wild speculation that attempted to run rampant in his mind. Two years among the Indians had shown him the growing number of bands populated by the old—bands whose young braves abandoned them to follow an upstart war chief claiming the protection of mighty medicine, or bands whose braves had been killed during skirmishes with the army.

Sucking down several breaths to quell the churning of his stomach, Clay stood. There was one way to find out what he needed. If worse came to worst, he had a fully loaded rifle and twelve more rounds for the Colt. He stepped from the cedars into the village, standing in plain sight.

Shock and fear twisted the faces of each Apache as he or she turned to him. Instead of charging him with upraised weapons, they cowered, slinking from him. He heard the name they whispered among themselves—"Fears-Not-Death."

An old squaw with braids of white offered the sole display of courage. She took five steps toward the rancher, lifted a hand, and beckoned him forward. "Crow-Who-Flies-Far told us that you would come. He said you would find us as surely as the sun chases the moon from the night sky."

"Crow-Who-Flies-Far spoke truth," Clay answered. He watched the tribe from the corners of his eyes. None of them made a move. They just stood there staring at him.

"I am called Strong Teeth." The squaw did not flinch when Clay approached. "I am wife to Crow-Who-Flies-Far. He would talk with you."

Clay nodded his acceptance. "I would talk with my old friend."

The rancher followed the squaw into a tipi. The ancient war chief lay on a bed of cedar boughs. A brightly colored blanket covered him from chest to feet. His eyes opened to peer up at the white man who squatted beside the bed.

"Fears-Not-Death, I felt we would meet one last time before I slept the sleep of forever." Crow-Who-Flies-Far's voice came strong. Yet, even in the dimness of the tipi, Clay discerned the warrior's sickly pallor.

"You will outlive braves three times younger than you," Clay said. He patted his shirt pockets, but found no tobacco.

"I will die—if not today then tomorrow. What the white man's bullets failed to do, the white man's beef did. I grew weak at Fort Stanton and a great fire began to burn in my stomach. Strong Teeth and her sisters brought me here, back to these mountains that have sheltered me throughout my life," Crow-Who-Flies-Far said. "It is right a man should die in a land that knows him."

Clay did not condemn the Lipan for seeking a place of solace to die.

"But you did not come to talk of my dying," Crow-Who-Flies-Far continued. "You wish to speak of Coyote Man."

Clay nodded. "Is he with your band?"

"Not my band." The old chief's head rolled from side to side. "His band. Ishpia died of a snakebite before he led his people to the Rio Penasco. Coyote Man took his place."

A cold shiver worked up Clay's back when he remembered the abandoned wickiup he found in the mountains above the river. The shelter might have belonged to Ishpia.

"Coyote Man knows you are in these lands, Fears-Not-Death. For a month he has watched you and the woman and the two children." Crow-Who-Flies-Far closed his eyes and swallowed hard. "He watched you and felt you sense him. He cannot understand why you have not come to fight him."

The fear Clay repressed earlier began to wriggle free. The Kiowa's eyes were the ones he had felt while helping Anna with her herd. That did not bother him. The fear stemmed from the fact the brave knew of Anna and her children and watched them.

"He sang his war songs and prayed to the spirits for medicine. But you did not come," Crow-Who-Flies-Far said as his eyes opened to Clay again. "He did not understand and that began to drive him mad. He felt shamed. He was certain you knew he was near, but you did not care enough to seek him out."

The old war chief's words shattered in a series of racking coughs that left his frail body shaking. With a moist rattle in his throat, he began where he had stopped. "It was then he began to understand your medicine, Fears-Not-Death. You became an evil spirit whose shadow stretched across the land before you. For Coyote Man it was you, not his own actions, that was responsible for his being driven from band after band. No enemy he had ever faced held such powerful medicine. He became a desperate man, uncertain how to deal with you and your power. Five days ago he took tobacco and a pipe and climbed atop this mountain to ask the spirits . . ."

Five days ago corresponded with Clay's departure for Texas. While he rode south, Coyote Man sought a medicine vision.

". . . Two days ago, he returned. A wild determination fired his eyes as he cleansed himself in the ways of his people," Crow-Who-Flies-Far went on. "Today he called the braves together and asked them to ride with him. The spirits had spoken to him, saying this was the day he should face you."

"He's ridden on Anna's ranch?" Panic constricted the rancher's chest while his heart and temples pounded. "How long ago? How many braves were with him?"

Crow-Who-Flies-Far rolled his eyes to Strong Teeth. The old squaw looked at the white man. "He and fifteen braves rode from the camp less than one hand before you came."

Clay twisted around and darted from the tent without glancing back at the dying war chief or his wife. A hand's width was the space the sun or moon moved in the sky during an hour. Coyote Man and his raiding party had ridden from the Indian village mere minutes before Clay sighted the smoke from the fires.

In a dead run he tore into the cedars. Branch and needles bit at his exposed face and hands. He paid them no heed. Anna and the children were in danger. He had to get to his horses!

CLAY HEARD THE CRACK of gunfire a mile from the ranch. He dug spurs into the buckskin's sides, demanding greater speed from the flagging horse. The animal responded; its long legs stretched out, hooves ripping into the sandy soil. Lathered sweat covered the gelding's chest when the rancher finally drew the horse to a halt atop a sandy hill south of the Grant home.

Clay did not require field glasses to take in the scene below him. Thirteen mounted Apaches, armed with rifles and bows, reined their horses in a wide circle around the small stone house. They held their fire for the front of the house, sending lead and arrows into the closed door and shattered glass window.

Theirs were not the only weapons that spoke. Clay caught the glint of light on a rifle barrel that barked time and again at the attacking Apaches. While he watched, a brave jerked under the impact of a bullet and rolled over the rump of his pony. He spilled to the ground and lay there unmoving, yards separating him from two other Indian bodies in the dirt. Anna gradually whittled down the numbers of her attackers.

What Clay did not see was the Appaloosa mare Coyote Man rode. He quickly scanned the area around the ranch. The Kiowa was nowhere in sight. The missing warrior would have to wait until later.

Dropping the rope lead that held the packhorse and brown mare, Clay again spurred the buckskin forward. There was no way to sneak closer and surprise the Apaches. Nor did he have some well-planned military strategy. He was a single man armed with rifle and pistol. There was but one approach to take—hit fast and hard.

So intent was the Apaches' attention on the stone house that he went unnoticed until he was fifty yards away and his Winchester opened up. In rapid-fire he pumped three rounds, one after another, into the chamber and squeezed them off. He pointed the rifle rather than aimed. Two of the shots went wide, completely missing their target. The third left a fourth brave dying in the sand.

Clay's fourth shot blasted directly into the chest of a brave as the buckskin lunged between two of the circling warriors. A scream of surprise tore from the Apache's lips when the bullet slammed into his body. From the corner of an eye, the rancher saw the brave slump and roll from his pony.

Wrenching hard on the reins, Clay wheeled the gelding around to face the attackers. Simultaneously, he dug his spurs into the buckskin's sides. The horse leaped forward, charging directly toward a brave mounted astride a war-painted pinto. The rancher cocked the Winchester and fired.

Throwing himself to the neck of the pony, the brave escaped death as hot lead sizzled harmlessly over his back. The Mescalero's rifle swung under the pinto's neck, muzzle jutting toward Clay.

Following the braves' suit, the rancher flung himself forward, stretching atop the buckskin's neck. The brave's shot sliced into empty air while the buckskin once more carried its rider through the circle of howling Apaches.

Clay saw a fifth warrior tumble from his mount when he wheeled the gelding about a second time. The braves no longer reined their mounts around the house but turned their undivided attention to the solitary man who had killed two of their number. Rifles whipped around, muzzles seeking the rancher.

A brave screamed, not in defiance, but in death. Anna opened up with a rapid-fire barrage from inside the house.

The volley Clay steeled himself for did not come. Panic twisted the braves' painted faces when Anna took another Mescalero in the back. Clay seized advantage of the Indians' uncertainty. He cocked the Winchester and slammed his spurs into the buckskin. Straight toward the Apaches he charged.

He squeezed off a shot. As quickly as arms and hands could work, he recocked the rifle to send two more bullets into the mounted warriors. One of the shots struck home, sending a brave to the ground, his body twitching spasmodically as life flowed from a crimson wound in his chest.

The bark of Anna's rifle died, but Clay fired three more shots, all going wide of their targets. It did not matter. The toll of death mounted too high for the Apaches. Their medicine gone sour, they jerked the heads of their ponies southward and fled. Clay spurred after them, pulling the buckskin up when the Winchester's hammer fell on an empty chamber.

He watched the raiders disappear in the distance while he reloaded the rifle and slipped it back into its saddle holster. He then turned the buckskin toward the stone house.

"They're gone," he called out as he approached the still-closed door. "We ran them off. It's over. They're gone!"

The relief and joy he expected to see on Anna's face were not there when she stepped from the house with Ben at her side. "Mary! He took Mary!"

"Mary?" Clay swung from the saddle and grasped Anna's shoulders. "Who took Mary?"

"The brave on the Appaloosa!" Anna managed through her sobs. She pointed to a patch of grass south of the house. "She was there, playing with Thelma Ruth when they rode down on us. The brave on the Appaloosa was leading them. He was beside Mary before I realized what was happening. He reached down and snatched her up. Then he rode south without ever firing a shot. He took her, Clay. He took my baby!"

"Damn!" The curse escaped Clay's clenched teeth as a hiss. The kidnapping, he was certain, was intended to be a final slap in the face from Coyote Man. The Kiowa had meant for him to suffer the agony of knowing the girl would be raised as an Indian—a tormenting knowledge to come just before the rancher's death.

Coyote Man had not reckoned on his medicine vision being flawed. As with his attack on Clay's own ranch, he had not considered the possibility of the rancher being elsewhere.

"I have to go after him," Clay said as he stared directly into Anna's eyes, "but I need your help. I have to do what I can to make certain the Apaches don't come back here after I leave. Are you in shape to help?"

Anna nodded, although tears still streamed down her cheeks.

"Good. First thing you do is reload your rifle and keep it with you until I get back." He watched the young woman nod again. "Next, I need you to saddle your bay for me. The buckskin wouldn't last five miles before he dropped out from under me."

"My rifle, then saddle the bay," Anna repeated.

Clay tilted his head in the affirmative. "Now do it." The rancher looked at Ben. "I need your help, too. Take my canteens and fill them. I'll need you to fill those two canteens in the tack room for me, also."

Handing the boy the canteens looped about the buckskin's saddle horn, the rancher ran to the tack room. He tossed Ben two more canteens and then took the rope he had retrieved from the barn and tied it to the ankles of the dead braves. It took three trips, but he dragged their bodies a mile south and left them piled there. Apaches were superstitious about leaving their dead in the hands of enemies. This way he ensured they would not return to the ranch for the bodies as soon as the sun went down.

Collecting the brown mare and packhorse, he returned to the house. There he placed the canteens Ben held over the saddle horn of the bay Anna had waiting for him.

"I don't like leaving you, but there's no other way." Clay took a box of cartridges from his saddlebags and handed it to Anna. "First see after the buckskin. He's the only horse I'm leaving you. You might need him. Then you and Ben gather whatever you need and lock yourselves in the house until I get back."

He reached into his shirt and withdrew the money pouch, which he also placed in Anna's hands. "If I'm not back in four days, the odds are Mary and I won't be coming back. Don't stay here. Saddle the buckskin, and then you and Ben ride for El Paso. There's enough in that pouch to stake you to a new start somewhere else."

"Clay, I won't—"

"Don't argue. This is no place for you now. Not with those young bucks holed up in the mountains. We hurt them bad today. I don't think they're likely to be back soon. But in a week or two, when they've had time to lick their wounds, they'll come again. This time they'll be wanting revenge. They won't be driven away."

Anna's body shuddered when she drew in a deep breath. "Four days and then ride for El Paso. If you don't come back here, I wait for you there."

There was no time to explain the futility in waiting. Each passing minute gave Coyote Man that much more of a lead.

Clay took Anna in his arms and kissed her. "I have to go. Keep your eyes and ears open. And remember, don't wait longer than four days."

She pulled him back to her when he turned to mount the bay. With desperation, her lips pressed to his mouth. "Take care of yourself, Clay Thorton. Please, take care of yourself."

He nodded. "No more than four days. Remember that. No more than four days."

He wanted to give her some word of reassurance that everything would be all right. He could not. Pivoting, he climbed into the saddle and spurred the bay to the south. He tugged the two other horses after him. The bay broke in an easy lope that stretched to a gallop, and then a full run under its rider's urging.

Twenty-two

THE WHITE-HAIRED SQUAW Strong Teeth stood on the edge of the cedar brake. She stared up at Clay with unblinking eyes when Clay drew to a halt.

"Crow-Who-Flies-Far sent me to say there has been enough killing for one day," she announced. "If you ride into our camp, the young warriors will face you and more will die—maybe even Fears-Not-Death."

"Release the girl Coyote Man stole and I will ride away," Clay answered. Strong Teeth's presence baffled him. His plan had been to ride into the camp and kill any who stood between him and Mary. He was certain the Apaches would not expect him to come so quickly after their attack. He misjudged Crow-Who-Flies-Far. The old chief prepared his braves for Clay's arrival.

"Coyote Man and the girl are no longer in the village." Strong Teeth pointed to two sets of hoofprints in the sand. "He has taken two ponies and ridden south. He knows fear in his heart. He knows Fears-Not-Death will follow."

Clay caught himself before he reined south. He stared at the old squaw. "Tell Crow-Who-Flies-Far and the young braves that Fears-Not-Death will not enter the camp this day. Tell them that they have felt Fears-Not-Death's strong medicine—a magic more powerful than any held by Apache, Comanche, or Kiowa."

"I will tell them, but there is no need. They learned this today," Strong Teeth said with a tilt of her head.

"And tell them there will be no escaping this medicine if any harm comes to the woman and boy who live in the house," Clay added. "If I find the woman and boy hurt when I return, I will hunt down every man, woman, and child in the village and kill them. Fears-Not-Death will show no mercy."

"I will repeat your words in the camp for all to hear." She turned and walked toward the dense growth of junipers. "I go now."

Clay watched the old squaw vanish into the brake, then spurred the bay south, following Coyote Man's trail.

THE THUNDERSTORM caught Clay in the low, alkaline flats separating the Guadalupe Mountains from their less-impressive cousins, the Hueco Mountains, to the southwest. Dismounting, he removed his hat and placed it crown down on the ground to collect a portion of the downpour while he pulled the saddle from Anna's bay and placed it on the brown mare's back.

He did not like leaving the bay in the middle of nowhere. Ridden to the point of exhaustion and left in this barren wasteland, the horse had little chance of survival. No animal that had served its rider as had the horse deserved such an ignoble end. But the rancher had no other choice. If he hoped to overtake Coyote Man, he could not allow the weary horse to slow him.

He watered the lathered bay from his hat first, hoping the water and coolness of the rain would provide the edge the animal needed to find grass and water before the desert leeched away the last of its strength. There was a chance, slim though it was, that the animal might make it.

Placing the hat back on the ground to catch more of the rain, he waited until it filled before he watered his own bay and the brown mare. He then mounted the mare. He studied the ground and found Coyote's trail washed away in the downpour. It did not matter. The Kiowa had committed himself when he rode southwest out of the mountains. There was but one waterhole between the flats and the Rio Grande to which he could head—Hueco Tanks.

Clay's eyes lifted to low-slung silhouettes on the horizon. At a distance the Huecos looked more like another gathering bank of storm clouds than mountains. He applied his spurs to the mare and rode for the mountains.

A COMANCHE with two fresh mustangs could cover a hundred miles in a night by riding one horse to exhaustion, then leaping onto the back of the second mount as the first collapsed.

Saddle-bred horses were not the rugged ponies of the plains.

Even riding Comanche style, it took Clay three horses to reach the three mountainous mounds of granite men gave the name Hueco Tanks.

A half mile from the northernmost pile of weather-smoothed rock, he eased back on the reins. The bay he had once used as a packhorse halted. The frosty light of a quarter moon rising in the east washed across the desert, illuminating the granite upthrusts. Although called mountains, Hueco Tanks appeared to be piles of gigantic smooth boulders that rose three hundred feet in the air.

The rancher's gaze moved along the eastern face of the northern mountain. Near a long, sloping face of rock sat a small adobe-and-rock building, a reminder of the Butterfield stagecoaches that in an earlier day used Hueco Tanks as a stop along the route to El Paso. Clay's eyes shifted from side to side while he perused the jumbled mound of granite.

Coyote Man was nowhere to be seen. He did not expect to find the Kiowa standing in the open waiting for him. It was a seven-mile circuit around the three mountains. Crevices, caves, and cracks in the rock offered hundreds of holes in which the brave might hide.

Pulling the Winchester free of the saddle holster, he cocked the rifle. His gaze centered on an elongated, triangular gash of blackness formed by overhanging rock twenty feet up the granite slope. Were he Coyote Man, that was where he would wait. Inside were three pools of water, and even in the daylight the deep recess in the rock was dark enough to conceal a man—and a five-year-old girl.

Clay clucked softly to the bay. The horse started forward, its steps unhurried as it moved toward the mounds of rock. Although the rancher's gaze constantly scanned the north mountain for any hint of movement, his attention centered on the dark recess. Moonlight edged back the blackness that filled the long slash, but it revealed nothing.

A quarter mile from the mountain, Clay again tugged on the reins. This time he dismounted. Using the animal as a partial shield, he walked the distance to the abandoned stage station. He tied the horse to a cedar hitching post and skirted behind the small building to peer around a corner. The triangle of black lay a hundred feet from his position.

Temples apound, he stared up at the gash in the rock. If the Kiowa hid there, he was liable to open fire the instant the rancher stepped away from the building. Clay repressed the impulse to shoulder the Winchester and squeeze off several rounds into the dark triangle. Coyote Man held Mary. A stray bullet was as likely to hit the girl as it was her captor. He could not afford the risk.

Which leaves—

He gave himself no time to consider the consequences. Circumstance demanded action, not thought. He had to find out if the Indian was above, then decide how to get him out of the hole.

Clay stepped into the open. He took a single stride, then lunged to the left. He hit the ground, rolling on sand and stone.

The explosive report of a rifle did not come. The sounds of insects and night predators on wing reached his ears. Clay's head lifted, eyes returning to the gash. Still he saw nothing.

Picking himself up from the ground, he moved forward in a crouch. Caution fell away when he reached the sloping granite. He scurried up the slope and ducked into the recess. He saw nothing. Coyote Man was not there. Squatting beside the nearest pool, he dipped a hand into the water and drank. The cool moisture did little to wash the bitter cotton from his mouth.

He rose, walked outside, and stood. Above and to each side he saw nothing except bare granite. Eroded pits, ranging in size from that of a thimble to a washtub, occasionally marred the rock. These pits, which collected rain and dew, gave the tanks their name. In Spanish *hueco* meant hollow or basin.

In a half-slide, half-walk, Clay descended the slope. The immensity of the Hueco Tanks pressed down on his shoulders like an invisible weight. During the long desert ride, he never considered more than reaching his destination. Now, he could not ignore the enormity of the three mountains. To circle the rough arrowhead formed by their bases would take the better part of two hours on horseback. All the time he would provide an open target for the Kiowa, who could be hiding anywhere among the rocks. It would take a week for a lone man to explore every nook and cranny in the granite mountains.

Where does a man begin?

He knew the answer to the unspoken question. He started the search where he stood. Leaving the bay hitched to the post, he edged eastward. His eyes and ears constantly alert, he darted from one shadow to the next, ran from the protection of one boulder to the smooth slab of rock that lay ahead of it.

He saw the flicker of light when he reached the narrow fissure that separated the north mountain from the tanks' east mountain. At first he thought his eyes and weariness conspired to produce the illusion of shifting shadows on the granite. The light remained, no matter from what angle he scrutinized it. Like pale moonlight filtered through the foliage of a heavy-boughed oak, it danced on the rock.

A campfire? Clay frowned. It verged on insanity for Coyote Man to light a fire, knowing that the rancher trailed him. Yet, Clay's mind could find no other explanation for the shifting light. *Why would he set a fire?*

Winchester leveled before him, the rancher entered the narrow passage that split the two mountains. Along the slight curve of the fissure he moved, his gaze searching the sloping rock walls that rose on each side.

Abruptly the passage ended, flaring wide to open on a grassy clearing that sat at the heart of Hueco Tanks. Clay stood at the northeastern corner of a lopsided rectangle bounded on three sides by mountains. The north and south sides of the clearing ran six hundred yards. The eastern edge of the rectangle collapsed inward by the outthrusting western face of the east mountain. The western side of the rectangle was a three-hundred-yard clear gap; desert spread to the horizon beyond it.

It was the fire at the center of the clearing that held Clay's attention. Mary, her wrists bound to a wooden stake driven into the ground, sat by the fire. The child's sobs echoed off the three mountains.

Damn! It took but one hasty glance for the rancher to grasp the insidious trap Coyote Man had laid. Apparently the Kiowa had recognized the immensity of the tanks before Clay. Playing cat and mouse among the rocks was not his intent. Somewhere out there, hidden amid the rocks of the mountains, the brave waited with rifle in hand. Mary was the bait to draw Clay into the open, into the light of the fire, where Coyote Man could easily pick him off.

Clay estimated the campfire's flames brightly illuminated a fifty-foot circle around Mary. The twenty-five feet beyond that were bathed in a subtler glow. The time required to cut Mary free and to cover those seventy-five feet, in and out, would be the most dangerous. Nothing, not even the night would obscure the Kiowa's aim.

A glance to the east mountain revealed the moon had yet to rise above it. The rancher had to make a move before it illuminated the whole clearing. Waiting until then, or until dawn, would be certain suicide.

Hugging close to the rocks that formed the western boundary of the east mountain, Clay cautiously worked his way to a point of granite that extended the deepest into the clearing. Mary, still sobbing, sat three hundred yards from where he stood in the shadows —closer than at the fissure, but a distance that might be a lifetime away.

Slow and easy, he told himself, discarding the idea of making a dash for the fire. Better to simply step forward and cover the majority of the ground step by step, saving his speed for the last seventy-five feet. After all—he bolstered his courage—the brave had as much terrain to watch as he. If he ran, the crunch of rock beneath his boots and the rustle of grass were certain to alert the Kiowa. Safer to move slowly and hope to be overlooked, no more than another shadow in the night's darkness.

His gaze making a complete circuit of the mountains one last time, Clay eased away from the granite. Like a man perched at the edge of a yawning precipice, he stood and waited for the rifle report that announced Coyote Man sighted him. The harsh bark of a rifle did not come.

He took another step, and another. The racing of his heart subsided. His shallow breaths deepened. By the time he completed his sixth stride, he allowed himself to consider the possibility of covering the ground to fire's fringe undetected.

The thought came too soon. A rifle spoke, its thunder ripping asunder the night's stillness.

An unseen sledgehammer slammed into Clay's left thigh. There was no pain, just the unexpected impact that spun the rancher around and threw him to the ground. He groaned as the air rushed from his lungs. Somewhere in the distance he heard the little girl scream her terror.

Dazed by the blow and fall, his confused brain did not grasp what had happened until the pain, burning like a red-hot branding iron, ignited in his thigh. He was hit. If the fiery agony in his thigh was not enough to confirm that, he felt blood flowing warm and sticky from the wound.

Holding back groans behind gritted teeth, he rolled to his belly and crawled toward the protection of Hueco Tanks' east mountain.

With each inch he covered he prepared himself for the second rifle shot that would tear into his exposed back.

When he pulled himself to his feet beside a pitted mound of granite, he realized why no other shot came. Coyote Man misjudged the accuracy of his aim. Clay's groan and fall served to enhance the misconception. The Kiowa believed him dead.

He'll come looking for my body. Coyote Man had to check his kill before the moon rose above the mountain. Doubt would gnaw at him. Had he missed, the Indian would realize, the moonlight left him as vulnerable as the man he hunted.

Ignoring the firebrand that jabbed deep into his left thigh, Clay stood, placing his weight on the injured leg. For an instant his head swirled dizzily and the leg threatened to give way under him. It didn't, nor did he faint from the pain. Instead, he hobbled back along the east mountain toward the fissure. Two hundred feet from where he had fallen, he found a wide crack in the granite and wedged inside it. He cocked the Winchester and waited. When Coyote Man finally came, Clay planned a little surprise for him.

An estimated ten minutes brought no hint of the brave's approach. Nor was the rancher certain from which direction Coyote Man would come. He had not seen the rifle's flash when the Kiowa fired his one shot.

What he did hear was Mary. The child's screams subsided to tearful sobs again.

Another five minutes crept by before the faint hiss of grass brushed by moccasined feet drew Clay's attention to the point of rock. Slowly he edged halfway out of the concealing crack and hefted the Winchester to his right shoulder. He slipped a finger around the trigger while he sighted down the barrel in an approximation of where he judged Coyote Man would step from the rocks.

A shadow separated itself from the mountain—a shadow in the shape of a long-braided Kiowa brave.

Too high! Clay lowered the rifle's muzzle. His finger squeezed the trigger. A startled cry of pain echoed above the Winchester's report. The shadow dropped to the ground.

Clay understood why Coyote Man had not followed up with a second shot. The grass concealed the Indian's body as it had hidden him when the Kiowa's bullet struck his thigh. Taking no chances, the rancher peppered the ground around the spot he had seen the brave fall with six shots. He then moved forward, a fresh cartridge ready in the Winchester's chamber.

The brave was nowhere to be found.

Clay's eyes narrowed when he crouched and perused the dark granite behind him. His certainty of mere seconds ago evaporated. Had he been wounded?

The toe of Clay's right boot stumbled into the answer two strides away. A Winchester lay on the ground.

He's hurt! No other reason would separate the Kiowa from his rifle; of that Clay was more than certain. Again the tables turned. He was once again the hunter, and he knew in which direction Coyote Man retreated.

Lifting the brave's fallen weapon, Clay twisted around and started to throw it as far into the clearing as he could. His arm gradually came down when he saw Mary crying by the fire. He had not ridden here to kill. He had come to return the girl to her mother. He looked at the Indian rifle in his hand. Wounded and without the weapon, the Kiowa brave no longer posed a danger.

Something dark tugged at his heart when he turned to the tanks' east mountain, watching the quarter moon push above its rounded crest. The advantage was his. He could search out Coyote Man and—

Clay thrust the temptation away. Two years of living had been lost to the desire for revenge. The little girl crying at the center of the clearing needed him, and she was a very large portion of his future.

Turning his back on the mountain and the Kiowa who hid somewhere among its rocks, Clay used the Indian's rifle as a makeshift cane to ease the pain in his left leg while he walked to the campfire. He knelt beside Mary, pulled a hunting knife from its scabbard, and freed the five-year-old girl's wrists. Taking her into his arms he held her quaking body close.

"Shhhh," he whispered and lightly kissed the side of her head. "It's all over now. I'm here. Everything is going to be all right. Everything is going to be all right."

He hugged her tightly until the tears subsided and her head pulled back so that she looked into his face. "I want to go home, Clay. Can we go home?"

He smiled and gently kissed her forehead. "Soon as I bandage this leg, that's exactly where I'm going to take you."

Placing the child on the ground beside him, Clay used the knife to cut away the bottom of his shirt. He straightened his left leg and examined it in the fire's light.

"You hurt yourself," Mary said, her eyes wide when she noticed the blood soaking the leg of his trousers.

"It looks worse than it is," he reassured her.

He did not lie. As painful as the wound was, Coyote Man's bullet had struck off center and come out an inch and a half from where it entered. The bullet had missed the bone, and the through-and-through wound was far cleaner than the messy job of trying to dig a slug out of his own flesh.

He tied the strip of cloth about the two wounds. The best he could hope for was to stanch the flow of blood temporarily. The bandage would hold him until he got back to the bay. There he would wash the wounds and doctor them with the sulfur he carried in the saddlebags.

He groaned when he stood. The leg was already stiffening on him. Leaning heavily on Coyote Man's rifle, he looked down at Mary. "Are you strong enough to walk? It would help a lot if I didn't have to carry you."

The girl nodded. "Nobody's carried me since I was little."

"Good." He smiled while he tucked the Winchester under his right arm. "Take hold of my hand. We've a piece to walk to get to my horse."

She took his hand and pointed. "What about that horse?"

Clay's gaze followed her fingertip to the north mountain of the Hueco Tanks. Tied to a stunted mesquite stood the Appaloosa mare. The corners of Clay's mouth rose. He had all but forgotten about Martin's mare. "Why don't we take that horse with us, too?"

"I think it's pretty," Mary said. "I've never seen a horse with spots like that."

"She is pretty," Clay agreed as he wobbled toward the Appaloosa. The mare was no more than three hundred feet from the fissure that led back to the outside of the tanks.

Reaching the mare, he untied the single-reined hackamore from the tree, then helped Mary onto the animal's back. "Hold tight to her mane and don't let go."

The five-year-old entangled her fingers in the mare's long mane. "I've ridden a horse before. I won't fall off."

Clay's smile grew, fueled by this unexpected twist of fate. Wounded, without horse and rifle, Coyote Man was stranded in a harsh oasis amid miles of desert that stretched around it in all directions. Over thirty miles separated Hueco Tanks from the Rio Grande. A man on foot with a supply of water might be able to make it. The Kiowa had no way to carry water. His water bag, made from a buffalo stomach, lay empty across the mare's neck.

The irony that concluded over two years of chasing the brave pleased Clay. Coyote Man's bloody ways had severed the cords that bound him to his own people. Those same ways now left him alone among three mountainous piles of granite stuck in the middle of the desert. The tanks were a natural prison for a man on foot.

The Kiowa could survive. The *huecos* would provide water. And game was plentiful for a man who could shape weapons from sticks and stones. Everything from lizards and snakes to mountain lions visited the tanks to quench their thirst.

One day, the rancher realized, Coyote Man might find a way to escape the prison. But to do so would require every iota of ingenuity he could find within his brain. Even the stages that stopped to partake of the water Hueco Tanks offered provided no serious avenue of escape for the brave. Drivers were well aware that Apaches and Comanches often visited the tanks, and they were alert for any attack. Rather than escaping, Coyote Man was more likely to get himself killed if he decided to take on a stagecoach.

"Let's go home." Clay handed Mary his rifle to hold while he took the mare's rein in his right hand and led her and her small rider toward the passage between the mountains.

"How long is it before we get home?" Mary asked, her fingers clutching the mare's mane and Winchester.

"Two days at the most." He mentally estimated the time it would take to water the Appaloosa and the bay, fill his four canteens, and tend his leg before heading north. He needed sleep, and rest would not hurt Mary either. However, he wanted to put an hour or two between them and the tanks before he camped for a few hours. Although the jerky in his saddlebags was enough for him, Mary needed a real meal. With luck he would sight a rabbit or two while they rode and solve that problem. All in all, he tallied, even with time for sleep and rest, they should arrive at the Grant ranch before the end of the four-day deadline he had given Anna and Ben.

When they reached the entrance to the passage dividing the two mountains, Clay's neck craned back to check the progress of the moon's ride in the sky. He heard the high-pitched yowl of a war cry a split second before a rock the size of a small watermelon hurled from the granite heights.

Releasing the hackamore's rein, he threw up an arm and shouted. While the mare wheeled and trotted away with Mary clinging to her neck, the rancher leaped in the opposite direction, throwing himself to the ground.

Solidly the rock thudded to the ground, half-burying itself in the soft sand where Clay had stood a moment ago. He rolled to his back. A screaming shadow launched itself from the rocks above. Moonlight glinted along the naked steel of a knife the shade held in its right hand.

Clay had no time to cock the Winchester or draw his Colt. Both his arms flew up, fingers locking around Coyote Man's right wrist when the Kiowa fell atop him to drive the air from his lungs in a painful gust.

The strength of his arms was not enough to stop the descending blade. The best Clay managed was to redirect its path by an inch. The knife bit into the sand beside the rancher's neck.

The brave screamed his rage. The balled fist of his left hand hammered into the side of Clay's face. His right hand wrenched back, pulling the blade from the dirt. "I will have your scalp this night, white eyes! It will hang on my belt beside the girl's!"

When the Kiowa threw his body weight behind the knife, intent on thrusting it into the rancher's throat, Clay twisted in the sand. His arms and body worked together as he rolled, unseating the brave and sending him tumbling to the right with another angry yowl.

Clay's right hand shot to the holster on his hip—and found it empty. The Colt had fallen out during the struggle!

While the Kiowa scrambled into a crouch, Clay wasted no time fumbling to find the pistol. The fingers of his left hand closed around the hilt of the hunting knife sheathed on his opposite hip.

Every muscle in Coyote Man's body tensed. A war cry howled from his chest and throat. He leaped, knife extended before him.

In a wide backhanded sweep, Clay's right arm slammed into the Kiowa's knife hand, jarring it far to the left. Simultaneously, the rancher's left hand drove upward. The tip of the hunting knife pierced the Kiowa's body just below his rib cage. Clay thrust the steel fang upward and inward, seeking the brave's heart—and found it.

In spite of the night shadows, Clay saw Coyote Man's eyes widen in confusion. The Kiowa's war cry abruptly died in a wet gurgle. For an instant the brave's body stiffened as though the warrior attempted to gather what life remained in him for one last act of defiance. In the space of a solitary heartbeat Coyote Man went limp, his body collapsing atop the rancher.

Clay allowed himself the luxury of a shaky breath, before he rolled the dead brave from him. Sheathing the hunting knife, he found the Colt in the sand and slipped it into the holster. When he once more leaned on the Kiowa's rifle, he stared down at the still body at his feet.

Unnoticed until this moment was the bloody bullet wound in the brave's left thigh. Both hunter and hunted had faced each other on equal ground.

The rancher felt no sense of triumph, no sensation of sated revenge, only a bewilderment. For over two years he had wasted his life for something that was over in seconds. It was done, and it meant nothing—less than nothing.

He looked up. Twenty feet away Mary sat on the back of the mare, staring at him. "It's all right. He's not going to hurt you anymore. He's not going to hurt anyone."

Mary's eyes shifted between the dead Kiowa and Clay. "I want to go home."

"So do I, Mary. So do I." He hobbled forward to gather the Appaloosa's dangling rein. "Why don't we do that right now?"

He led the mare and girl past Coyote Man's sprawled body without looking back.

Twenty-three

THE DOOR to the small stone house opened when Clay drew up the Appaloosa. Anna, with Ben at her heels, stepped across the threshold. Mother and son stared at the rancher, disbelief on their faces.

Clay lifted Mary from where she sat in the saddle in front of him and gently lowered her to the ground. "Go say hello to your ma and brother."

The five-year-old girl did not hesitate. With arms held wide, she ran forward. "Momma! Momma! Momma!"

Anna leaned down and swept her daughter into her arms. She lifted the girl into the air, hugging her close while she smothered her face with kisses and tears.

Smiling, Clay managed to swing his right leg over the saddle horn and slid to the ground without cursing when the throbbing reawoke in his left thigh. Ben ran to him. "You're hurt!"

Clay tilted his head and shrugged. "Not bad. I'll—"

"Clay!" Anna put Mary on the ground and hastened to him. "Your leg. You've been—"

"I'm all right," he assured her. "It's stiff, but—"

She cut off his words when her mouth covered his. Her arms encircled his neck. He did not mind. He returned her passion, his own arms sliding about her slender waist and drawing her close.

"I didn't think we'd ever see you—"

This time he cut her short with a kiss. When their lips parted, he said, "It's over. We're both safe—and we're back. For the moment that's enough. Right now, we've got to talk about getting all of us out of here."

"Out?" Anna stared at him, puzzlement in her aquamarine eyes.

"It's not safe here." He told her of the Mescalero band camped less than ten miles away. "Sooner or later, they will be coming back."

"But this is our home," Anna answered. "We've no place else to go."

"That's something else I need to talk to you about," Clay said. "There's a ranch across the border in Texas that's been in need of a family to tend it for the past two years. I think the four of us might be able to make a go of it."

Anna's eyes brightened, and just as abruptly she frowned. "Do you realize what you're asking?"

"I'm asking you to marry me." Clay kissed her.

"A ready-made family is not something most men want to be burdened with." Uncertainty still colored her tone. "Are you sure you know what you're doing?"

"More sure than I've been of anything in a long time."

Anna's arms tightened around his neck. "Then, Mr. Clay Thorton, I would be honored to be your wife." With that, she kissed him long and hard. When her lips reluctantly eased from his, she said, "As much as I want to stand here all day letting you hold me, I think I'd better get things ready for the ride to Texas."

"Take only the things you need," he said. "The lighter we travel, the better time we'll make."

"Clothes and a few keepsakes, that's all we'll need." She turned to her children. "Ben, Mary, come along. We've got to get ready. We're going to a new home in Texas."

Clay watched them as they walked into the house, savoring the feelings that swelled inside him. Then he limped toward the open door to join his family.

ABOUT THE AUTHOR

GEO. W. PROCTOR, a prolific Western writer and lifelong Texas resident, is the author of the critically acclaimed Double D Westerns *Enemies* and *Walks Without a Soul*. He and his wife currently reside in Arlington, Texas.